Barston Falls in 1822

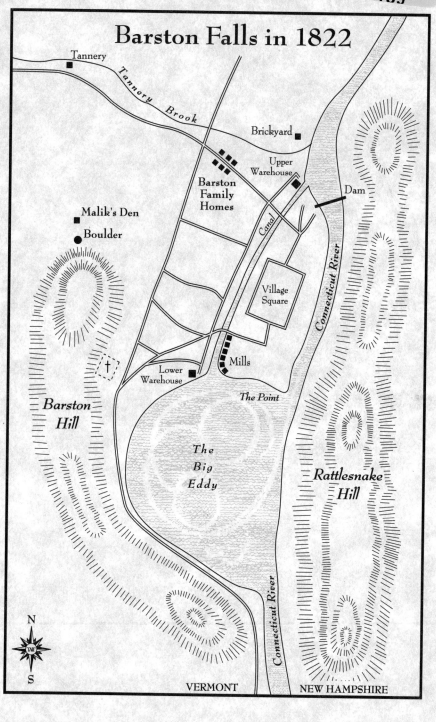

Tannery

Tannery Brook

Brickyard

Upper Warehouse

Dam

Barston Family Homes

Canal

Malik's Den

Boulder

Connecticut River

Village Square

Mills

Lower Warehouse

The Point

Barston Hill

The Big Eddy

Rattlesnake Hill

N

S

Connecticut River

VERMONT

NEW HAMPSHIRE

The Big Fish
of Barston Falls

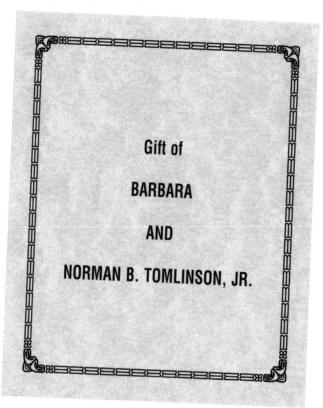

The Big Fish
of Barston Falls

by Jack Noon

Jack Noon

Moose Country Press

1995

Moose Country Press
Warner, A.H.

ISBN 0-9642213-2-2

Library of Congress Cataloging-in-Publication Data

Noon, Jack, 1946–
    The big fish of Barston Falls / by Jack Noon.
        p.   cm.
    ISBN 0-9642213-2-2 (cloth : alk. paper).
    1. Indians of North America – Vermont – Fiction.
    2. Vermont – History – 1775-1865 – Fiction. 3. Abnaki
    Indians – Fiction. I. Title.
PS3564.0489B5 1995
813'.54 --dc20   95-17828
                                                                      CIP

10 9 8 7 6 5 4 3 2 1

Cover & illustrations by Walt Cudnohufsky
Maps by Alex Tait

Printed in the United States of America

To my parents,
Ted and Marjorie Noon

Part One

1794

I

South Hadley Falls, Massachusetts
May, 1794

"They're set deep enough," Henry said to the kneeling boy, waving him aside.

Henry swung the sledgehammer hard and accurately, sinking an oak peg several inches into an auger hole with his blow. Recovering and controlling the weight of the sledge, he raised it behind him in a slow arc and again struck the peg hard. Five blows forced the peg through one squared timber and well into another lying perpendicularly beneath it; squeezed grease out onto the top of the peg as it disappeared. Without breaking his rhythm, Henry drove three more pegs into auger holes, each within a foot of the first.

"I need more grease," the boy said. "Be right back."

Henry nodded, laid the sledge down on top of the timber he had just pounded the pegs into, and threw his shoulders back to ease the tightness. He watched the boy for a moment working his way along the cribwork towards the riverbank with his grease bucket in hand; threading his way among the men boring auger holes, greasing and setting pegs, driving pegs, raising timbers from the Connecticut with ropes and setting them into place, filling the hollow cribbing with rocks windlassed up on gin poles from the rock barges on the downriver side of the cribbing. He guessed there were at least fifty men in front of him working on the dam. He watched the boy walk the last ten yards to the riverbank. The cribwork there next to the bank would be the highest on the dam — fourteen feet tall — and had been finished. Already men were pegging planks to it, beginning the sheathing which during the next few months would spread all the way across the river and hold back the water.

The boy walked a short distance up along the riverbank to a flatboat resting in the slot of the guard lock, which marked the beginning of the canal. The grease was on the boat in a barrel. Henry watched the boy hop on board, then gazed for a moment at what he could see of the canal. He was glad to be working on the dam rather than on the canal. Close to two hundred men spent all their working days digging a twenty-foot-wide ditch — a ditch which would be over two miles long when it was finished. Building the dam was hard work, but it was cleaner than digging the canal, and there was more variety in the work.

Henry turned to look the other way. His eyes followed the continuation of the ledge the cribwork was being built on. It ran up diagonally out into the river, disappearing under water here and there and then surfacing beyond. He fixed his gaze on the tallest of the outcroppings, which had been pointed out to him many times. The leg of the dam he was working on would run all the way to that outcropping, a distance of a hundred rods. Already the crew working from the other side of the Connecticut had pushed its cribwork out half the distance to that same outcropping. Those men would finish their leg of sixty rods and then angle down to join the leg Henry was working on. Half a mile of cribwork, stones, and planking in the dam! A canal ditch more than two miles long! Henry had been staggered at first by the scope of the project, thinking that it was impossibly huge, but then he had labored the previous year with two hundred and fifty hard-working men, and they had accomplished a great deal. The more than three hundred men working that summer would finish the dam and canal, Henry thought, if they kept working steadily. The plan was to finish the middle of the dam in August, when the water would be at its lowest. Then as soon as the river filled up behind the dam, the canal could be put into operation — assuming, of course, that the diggers finished their work on time. There was a question in Henry's mind too of whether the special cart for the canal would work on its incline the way it was supposed to. Rather than building a series of locks to raise or lower flatboats the fifty-five foot difference between the upper and lower ends of the canal, the plan had been to cradle each flatboat in a monstrous wheeled cart raised or lowered along a 275-foot-long incline by means of chains and water-powered capstans. The six-wheeled cart had already been built — fifty feet long and twenty feet wide. It had tall wheels at its lower end and short wheels at its upper end so as to keep a flatboat level as it was raised or lowered over the incline, which was being paved with hewn stone. If the incline and cart system failed to work, then many locks would have to be built, and the canal would have to be deepened.

As Henry waited for the boy to return with the grease, he continued to gaze out over the river, squinting because of the brightness of sunlight on the water; oblivious to the sounds of many men working because he had been surrounded by them for so long. Suddenly Henry gave a start. He jerked both hands up to shade his eyes and stared hard out at one of the gaps in the line of ledges. He had seen — or thought he had seen — a dark body heave up out of the water for a moment, headed upriver through the gap. Even in the distance it had looked huge. Then there was another. Henry dropped his right hand from his forehead and pointed out to the gap as he shouted to the men closest to him. They stopped their work and stared out hard with him, shifting their eyes here and there as Henry tried to explain which gap he was looking at. There was nothing to see. The men stood and watched for a moment. Then most of them got back to work. Three, however, lingered a moment longer. Suddenly they too were pointing and shouting with Henry. The others, a dozen or more, again stopped working, shaded their eyes, and stared out at the river. They stared for close to five minutes as Henry and the other three men described the hugeness of whatever they thought they'd seen swim up through the gap. They stared out at the river until one of the overseers shouted for everyone to get back to work, but none of them except for Henry and the other three claimed to have seen anything.

Later, as the boy knelt greasing pegs and twisting them to stand upright in the next set of auger holes, he listened to Henry describe something with a dark, shiny back which had risen out of the water for a moment as it had passed the gap on its way upriver; something larger than a sheep. The boy guessed it might have been two or three salmon coming out of the water at the same time. Henry didn't know what to think and kept wondering out loud, drawing some teasing from several men about his "sea monster." Finally he shut his mouth and set himself back at driving pegs to anchor together the cribwork timbers. He thought as he worked.

An hour later, when it was time to walk over to the riverbank and eat, Henry had nearly convinced himself that what he had seen must have been several salmon rising together. However, after the other three men who also claimed to have seen something swimming through the gap sought him out and began talking, he wasn't so certain. Though the glare on the water had been strong and the gap a good distance from where they had been standing, all three men spoke of the clear image of a single, massive creature rolling slowly above the surface in the gap between the outcroppings of the ledges. When Henry spoke of the possibility of salmon rolling together to give the same impression, they scoffed at him. Once again Henry began to believe the images pressed into his memory. No, it hadn't been salmon rolling together. It had been something else, but Henry was incapable of saying what. None of the other three had any idea of what it might have been either.

For several days the four men watched the gap closely when they could. They tried to have others with them as they watched, but no one saw a thing. The four men stopped speaking to others about what they thought they had seen, but throughout the rest of the summer, as the two sides of the dam grew towards each other, those four often stared out over the remaining undammed area.

The dam was completed that fall. The huge cart and the incline were a success. In December, Henry and many others rode up and down the incline repeatedly in the cart. The following April the cart easily bore the weight of a loaded flatboat and again worked well on the stone incline.

Henry was proud to have worked building the dam. In later years he liked to think back to his work at South Hadley Falls. Whenever the image of something huge swimming up through a gap between river ledges came to mind, however, he simply shook his head and smiled to himself, powerless to explain.

II

Bellows' Falls, Vermont
June, 1794

Reuben White sat in a chair hanging from ropes tied to Colonel Hale's bridge across the Connecticut. He was deeply content as he held his salmon spear ready and kept an eye on the water rushing inches beneath his dangling feet. The river, though down from its earlier spring levels, still surged over the ledges with tremendous force. A fall from the chair would have been certain death, but Reuben wasn't concerned. The chair hung from four new ropes and was itself so tightly overlaced with cord that even if every wooden part in it broke, it would still hold together. In addition a separate rope knotted around Reuben's chest was tied to the bridge timbers above. Finally, his brother and two cousins waited up on the bridge to give whatever help he might need. Reuben felt so secure that he didn't worry even about getting wet. He thought only of spearing salmon.

He remembered stories his father and Uncle Douglas frequently told of how plentiful salmon had been nearly thirty years earlier, when they had been boys. They hadn't had Hale's bridge to spear from then and had worked from the ledges on the Vermont side of the river or from rafts anchored out in the eddy below the fast water. Tremendous numbers of salmon had come up the river then, they said, and shad had been even more plentiful than salmon. Shad couldn't ascend the fast water; never got further up the Connecticut than the huge eddy below the falls, where they were netted easily. Though it had been common for several hundred people to be fishing at the Great Falls, as Bellows' Falls had then been called, there had always been plenty of salmon and shad for everyone. But over the years Reuben's father and uncle had grumbled increasingly about the worsening fishing, blaming the greed of those people down in Massachusetts and Connecticut who weren't content simply with catching enough fish to last their families through the year, but who instead wanted to get rich selling fish. There was a sure market in the West Indies for all smoked or pickled fish: food for slaves on the sugar plantations. Massachusetts and Connecticut fishermen, Reuben's uncle claimed, wanted every single fish; would never be happy as long as anyone up the Connecticut in Vermont or New Hampshire was still catching any. There were far fewer salmon now, his uncle said, and they were a lot smaller than they had been in the early days. When Uncle Douglas's own sister, Reuben's Aunt Molly, was sixteen, hadn't she speared one herself from the ledges that had weighed forty-eight pounds on the flour scales in the Whites' gristmill? And in recent years a fish half that size had been thought an unusual catch.

A salmon arched out of the water fifty feet down below Reuben. Instantly his hand tightened on the spear shaft. He scanned the water below his feet carefully, waiting. Then the salmon appeared over to his left, but out of range. Reuben muttered at it.

A few minutes later a salmon struggled up against the current and headed directly towards the hanging chair. Reuben plunged the prongs of the spear down hard over the salmon's back. The salmon tore the spear from Reuben's grasp, but he quickly pulled it back with the long cord tied between the chair and the end of the spear. He wrestled in the salmon hand-over-hand until he could grab its gills. Then he shouted for his brother and his cousins. He shouted repeatedly to make himself heard over the roar of the water. Finally one of his cousins looked down from the railing of the bridge. Then Reuben's brother and his other cousin appeared. They lowered the end of a rope to him. Carefully he threaded the rope through the salmon's gills and knotted it. Then he freed the prongs of the spear and motioned for someone to haul the salmon up. Fifteen pounds, he guessed as he turned his attention back to the river.

A moment later a jug hanging beside his elbow gave him a start. He looked up to see his brother laughing. Reuben let the spear drag in the current as he drank three long swallows of rum. He waved to his brother and put the stopper back into the jug, which then rose up and disappeared over the railing. There were no salmon for the next half hour. Occasionally Reuben's brother or his two cousins glanced over the bridge railing and gave the river down below a look to see if they could spot any salmon for Reuben, but then they lost interest. They sat leaning against the railing, drinking rum, and watching the bridge traffic pass.

Reuben himself all but lost interest in the fishing. His swallows of rum had made him feel good inside for a little while as he continued to watch for salmon. However, as the minutes passed and he saw no more salmon, he grew bored and then sleepy. He shook his head to ward off the sleepiness and yawned repeatedly. He shut one eye and let the other droop until it was nearly shut. Several times as his chin fell down onto his chest he lurched back into being half awake, but his drowsiness gave every promise of having him fall asleep in the chair.

Then, without knowing why, he was suddenly wide awake and staring hard at the river. He was scarcely breathing, his heart was beating wildly, his hand clenched the spear hard, and still he didn't know why. He looked right and left and straight at the river down below him, ready for any salmon.

Reuben jerked his head hard to the left and caught only the shortest glimpse of an enormous dark shape.

"A log. Had to be a log," he said to himself, but confusion flooded over him. The shape had been too big to have been anything but a log. His eyes had been tricked, however, into thinking that it had been headed up the river and, as he gazed down below to where the current would have carried a log, it hadn't risen again. He couldn't explain why he kept looking for the log long after it would have washed down into the eddy below. Nor could he explain the prickly feeling on the back of his neck and his overwhelming anxiety.

Then fifty yards below he saw a dark back roll up out of the water and disappear. Reuben gasped at the size, then felt foolish that he had let his eyes trick him into believing he had seen something bigger than a man and ten times the size of any salmon. He took a deep breath, trying to calm himself. Suddenly, twenty yards below, the broad back rolled up again out of the white water, right in the heart of the current. All the air rushed out of Reuben's lungs in a moan. His spear dragged on the surface of the swift water, and he found himself standing in the chair and trying to claw and thrash his way up the ropes, which were too thin to get a good grip on. He held himself in the air above the chair, both hands clenched around three ropes bunched together; the fists one on top of the other right at his chin and the ropes pressed against his cheek. Just beneath him he saw the dark, wide, scaleless back roll again — the back larger than Reuben himself — and then an enormous sickle tail rise and disappear beneath the white froth of current. An uncontrollable moan rattled in his throat — continuous except for Reuben's sharp gasps for air. His whole body clenched tight. Then, in a quickly moving procession, he saw four more of the great backs and sickle tails rise and fall in and out of sight down below, right beneath him, and then up above the bridge. Finally they were gone, and Reuben was shrieking hysterically. He didn't stop until his brother and cousins had pulled him and the chair up onto Hale's bridge.

No one believed Reuben, and after a few days he himself doubted what he thought he had seen. Nonetheless he never again tried to spear salmon from the hanging chair. It was over a year before he had another drink of rum. His brother, cousins, and others he later regretted telling his fish story to teased him mercilessly. It wasn't until he mocked himself better than the others did — shaking his head and laughing and using the story to caution others about drinking too much rum — that the teasing eased.

Secretly Reuben hoped that someone else fishing from Hale's bridge might see what he thought he had seen. It had seemed so real to him that he always kept a picture in his mind of the backs and the tails of the fish. If two or three other people could see the same sight, that would prove it hadn't been just a rum hallucination. Other men that spring and early summer hung in the salmon chair and speared fish, but they saw nothing but salmon. The following year the chair was used briefly, but then never again because there were no more salmon coming up the river. Someone had built a dam down in Massachusetts, and the salmon couldn't get by it. Young salmon, trapped up above the dam, lingered for a few years and were caught on baited hooks, but they were never of any size. They were no bigger than trout. The big salmon were gone from the Connecticut. Most people thought they'd be gone forever.

Nearly thirty years later Reuben chanced to read something in a newspaper that caused him to think hard remembering that last day he had speared salmon from the hanging chair.

Part Two

1822

III

Barston Falls, Vermont
June, 1822

The three boys sneaked down through the growth of short trees. Right at the edge of an expanse of broken ledges and small bushes leading down to the Connecticut River they stopped. From where they stood, if they had turned their heads to the left, they could have had a good view of the last surges of swift water from the outrun of the falls. Or, if they had lifted their eyes, they might have gazed out over the vast bay down the river and at the furthest limits of the view seen a flatboat crew poling up towards the lower end of the canal which passed through the village of Barston Falls. However, their attention was firmly fixed on the prostrate figure of an old man down below them at what was known locally as "the point," a protrusion of ledge right where the Connecticut widened abruptly into a huge bay. They stood and stared. Two of the boys were empty-handed. The third — Benjie — carried a dead woodchuck by a cord around its neck. They whispered among themselves, just loudly enough to be heard over the background rush of the falls.

"Asleep, ain't he?"

"Asleep or dead. Anyways he don't move. Can't see how he expects to catch fish like that."

"He's just drunk again. Just a drunk old Injun. He don't trade his fish for nothin' but rum and whiskey. My pa says you can tell how good the fishin' was by how drunk he is the next day."

"How much rum you s'pose a woodchuck might bring him?"

The three stifled their laughter.

"Come on. Let's do it. Let's give the old Injun his surprise."

With great care not to make any noise, the three boys stalked down the ledges to where the Abenaki Indian lay. Ten feet from him they stopped and studied his slow breathing. Then one of them walked ahead and motioned to Benjie, who followed him the few feet to the water's edge. Benjie stood there with the woodchuck and stared back over his shoulder at the sleeping Abenaki. The other — Tom — pulled the man's fishline in hand-over-hand until he came to the hook and weight. He knelt down, stripped the mussel bait from the hook, and hurriedly beckoned for the woodchuck. He twisted around as he beckoned again and looked up at the back of Benjie's head. The third boy — Foss, standing by the old man — mirrored Tom's signals and then, impatient, strode ahead and jostled Benjie over to Tom. The three boys together hooked the woodchuck firmly in its mouth. Then they stood with it dangling, each of them with one hand on the line. They gestured with their free hands as they spoke in rasped whispers.

"No!" Tom said. "Don't throw it or the splash 'll wake him up!"

"Shush, Tom! He'll hear you!" said Benjie.

"Shush yourself, Benjie, or you'll wake him with your shushin'!" Foss said.

"Well go find us somethin' to push it out with then if we ain't goin' to throw it," Benjie said. "Hurry up. I don't want him openin' his eyes and findin' me standin' here. Go on!"

Tom and Foss let go of the line and together went around the point and began searching the bank of the great bay. Halfway over towards the entrance to the canal they found a good pole and dragged it back to where Benjie stood with the woodchuck. With it they pushed the woodchuck out into the current. Then the three of them retreated quickly back up to the spot where they had first stared down at the Indian. There they spoke in more normal tones, the urgency gone from their voices.

"A fine day for woodchuck fishin'," Benjie said, "and a perfect job on old Malik. And good work to you, Tom, for findin' us a good, fresh, sinkin' woodchuck."

"All we need now is for him to wake up," Tom said.

The three stood and watched for a few moments as the Abenaki continued to sleep.

"Maybe we should give a good sideways tug so the line touches him," Foss suggested.

"No. He'd see us right there and know," Benjie said. "Here's a better way."

Benjie picked up a rock, walked a few steps towards the river, and gave the rock a heave. It splashed about thirty feet from the old Indian.

"Still asleep," Tom said.

All three of them got rocks. When Benjie gave the signal, they flung them together out into the river. The old man didn't move. Then the boys commenced a random barrage, throwing into the river as close to the old Abenaki as they dared, but still failed to wake him. One of the rocks fell short and clattered no more than five feet from him. He slept on.

"Drunker than we thought," Benjie said. Then he gave several short yells as loudly as he could. The Indian never stirred.

"Well I'm disgusted," Foss said. "All the trouble we went to and we prob'ly could of scalped the old Injun and he never would of woke up. Drunk as a skunk."

"My woodchuck 'll bloat and float 'fore that old cuss wakes up," Tom said. "We just went and wasted the whole mornin'. Ungrateful Injun. Might just as well leave. Might just as well go do somethin' to somebody who can appreciate it."

Still they stood side-by-side for another five minutes, wishing out loud for the Indian to wake up, to check his fishline, to pull the dead woodchuck in and be surprised. At last, however, their patience wore through, and they left to seek other entertainment.

IV

Sue Reckford finished chopping to length the last of the sticks. It was driftwood she had hauled from the bank of the wide bay down below Barston Falls up to the small, brick house she and her father rented in the village. She set aside the axe and began picking up the smaller sticks and stacking them on the pile against the house. When all the small wood was stacked, she turned to the thicker pieces, which had to be split. She took the first of them, leaned it into the notch of her splitting log, picked up the axe, and struck as hard as she could. When the wood popped apart cleanly, she laid one of the halves against her splitting log and smashed that in two. Log by log she worked steadily until all the wood was split and stacked — all except for three pieces she had savaged with the axe without result. She saved those for her father's efforts when he got back from work.

Tired and hot, Sue sat on the ground and sprawled back against her splitting log. She wiped trickles of sweat from her forehead and dried her hands on her britches. As she rested, a familiar heaviness settled over her — the leaden unhappiness which came most often during nights when she lay awake and thought about the tricks life had played on her. She studied what she considered to be the hugeness of her hands and feet, more like those of a man than of a girl, she thought. At twelve years old she hated being taller than many men (a scant three inches shy of six feet) and heavier and stronger than some. She hated not having a mother — the cruelest trick of all. She remembered only vaguely the woman who had died in childbirth before Sue was three years old. Since that time she and her father had lived in many places. Her father had kept seeking work and a new wife. He always found work easily, but mainly because of his shyness he hadn't found another wife. Sue's own shyness seemed like a prison to her. On the few occasions over the past decade when she had begun to make progress in getting out of that prison, her father had abruptly moved her away — to his new work in a new village. And then it had begun all over again, just the way it had been in Barston Falls: the loneliness and isolation among complete strangers. They had moved to the village six weeks earlier, and after six weeks Sue felt just as out of place as when she had arrived. In that time perhaps a dozen people had asked her name. Of those, a few greeted her from time to time as they passed in the streets, but there were never more than a few words. Otherwise she felt lost and alone amid the general bustle of activity. If she were more at ease with strangers, she told herself, she could have friends and not be so lonely, but her reluctance to talk with people she didn't know was deeply rooted, and she despaired of ever being able to overcome it. It would be up to others to break through the shyness, she knew. She couldn't do it by herself.

Her unfortunate size, she was sure, kept people at a distance, but more than size was to blame. If she'd had anything even approaching beauty, people might have paid more attention to her, but she knew she was coarse-featured: a wide, solid, muscular plainness to her face; drab, ordinary hair cropped above her shoulders. Shyness. Size. Coarse features. She began the familiar enumeration of the five things she had decided kept her from being happy. The fourth was clothes. She could never remember having worn a dress, but always britches and shirts. Though she considered dresses impractical and confining, she sometimes caught herself wishing that she had grown up feeling comfortable wearing them. She guessed that people looked askance at a girl who wore britches. Other girls her age felt nothing in common with her and never approached her in attempts to begin friendships. If her mother had lived, Sue most likely would have grown up wearing dresses, would have been raised to be comfortable in the ways of women, and would have had someone to talk to about things she could never talk to her father about. But her mother had died.

The fifth reason which kept Sue from being happy was her father, Joe Reckford. She always felt uncomfortable tolling off the fifth reason; admitting that her father, whom she loved, was a reason she was unhappy. His overwhelming shyness — even worse than her own — kept her isolated from people. For ten years he had claimed he was looking for a second wife and had moved from place to place to maintain the fiction that he was searching. In those ten years there had been young widows and unmarried women who would have made fine wives, but Joe would scarcely have begun a courtship — more from a feeling of obligation to provide Sue with a mother than for his own happiness — before his nerve would flee. The courtship would abruptly cease, and Joe would begin the vigilance of avoiding whomever it was he had once been courting. Occasionally Sue and her father would stay in one place long enough for Joe to begin — and end — three or four such lost-nerve courtships. But soon the multiple vigilance would become too much of a chore for Joe to keep up. The excuse then would be that he had to find new work, and they would leave for somewhere else so Joe could begin fresh. The longest they had ever lived in one place had been a year. Thusfar they had been living in Barston Falls for six weeks, renting a small house from Tom Barston. Joe paid the rent and bought food with money he earned from loading and unloading flatboat cargoes at the lower wharf and warehouse, delivering goods from the warehouse to various merchants in the village, and taking flatboats up or down through the canal and locks. Much of Joe Reckford's work during the past decade had been like that — menial, unthinking work generally involving moving things from one place to another. He had worked in lumber mills, brickyards, a tannery, and a shingle mill. Sue thought further that if they had been in the habit of going to church, that would have been a way to meet people. Joe Reckford, however, saw church as a waste of time. Although he was a religious man, his religion was personal — a church of one. He read the scriptures by himself on Sunday mornings, feeling that no minister had the right to come between him and the God he believed in; that joining a church and all the particular beliefs attached to it was the first step to hypocrisy. Joe Reckford was a good man, Sue thought, and yet she couldn't help wishing that his ways had put more people into both their lives rather than keeping them so isolated.

Sue stood up and wondered what to cook her father for supper that night. After a few moments she decided she would go down to the river and try to catch a few fish. She left the axe inside the doorway, out of sight of passersby, took the fishpole from where it leaned against the side of the house, and walked down towards the Connecticut. She would wade briefly in the slack water of the bay to get enough mussels for bait. Then she planned to fish at the point.

V

Malik, the old Abenaki, lay in the afternoon sun. Without opening his eyes he brushed clumsily at flies on his face. Then he settled back into his torpor.

Sue Reckford studied the old man as she sat on a ledge next to the river holding her long fishpole straight out. She wanted to keep her bait right in the swirl where the current met the eddy coming back. Now and then she would lift the tip of the pole a few inches; then slowly let it back down again. Most of the time she kept her eyes on the old Indian.

She had seen him many times before. She remembered first noticing him a month earlier — a thin and wrinkled old man who had perhaps two dozen baskets to trade and a few furs. He had simply set down the baskets and furs on one side of the village square, had sat down beside them, and had waited for people to come. The baskets were well made. Sue had admired them without having anything to trade. The next time she saw the old Indian he had no baskets, but only the furs. A few days after that he was offering fish. Since then she had seen him either fishing in the Connecticut or else trying to trade perch, eels, pickerel, or horned pout in the village. Sue had no idea where he lived. His thinness made her wonder how often he ate anything. However, it was clear to her that he drank a great deal of rum. He had woven a basket over a bottle and carried it on a sling around his neck and over one shoulder. He drank from it frequently when he was fishing or trading. Beyond those few details Sue knew nothing of the old Indian, not even his name. She wondered about him as she watched him sleeping.

Sue felt a strike at her bait, gave a quick jerk on her pole, and hoisted in a yellow perch of about nine inches. Nine or ten more like it, she thought, would make a decent meal for her father and her. She twisted the perch off the hook and left it flopping on the ledge behind her.

As Sue was rebaiting her hook, she noticed three boys watching her. She had seen the boys often before. They were all about her own age, but she was taller than any of them by almost a head and a good deal heavier. The three were always together when she saw them, always roaming, carrying fishpoles or spears through the village or berry baskets or crude bows and arrows. They were together so much that they might as well have been linked with ropes. She had watched them with fish they had caught and once with a dead raccoon — parading it through the village simply to show off. For three days in a row they had taken turns carrying that same raccoon, which one of them claimed to have shot with the arrow stuck in its body. Probably there wasn't a single person in the village who hadn't seen the three of them with that raccoon. Sue finished putting the mussel onto her hook; looked up at the three boys and smiled, but when there was no response, she lowered her eyes and pretended not to notice them.

The old man stirred. He sat up, rubbed his eyes, and gazed about him. He looked at Sue as he yawned. Then he reached over to his fishing line, which was wrapped around a rock beside him, and began pulling it in hand-over-hand. Sue watched with interest and then with great curiosity as the brown, furry body of a woodchuck broke the surface. The Abenaki stood up, hauled the woodchuck out of the water, and stared down at it in confusion as it dangled from his hook.

Sue turned towards the sound of the laughter up above; saw the three boys slapping one another on their backs and holding themselves in exaggerated hilarity.

"Hey Malik!" one of them shouted. "How's the wood-chuck fishin' today?"

"How much rum's it worth?" called another.

Malik looked up at the three boys for a moment, then bent over the woodchuck. The boys called out other things to him, but he ignored them. Taking his knife out of its sheath, he quickly skinned, gutted, and beheaded the wood-chuck. He tore free the usable meat, threw the offal out into the river, and rinsed the meat well before he put it into his basket. He coiled his fishing line as the boys continued to taunt him and put it in on top of the woodchuck. Then, hanging the straps of the basket over one shoulder and the strap of his rum bottle over the other, he left the river.

Sue watched Malik leave; ignored the boys as they glanced at her. After they had left, she turned her attention fully to fishing.

* * * * *

The skin of the woodchuck and the offal still attached to it tumbled freely in the currents. Erratic underwater swirls where the vast eddy came back to meet the main current of the river kept the skin drifting over the same irregular ledges for several hours without making much progress down the Connecticut. Then at last the current lost its hold on the skin, and it settled into the still water, coming to rest on the ledge at the bottom of the deepest hole below the falls. Each spring the surge of high water coming down through the falls scoured out the hole right to bare ledge, but in the low water of the summer there was no current there in the deepest hole.

The skin lay at the bottom of the hole until late evening. Then an enormous, shadowy bulk passing methodically over the riverbottom paused for a brief moment, and the skin was gone.

VI

Joe Reckford was tired. He had worked all morning and the first part of the afternoon loading boxes, crates, kegs, and barrels from Tom Barston's lower warehouse into the delivery wagon and unloading them by himself at their destinations in the village. When he had returned to the lower warehouse, Jared Barston — Tom's son — had told him to work with Mark Hosmer and the crew of a flatboat tied to the lower wharf. Joe had joined them in loading goods into a pair of handcarts. Jared stood on the flatboat with the head poleman and pointed out what to take from the cargo. After the handcarts were loaded, Jared listed the items remaining on the flatboat so that he could reckon the toll for the passage up through the canal. While he was doing that, Joe and Mark pulled the handcarts up through the double doors of the warehouse and began unloading them. They were still putting away the goods when Jared came in.

"All right, boys," Jared said. "Toll's paid, and you can take her up through."

The men nodded to Jared. Mark left to unhitch the two horses from the delivery wagon and lead them to the towpath at the head of the first lock. Joe went out to the wharf and stepped aboard the flatboat. The polemen pulled in their bow and stern lines, leaned against their twenty-foot ash poles with patient firmness, and slowly set the flatboat into motion towards the canal. They worked without haste, moved the flatboat a few rods up along the riverbank, and then skillfully pivoted it to enter the canal. They continued poling until the flatboat neared the gates of the first lock.

"No poles past the gates," Joe said. "Poles aboard after the gates."

The polemen knew without being told, but Joe had reminded them anyway lest the iron socket-spikes on the ends of their poles poke leaks in the canal lining. One of the polemen threw the bow-line to Mark Hosmer as the others were laying down their poles and starting to sprawl out over the deck of the flatboat. Mark hitched the line to the harnesses and then urged the horses forward. The flatboat eased the rest of the way through the gates with half a foot of space on either side. When the stern of the flatboat was far enough up into the lock to allow for the swing of the gates, Joe waved. Mark halted the horses.

Joe climbed the short ladder onto the east bank of the canal and looked down at the four-foot-wide sluiceway which ran parallel to the canal along its east side. He walked between the empty sluiceway and the canal the few feet to the closed canal gates at the head of the lock. There, by turning two horizontal wheels, he raised one sluicegate feeding into the canal and lowered another across the sluiceway. Water trickled into the upper end of the lock from a port low in the canal wall.

Mark waited for Joe at the foot of the lock, leaning over the balance beam on his side of the lock gates. When Joe stood at the other balance beam, Mark gave him a nod, and the two men pushed the heavy gates shut. Mark then walked across the tops of the two gates, which came together in a slight V pointed up the canal. He followed Joe up along the sluiceway, passed him where he had stopped to shut off water to the first mill, and himself shut off water to the second mill. The two men kept passing each other until they were beyond the lower bridge and above the third set of canal gates and had finished shutting off water to all six mills which stood between the canal and the Connecticut River. Then they walked back down beside the full sluiceway and waited as the first lock filled and floated the flatboat up to the level of the second lock. All the polemen were sound asleep; scarcely stirred as Mark and Joe kept at their work of moving the flatboat up through the canal.

The canal ran right through the village of Barston Falls, making an island of the land between it and the Connecticut. The village square lay in the middle of the island. Most of the stores and businesses of Barston Falls were located on the island, including the six mills on its south end. Flatboats and timber rafts went through three locks in their canal passage. The so-called lower and middle locks lay close together at the lower end of the canal. The upper lock was right at the head of the canal. A bridge passing over the middle lock and a second bridge crossing about two-thirds of the way up the canal over the long, flat stretch of water between the middle and upper locks made necessary the unhitching and re-hitching of the tow rope so that horses on the towpath might draw flatboats and lumber rafts under the bridges. The lower bridge had never been called anything but "the lower bridge." The upper bridge, however, in addition to being called "the upper bridge," was known as "Tannery Bridge" because the road crossing it was called Tannery Road.

Most of the buildings in the village of Barston Falls were of brick: all but one of the six mills on the south end of the island, Tom Barston's two warehouses at the head and the foot of the canal, stores, hotels, taverns, stables, a school, a blacksmith shop, the shed for the fire carriage, some small houses, a pair of churches. The block of six Barston family homes (three on each side of Tannery Road about thirty rods west of the bridge, including Tom Barston's home, which was the largest in the village) and even Old Sam Barston's tannery (half a mile out beyond the houses and on the south side of Tannery Brook) were also brick buildings.

Israel Barston, until he had died two years earlier, had lived where his son, Tom, now lived. He'd had all the brick buildings built and had planned and overseen the digging of the canal as well. The original village of Barston Falls, which Israel, Old Sam, and their brothers had built, had consisted of only wooden buildings — all owned by the Barstons (particularly Israel) and rented out to anyone who would pay to run businesses or to live in them. In the early years Israel Barston had operated a carry business around the falls and had done well. All the owners of cargoes bound upriver depended on him. The downriver traffic at first floated by the village without a carry fee and without great difficulty if it hung to the east side of the river, for there seemed to have been plenty of water in the early days. However, over the years the summertime level of the river kept dropping. (Old Sam, who was well up into his seventies and the only survivor of the five brothers who had given their name to the town and to the Falls, claimed that in his youth there had been twice as much water in the river.) Because of the lowering water, the ledges at Barston Falls began to be a problem for the river traffic, and Israel gradually picked up most of the downriver business as well. Except for running logs and sometimes lumber rafts downriver, people used Israel's carry service rather than risk being wrecked on the increasingly exposed ledges. At the turn of the century rafts and flatboats ran down through Barston Falls only during the highest water of the spring run-off. The rest of the time they used Israel's carry, and he was rich many times over. By then, with the help of his brothers, he had built several dozen wooden structures — houses, stores, taverns, stables, warehouses, and the like — all of which he had kept title to and rented to those willing to pay his fees; a church and school, which he had built for the use of any who lived in the village. More buildings had been crowded in over the years without any particular regard for how they were located in the village. The old carry was the only real road. Near its head and foot it joined the route to towns up and down the river.

Then one dry and windy day in 1804 a fire began in a stable on the west side of the village. It spread quickly to other buildings. People fought it with buckets and brooms and wet rugs until they saw it was hopeless. They fled up onto the side of Barston Hill and, with the wind safely at their backs, watched the village burn all the way to the Connecticut, leaving a blackened wasteland — all of it owned by Israel Barston or his brothers. Only a few houses on the western edge of the village were spared.

Israel's shock was great, but within a few days he had recovered sufficiently to think about rebuilding the town. He even began to see some advantages to his loss. A week after the fire, he started driving stakes all over the charred land, studied the arrangement of the stakes and moved them several times, and then announced his plans for the new village of Barston Falls: new roads here and there, a central square, warehouses and wharves at the head and the foot of the carry, sites for many different buildings wherever they could fit among the ledges. The most significant change, however, was the land he left untouched in a wide swath through the middle of his new-planned village. Surely inspired by what others had done down the river, particularly at Bellows' Falls, he decided that the village would have a canal and a dam across the Connecticut just high enough to put water into the canal. He went down the river and made close inquiries about investors who had made possible the building of the canals at Bellows' Falls, Turner's Falls, and South Hadley Falls. It took him over two years to arrange backers for his project, but at last he found them — wealthy British and Dutch investors who were convinced of the continued growth of trade throughout the upper Connecticut valley.

Israel, it is to be noted, was careful to keep his own money out of the dam and canal project. He would spend it to erect the new buildings of Barston Falls, all of which he decided would be of brick. In spite of the extra time and expense involved in building with brick, he went ahead — determined that the new village never burn down. With the money he kept earning from his carry business he set up a brickyard on the north side of Tannery Brook, near where it emptied into the Connecticut and right beside a seemingly inexhaustible bank of hard, blue clay. Sand of a sufficient fineness for bricks was to be had from a few dozen rods up the west bank of the Connecticut. Cordwood to fire the bricks came at first from the Barston family land on both sides of Tannery Brook, but later had to be rafted down the Connecticut from wherever Israel could buy it cheaply. Over the years Israel and his brothers made tremendous quantities of bricks in the brickyard. At considerable expense Israel brought flatboat loads of lime to the village site for his mortar. He went deeply into debt putting bricklayers to work on the buildings he'd planned, borrowing from whomever he could. By the time work commenced on the canal in the spring of 1807, many of the buildings around the new village square had been completed. Israel sold most of them and with that money paid off his debts and kept his brickyard workers and bricklayers busy. By the end of 1808 the upper and lower warehouses had been finished.

The first flatboat passed through the canal and locks in 1810. Israel, as had been his arrangement with the British and Dutch investors, kept one-tenth of the toll fees for himself as compensation for his land, work, and maintenance of the canal and paid nine-tenths to the investors — and would continue to pay that nine-tenths forever, as nearly as anyone could tell. Many thought that it was too little return for Israel, considering all the work he'd had to do and considering that the opening of the canal had killed his carry business, but eventually his shrewdness became apparent. In the dozen years the canal had been open the investors had gotten back only about a fifth of what they'd invested. Their grandchildren, it seemed, would be the first to see any profit. Meanwhile Israel, in the decade before his death had done well, even though his tenth part of the tolls hadn't amounted to much. In the village he sold brick buildings and the land they were on; bought and sold land elsewhere in Barston and in Wheelock, across the river in New Hampshire. He had raised four mills on the south end of the island between the canal and the Connecticut — built of brick, of course. Israel powered the mills with water from the canal sluiceway. Having shown others the possibilities, he then sold two of the mills and sold two undeveloped millsites along with a share of water rights to the sluiceway. With the money from those sales in hand he set bricklayers to work on the six Barston homes and afterwards on a new building at Sam Barston's tannery.

Israel's brickyard had ceased making bricks about six months before he died in 1820. (Joe Reckford had occasionally wandered through the tall weeds by the brick-drying sheds and the kiln shed and had examined carefully the brick-making machine, the wooden brick molds made out of cherry, and the quality of the clay in the bank. He wondered why the brickyard was no longer in operation — selling bricks up or down the Connecticut if they weren't needed in the village, but such was the isolation imposed by his shyness that he never asked anyone about it.) After the tannery had been finished, Israel sold bricks cheaply to home or business owners in the village who would use them to build outbuildings or additions. He refused to sell empty houselots in the village, for he feared that buyers might build houses of wood — cheaper, easier to build, and burnable. Instead, he hired men to raise small, brick houses west of the canal. He sold some of these houses; kept others to rent, including the one Joe Reckford and his daughter now lived in. Israel viewed with horror the fulling-mill which had been built of wood on one of the two mill sites he had sold and predicted it would be only a matter of time before it lay in ashes. While Israel had been alive, the fulling-mill was the only wooden building of any consequence in Barston Falls aside from the few on the extreme west side which had survived the fire of 1804. Tom Barston, however, sold many empty lots soon after his father's death, and wooden buildings sprang up on them quickly.

Tom Barston now suffered from poor health and rarely left his house. According to village sentiment, even in his prime he hadn't been even one-tenth the man his father had been. Nonetheless, he had a great deal of money. It took little sharpness to see that tenants in the brick houses paid their rents, to sell land or buildings he had inherited, or to have two of his sons — Seth and Jared — collect the canal tolls and charge merchants fees for unloading, storing, and delivering goods they had ordered from up or down the river. As a young man, Tom had made a brief attempt to move out from under the shadow of his father and show off his sharpness in general trade on the river. However, his experience there had proven only that many others were sharper than he. As an excuse for abandoning his foray into trade on the river, he had cited the persistent ailment in his lungs, which indeed in later years made a near invalid of him. His father would have continued to use his landholdings in the village to build more brick houses on or to develop new businesses he could either run or sell, but that approach evidently struck Tom Barston as too much work. He was content to sell land as it was and let others worry about developing it. In the two years since Israel's death Tom had thus parted with much of the land east of Barston Hill and became easily the richest man in the village. He gave Seth and Jared the responsibility of running the warehouses at the head and the foot of the canal and generally stayed at home in idleness and increasingly ill health.

Joe Reckford sensed that there were a lot of Barstons in Barston Falls, but hadn't broken out of his reticence enough to ask about them. He was sure of only a few. He could recognize Tom Barston, of course, and his uncle, Old Sam, who owned the tannery. Jared, Tom's son, took care of the lower warehouse; Seth, another son, ran the upper warehouse. Joe also knew a boy named Benjie, who was Jared's son. Beyond that, however, he didn't know the names of the others he suspected of being Barstons.

Joe and Mark kept the flatboat moving up through the canal, a routine so familiar that nods or glances were sufficient for them to work together. As they left the middle lock, mill workers reset the gates for the sluices that carried water down to the mills.

From the flatboat Joe glanced across the canal at what he could see of the main square of the village, his view mostly obscured by the backs of buildings fronting onto the square, and then watched Mark leading the horses up the towpath on the west side of the canal. It occurred to him that he knew very little about Mark Hosmer, though the two of them had worked a month and a half together for Tom Barston. Mark was about forty. He was heavier than Joe and nearly as strong — a great surprise to Joe, who had never met a man stronger than he was himself and few who came close. Mark and his wife had lived in Barston Falls for a long time and, like Joe, rented one of Tom Barston's brick houses. Joe knew nothing else about Mark, not even if he had any children, and felt a little ashamed that he didn't know him better.

Joe interrupted his thoughts to unhitch and rehitch the tow line so that the flatboat could pass beneath Tannery

Bridge. Then he lay back and rested until the flatboat was in the upper lock. There he climbed the ladder on the side of the lock, with Mark closed the lower gates, and walked up to the floodgates thirty feet from the head of the canal.

The floodgates were far taller and thicker than the other gates on the canal — too large to be pushed open and shut with balance beams. They had capstans and sturdy ropes instead. The floodgates had been built to be stronger than the other gates so that they could withstand the high water and grinding ice of early spring. They stayed closed all winter and kept the canal empty — except for creeping fingers of ice from isolated tricklings — so that repairs could be done then on the walls and floor of the canal. While Israel Barston was alive, the floodgates had been inspected constantly. More than once Israel had dreamed in nightmares that the floodgates had failed; that surging water had breeched the other gates below and had washed out the canal and much of the village. Tom Barston wasn't as concerned about the floodgates as his father had been. The past fall he had looked them over and had had Jared tighten a turnbuckle or two. Otherwise he had left them alone.

As the upper lock was filling, Mark and Joe turned their attention to the capstans. On each side of the canal there was a pair of capstans for the floodgate: one to open it and one to close it. A large eyebolt out at the end of each floodgate anchored a rope long enough to reach either capstan on its side of the canal.

Joe unwrapped the rope from the capstan beside the upper lock and hauled its free end up past the floodgates to the other capstan, which sat near where the canal rejoined the Connecticut. He pulled the rope taut and threw several wraps of it around that capstan. Then as he stood by the lock watching the water and the flatboat rise, he leaned against the ironwood pole thrust horizontally through the drumhead of the capstan. At last Mark called out to him.

"She's full over this side! How about over there, Joe?"

Mark laughed, but Joe simply nodded. He heaved hard against the ironwood pole and began trudging around on the ring of well-packed dirt, pausing in each circuit to step over the rope. The rope creaked as it wound in around the capstan. The floodgate eased open. Joe put a bow into the ironwood pole and soon had the floodgate open all the way. He glanced up then and watched Mark finish opening the other floodgate.

As Joe was crossing the canal on the flatboat, he gave a start at the sound of a shrill whistle, but it was only Mark waking the crew of the flatboat. Mark said a few words to the men. They arose and stretched and then grabbed their poles as Mark led the horses out onto the upper wharf, stopped them close to the end, and untied the bow-line. One of the polemen coiled the bow-line neatly and left it on the deck. He and the others nodded to Mark and Joe and got right to work poling the flatboat up the Connecticut.

Seth Barston shuffled out of the upper warehouse and approached Joe and Mark on the wharf. From the look on his face, Joe guessed he'd been sleeping. Seth was about the same age as Joe, but didn't carry his years as well: bald, fat, and pale; always with an air of unwashed shabbiness about him. He was in charge of the upper warehouse, but did little real work; spent most of his time dozing or otherwise idling. He was a lazy man, but quick to order Joe or Mark or others to one chore or another, and Joe didn't like him. Seth stopped in front of Mark and Joe and streaked the wharf with his tobacco spittle.

"Might as well take a box down through," Seth said. "Guess I'll have you two do that."

"All right," Mark said.

Rafts of boards floated along the shore in the space between the wharf and the mouth of Tannery Brook. They were put together in units called "boxes." Each box was long and thin so as to fit the dimensions of the canal locks not only at Barston Falls, but all the way down the river. A box could thus be sent intact down to tidewater. The Barstons owned the boards there by the upper wharf through their trading. Though there was no urgency in getting them down the river to sell, Joe thought it obvious that whenever he and Mark took a flatboat up through the canal they should take a box back down to take advantage of the way the canal gates had been left by the upward passage. Joe and Mark would have taken one of the boxes down through the canal even if Seth hadn't told them to. Joe kept his thoughts to himself, but considered it a measure of Seth's uselessness that he felt a need to order them to take a box on their way back down. Joe liked working with Seth's brother, Jared, at the lower warehouse much better.

Mark followed Seth into the warehouse and returned alone with a raft pole and a coil of rope. He walked up along the riverbank, hopped out onto the nearest box and untied it from the others, and with the raft pole launched the box far enough out to clear the end of the wharf. He tied the rope to the box and threw the free end to Joe, who hitched it to the horses. Then with the pole and the horses the two men nosed the box of lumber in between the hewn-stone walls of the canal entrance, through the floodgates, and into the upper lock. Mark jumped from the box over to the east side of the canal and went to reset the gates for the sluiceway so that no more water would flow into the upper lock, but found that someone from one of the mills had already done it.

After the box was in the lock and Mark and Joe had closed the floodgates, Mark stepped out onto the lower gate on the east side of the lock and opened the drain port there by turning a short, horizontal wheel on top of the gate. As the upper lock was draining, three boys appeared on the side of the canal. Each carried an eel spear.

"Is it all right if we go down with you again?" one of them asked.

"Sure Foss," Mark said. "Hop aboard and keep a sharp eye out, for we'll soon be drained down to nothin'."

The three leaped down onto the box and crowded together at the lower end. They held up their spears in readiness and stared hard at the ten-foot expanse of water between them and the closed gates, eager for a glimpse of whatever fish might appear as the water drained. The three boys often rode down on the lumber boxes. Though most fish trapped in a draining lock retired to safety in the shadows under the boxes or else swam down through the drain port, the boys occasionally speared them, particularly eels. Each time they rode down with a cargo, Mark reminded them sternly that they were to stay out from underfoot and that they weren't to beg him to leave the gates closed after the lock had drained. He repeated his threat to heave them into the canal if they didn't heed him. No matter how big a fish they claimed might be trapped in an emptied lock, they weren't to interfere with the work.

Joe and Mark leaned into the balance beams and swung open the gates at the foot of the upper lock. As the horses began to move the box, the three boys ran quickly over the lumber to the other end and stood ready for the moment when the cover an unwary fish had sought under the lumber box might slide away and give them a chance with their spears. They rode that way all the way down the flat section of canal past the center of the village and into the middle lock. When Joe and Mark swung the gates shut behind the box, the boys moved back to the front end and waited as Mark turned the wheel on top of the gate to open the drain port.

Joe watched the boys with their spears as the water drained from the lock. Benjie Barston he recognized — Jared's boy and Tom Barston's grandson. The one with red hair was named Foss Richardson, he was fairly certain. Tom Peasley — or Beasley — was the third. They were all about the same age and size and, though their looks were different, they might as well have been triplets, for all Joe Reckford could see. They were always together, he supposed, from the first thing in the morning until the last thing at night: paraded together with dead fish or animals whenever they managed to get them, skipped rocks together in the Connecticut, carried their puny bows and arrows together, played at Rogers' Rangers together with long sticks serving as muskets, threw rocks together at birds or cats or tree stumps or floating logs or whatever else might be the target of the moment. If one had britches caked with mud to the knees, then the other two did as well. If one smelled of something old and dead, so did the other two. They sought entertainment constantly and always sought it together. Sometimes it was harmless; sometimes mischievous. None of them, Joe was certain, would grow up to be as lazy as Seth Barston, Benjie's uncle. At twelve or thirteen years old — about the same age as his daughter, he reflected — they had already built up too much momentum ever to settle into such laziness.

Benjie speared an eel just before Joe and Mark swung open the gates between the lower and the middle lock, and the three boys were quite pleased with themselves. They set down their spears and crowed over it. As soon as they were down in the lower lock, they climbed over onto the towpath, stretched the eel out on the ground, and fussed considerably over it. As the lower lock drained, Joe watched the three boys head up the towpath and cross the bridge over the canal — headed into the village square to show off the eel, he guessed.

Joe and Mark swung open the last set of gates. Mark closed the drain port and then hopped down onto the box to wield his pole. Joe led the horses. Together the two men worked the box of lumber over to the lower wharf. Then they went into the lower warehouse to ask Jared Barston about their work for the rest of the day.

VII

Joe broke another piece of bread from the loaf, dabbed it at the last of the grease among the fishbones on his wooden plate, and ate it. Then he pushed his chair back from the table and stretched out his legs. Sue rose from her side of the table and carried their plates to the dry sink, which stood in the corner of the single downstairs room in their house.

"Good meal, Sue," Joe called over to her. "Always did like perch."

"So don't I," Sue said, returning with a wet cloth to wipe the table. "But sometime I want to catch you somethin' big enough so you ain't got to fuss with all the little bones."

"Oh, I don't mind the bones much. But a big fish would be nice. Just make sure it ain't a woodchuck, but a fish for sure."

Joe smiled at his own words. He had laughed when Sue had told him of the woodchuck on the old Indian's line, his only laughter of the day. He knew the three boys were Benjie, Tom, and Foss, had said to Sue that it couldn't have been anyone else, and had told her about the eel they had speared that afternoon.

"I couldn't believe it, Pa, when I watched him clean the woodchuck and take it with him," Sue said.

"I've ate a lot of woodchucks," Joe said. "And there ain't anythin' wrong with ..."

"But that one he should of pitched right back in the river, Pa. No tellin' how long those boys had it 'fore they put it on his hook."

"Injuns eat lots of things you wouldn't even think about eatin'. They're raised that way. And I don't feel sorry for that Injun on account of he could eat just about any kind of food he wanted."

"What do you mean?" Sue asked.

"The furs and baskets he trades, for one thing. And he's always got fish to eat or trade for other food. He wouldn't stay so skinny if he drank less rum and ate more food, but that's his business. He don't have to eat woodchucks — either rotten or fresh. If he traded his stuff for food, he could eat just as good as us."

"You're right, Pa. He drinks a lot from that bottle he carries with the basket wove around it, and I think he's drunk most of the time. You know much about him?"

"Nope. Not much. A couple things I heard Mark Hosmer say to somebody the other day. The Injun knows Old Sam Barston from years ago and comes to Barston Falls every summer to fish and trade. I guess he likes to fish. Likely he could teach you a thing or two, Sue."

"I'll wait and see if he catches any himself first. I'm doin' fine fishin' the way I am."

Joe rose from the table and followed Sue to the sink.

"Course you are, Sue. Didn't mean to say you wasn't. Here. Let me have the fish bones, and I'll give 'em a heave. Hand me the bucket while you're at it so I can get more water."

"I got enough for the dishes here," Sue said.

"We'll need it in the mornin' anyway."

"All right."

Sue washed the few dishes and worried about her father after he had left with the bucket. He looked tired, she thought, and his laughter at her story about the woodchuck on the old Indian's hook had been the first she'd heard from him in a long time. There wasn't much joy in life for him. In his six weeks working in the village he had made no friends. He scarcely ever talked to anyone but her, and it surprised her that he knew anything about the old Indian. Everywhere he and Sue had been, Joe had been ignorant of nearly all common-knowledge village gossip simply because he didn't talk to people. If in Barston Falls he followed the same patterns as in the many other villages where they had lived over the years, Sue guessed that before long his festering loneliness would boost his courage just enough to send him in faltering pursuit of some woman or other. Then, about the time that Sue's hopes arose that he might at last remarry, the halfhearted courtship would end. At home there would be no more mention of the woman. If he chanced to see the woman in the village, he would cross the street, turn a corner, or cast down his gaze and pretend not to notice her. He might repeat several tentative courtships in Barston Falls, but then within the year they would surely move on to other work in another village. It had happened so many times before. She wondered if they would ever find a place to settle down in; whether they would continually keep moving; whether her father would ever be happy. Joe's return pulled her from her thoughts.

"Here's your water, Sue, and the plate to wash."

"Thanks Pa."

"I was thinkin'," he began. "You like fishin' so much I thought you might like fishin' with Benjie Barston and his two friends — give you somebody your own age to be with. They always ride down through the canal on the lumber boxes just for the chance to spear whatever they can find when the locks drain. Got that big eel today. I s'pose they must fish with hooks and lines too. It'd give you a chance to ..."

"They was pretty mean to the old Injun," Sue said.

"Just boys full of it, Sue. Always up to somethin', but I can't see the harm in it — not like they'd stole or broke anythin'. The Injun got his supper from the boys if you look at it that way. I wouldn't call 'em bad boys, and you should have someone you could ..."

"I don't like 'em, Pa."

"You might get to know 'em some 'fore you decide that, one way or the other."

"Well, I don't know."

"I won't push it on you," Joe said quietly. "But you need some friends your own age. You got the curse of my shyness, Sue. It always was a pain and a hindrance to me 'til I met your ma, and then it was again after she died. I wish you could of known her better, Sue."

"Yes Pa. And I wish you could find somebody to take her place."

"If it's God's will, maybe we'll find somebody here at Barston Falls."

Sue finished cleaning up from supper as her father sat in his comfortable chair. She glanced at him from time to time and saw him staring at the reflections of candles in the window, evidently lost in thought. He yawned repeatedly. His face was sad and drawn. Sue leaned over and put her hand on his shoulder.

"Oh," he said rising to his feet. "Guess I was off driftin'. Long day today, and likely another long one tomorrow. I'm off to bed now." He leaned over and kissed Sue on the forehead. "Rest well."

Joe yawned and stretched and went upstairs to his room. Sue blew out the candles and for a time stared out the window into the twilight, watching darkness creep in among the mill buildings and gradually swallow up her view of the eddy down below the falls. Then at last with scarcely any twilight left she groped her way to the stairs, went up to her room, and undressed for bed.

* * * * *

Sue lay in bed wiping away tears with the sleeve of her nightshirt. Thoughts of her father's loneliness and unhappiness and then of her own misery raced around in her head, as they did nearly every night. Only by praying, she had discovered, could she still the chaos of thoughts, restore at least the hope that future days would be happier, and with that happier vision in mind drift off to sleep. She prayed first for her father in a whisper so low that the sound scarcely got beyond her lips; prayed that he might have friends from among the men in the village and that he find a good woman to be his wife. Then she prayed for a way out of her own miseries: mainly that she stop growing and, if possible, lose six inches or so of her great height.

Her prayers generally ended there, after she had prayed for her father and for herself. Usually her mind was stilled then, and she could fall asleep. That night, however, she found herself thinking about the old Abenaki Indian.

"And please help the old Injun who fishes down by the river. Make him trade for food with his fish and baskets and furs and not waste it all on rum. He don't have to eat old rotten woodchucks. Let him eat good food, and make those three boys be nice to him. And if he don't have a good place to sleep, find him one where he can be warm and dry and not plagued with the bugs. Thank you for listenin'. Amen."

Sue felt good having remembered to pray for the old man. Her mind emptied of its worries, she fell asleep.

* * * * *

Joe turned restlessly in his bed, very tired from his day's labors, but unable to sleep. He thought of Sue and of his continuing failure to end her unhappiness; wished she had friends. He regretted that in the decade past he had been unable to find a woman to replace the mother Sue had lost.

If in one of the many villages where they had lived during that decade he had found someone, Sue would have had a better and happier childhood. Now perhaps it was too late. In a few years Sue would be a grown woman. The marks of her unhappiness as a child might be etched into her too deeply ever to be changed. The unhappy child would become an unhappy woman. He had failed badly, he told himself, in his attempt to be both father and mother to her.

He thought of Betsy, his dead wife, as he had thought of her every day and night since she had died ten years before. She'd had such strength and such a vibrant force of life within her that just being near her had made Joe content. The first time he met her she had seemed nothing but a large, plain-featured woman, remarkable only in being taller and sturdier than other women. But then she had smiled in her all-embracing way, and those dimples had shown in her cheeks. She had easily pulled him from his shyness. Her hearty laughter had quickly affected him. Suddenly he had felt light and free and happy. Through some miracle he had won her hand. They had married, and his happiness had known no bounds.

When Sue had been born, Joe had been astounded at the changes in Betsy. It was as if he had discovered for the first time a door in a house he had lived in for years, had opened it, and had found a beautiful new room, whose existence he had never before suspected. She had been such a mother. The two of them had doted on Sue. Betsy had shown such patience, such strength, and such love that the men Joe worked with at the brickyard had teased him about his singing and whistling and smiling all the time. And Joe had laughed at their teasings.

Then a year after Sue's birth Betsy had fallen ill while carrying their second child. Joe's fear gnawed at him day and night. Betsy at last miscarried. The laughter was gone from her for weeks, and it had taken her several months to regain her strength. Later, when Sue was two, Betsy was ill again in a pregnancy — another time of great dread for Joe. She had carried the child to full term, but it had been born dead. Joe and Betsy had grieved together those moments after they had realized the futility of the midwife's efforts to shake, slap, or breathe life into their tiny son. Joe remembered well the pathetic scrawniness and the blueness of his stillborn child and the leaden despair in his chest. Then the afterbirth had come and with it the bleeding that wouldn't stop: the slow but inexorable trickle; the ebbing-out of life hour after hour. They had realized with Betsy's growing weakness and pallor the possibility that she might die and then, at last, the inevitability that she would die. They had had two hours together at the end — two hours to speak of their love for each other, to plan together for Sue's upbringing; two hours to use as best they could as a substitute for the many years of life together they would lose, for the other children they would never have, for the happiness they were being cheated out of. She had told him he should remarry so that Sue would have a mother. Amid many tears they had spoken a final time of their love for each other. Then Betsy had lapsed into unconsciousness, her breathing had slowed to nothing, and she had died.

Joe had raged for weeks then: utterly distracted; verging on madness. He had cursed everyone who had tried to comfort him — old friends, ministers, neighbors. At last, however, his rage had spent itself. He entered a long period of depression, growing increasingly silent and bitter because his surroundings reminded him constantly of Betsy. Finally, in an attempt to run away from those reminders, he had set out with Sue for what had proven to be a decade of wandering. He had taken many different jobs in succession. Betsy's deathbed wishes and his own feelings of responsibility for Sue had set him on a halfhearted and intermittent search for a new wife. Joe seemed joyless in the pursuit, however; never in love with any of the women; perhaps incapable of ever falling in love again. That joylessness had put off many of the women. The few who remained interested in him always found that without warning he would abruptly stop courting them, to the extent of avoiding them completely. If they sought him out and confronted him directly, they found Joe embarrassed as he stood before them mumbling unsatisfactory excuses and regarding the ground at his feet. Then shortly afterwards they would learn that he had left town with his daughter without telling anyone where he was going. That had become the pattern. In the back of his mind Sue's need for a mother always nagged at Joe. If he ever found anyone like Betsy, he told himself, he would marry her in an instant. Unfortunately he had never found anyone like Betsy. During that decade Sue had been without a mother; he without a wife.

Joe and Sue had arrived at Barston Falls six weeks earlier, Joe looking for work and a place to live. He had sought out Barston Falls because he had heard of its brickyard. His favorite work of the many jobs he had had over the years had been his brickyard work, and he was hoping to get work at the Barston Falls brickyard. Unfortunately his information had been old: the yard hadn't been used for two years, and there was no prospect of its re-opening. He was disappointed at that discovery, but had stayed in the village anyway, telling himself that Barston Falls would likely be no worse than anywhere else he might travel to. He had found work on the canal and in the lower warehouse and had rented, at a reasonable price, a small brick house he liked the looks of. He had worked the way he usually did: a steady and reliable man capable of any task involving either endurance or great strength, but silent and withdrawn enough to discourage others from getting to

know him; to keep them from going beyond the most su-
perficial of greetings.

As he lay in bed, Joe reflected on his dim prospects of
finding a wife in the village. During his first week in Barston
Falls, two women had caught his attention. One, about his
own age, was married to Jared Barston; the other, perhaps
ten years younger, to the blacksmith. Both had reminded
him of Betsy. He had spoken to neither of them, refusing to
put himself into a situation where he might be attracted to
a married woman. He admired the luck of their husbands
and kept an eye out for the other women of the village,
none of whom had thusfar appealed to him. He couldn't,
by looking at them, imagine any of them as Sue's step-
mother. Once again, in yet another village, he felt he had
failed Sue; had failed Betsy in her deathbed wishes. For at
least a while longer he would have to continue his bun-
gling attempts to be both father and mother to Sue. There
were so many times she needed a mother's touch, a
mother's sympathy, a mother's listening ear, and she did
without.

Joe's thoughts of his failures roved through his mind
until the early hours of the morning. Finally, however, he
fell asleep.

VIII

Pole in hand, Sue stood knee deep off the point in the afternoon sun and fished where the outrun of the falls met the slow eddy from the bay. It was where she usually fished, but this time, with a slightly different way of fishing, she had caught more fish than ever before. It pleased her to see the old Indian's interest grow as she hauled in one perch after another and a pickerel, which had hooked itself by grabbing one of the perch before she could pull it in. A sizeable scattering of fish was beginning to accumulate on the ledges and rocks up behind her. Each time she caught another, the old man gave her a slow nod of approval.

Her innovations had been simply to tie twenty feet more line to her fishing pole and to wade out to her knees. That let her fish out further than before. She would hold the pole in one hand, heave out the bait and weight with the other, and reach out as far as she could with the pole as the bait drifted with the current, swung around into the edge of the eddy, and settled towards the bottom. Then she would wait, occasionally twitching the pole to move the bait. From the way the bait settled after casts of different lengths, Sue guessed there was a drop-off out beyond a ledge shelf. She was catching her fish just beyond the drop-off: letting them tap at the bait long enough to get it into their mouths before she set the hook and then dropping the pole into the water as she pulled the fish in hand-over-hand. The first six fish had come quickly. The rest had been slow enough for her to enjoy the views of the river, of Barston Hill, and of Rattlesnake Hill over in New Hampshire. The pickerel had put quite a bend in the pole when she'd set the hook, and she was glad to get it in. It weighed over two pounds, Sue was certain. She wished she'd added the extra line to her pole much earlier and, as she waited for more fish to bite, tried to decide just how much additional line she might be able to manage. Looking out over the wide bay, she wondered how deep the water was out there; how many more ledge shelves and drop-offs there might be. Probably, she thought, there were great expanses of the eddy where no one had ever fished; depths where no baited hook had ever been. There were fish out there somewhere that would weigh as much as all the fish she had caught that afternoon combined. Perhaps if she could get a raft and fish from it, she might catch a fish as long as her arm. Her heart started to race a little at the thought. Perhaps, if she could only ...

A tug at her line abruptly ended her reveries. She struck hard with the pole — so hard, in fact, that she stumbled and barely avoided sprawling backwards in the water. As Sue pulled the line in hand-over-hand, she was conscious of laughter up behind her. The fish was a six-inch perch. She turned towards the laughter and saw the three boys, together yet again.

"That's right, girl. Don't let those great big ones pull you in."

The three roared out their laughter, and Sue reddened. She saw the old Indian watching her.

"Hey Malik," one of the boys shouted. "Ain't got any good woodchuck bait today, do you?"

"No," the Indian said. "But come down here, Benjie Barston, and learn to take scalps quickly. Three scalps."

Benjie turned to his friends.

"Anybody need a scalpin' today?"

They shook their heads.

"Foss and Tom say 'not today' and I can't spare the time neither, but maybe that girl's interested. We got to go, Malik. Find somebody else to scalp."

As the boys started to walk towards the canal, Foss Richardson shouted back over his shoulder.

"Tie yourself to a tree, girl, and the big ones won't pull you in."

He laughed with Benjie and Tom. Sue was glad when the three of them were finally out of sight. Malik turned back to his fishing. Sue thought of fishing more, but realized as she was unhooking the small perch how many fish she had already caught. She and her father would have to eat them three or four meals in a row or else some of them would spoil.

Before she set to work cleaning the fish, she remembered the dinner she had brought. She should have eaten it hours earlier. Rummaging through her sack, she took out bread and cheese. As she ate, she studied the Indian. Looking old and thin and tired, he sat staring at the spot where his hand-line entered the water. She hadn't noticed him catching many fish that day and smiled to think that she had out-fished a man who'd likely had years of experience fishing at Barston Falls. She wondered how he felt about that. Then she realized that she hadn't seen him drinking that day, nor had she seen him eat anything. She thought about him further and of how drunk he had been the day before, when the boys had put a woodchuck on his hook. The day before that, she decided, he must have caught fish and traded them for rum. Then he had stayed drunk until he had run out of rum. Now sober, he was fishing so he could trade for more rum. She wondered how long it had been since he'd had anything to eat besides that woodchuck.

Sue looked down at her cheese in one hand and bread in the other. She could easily have finished them, but the edge was off her hunger. She put the cheese on top of the bread and carried the food over to the old man, who turned towards her as she approached.

"For you if you want it," she said.

In surprise he looked up at her with his dark, unmoving eyes. For a moment she was aware of the calmness in those eyes, the depth of the wrinkles in his leathery face, and the stark contrast of his hair with his dark skin. Then the thin, old hand came up, and he took the bread and cheese.

"Thank you," he said.

"I thought ... thought you might like it. That's all."

Flustered, Sue turned and went quickly back to her pole. She stripped the remaining bit of mussel from her hook and tossed it into the water. Next she wrapped the line around the pole, finishing by sinking the hook into the butt end deeply enough so that it wouldn't work free while she was walking home. Then she took a short knife from the sack her dinner had been in and with a sigh set to work cleaning fish. She took up one of the perch, long since stilled in its floppings. Setting the fish on its side, she commenced scraping it with the back of the blade. The skin had dried in the sun, and the scales clung tightly, but finally she finished getting the last of them off. Then she gutted the perch and cut off the head, the tail, and the dorsal fin. With a tremendous sigh she realized how long it might take her to clean the rest of the fish. She had a second perch in hand when Malik appeared beside her holding his own knife. He picked up the perch she had just finished cleaning, looked at it for a moment, and shook his head as he set it down.

"Here," he said. He took the perch from her hand. "Cut so." He made a cut on the back all the way along one side of the dorsal fin. "And so," he continued, cutting on the other side of the fin. He stripped out the fin with his fingers and threw it into the river. "Now see — an opening to skin it." He ran his knife blade between the flesh and the skin first on one side of the fish and then on the other. Next he pulled a short piece of driftwood over beside him. "Cut the head on wood." He slid the knife point inside the skin and cut through the backbone up by the head, but left the skin on the outside intact. When he pulled the head, the skin and guts came with it. He peeled the skin down nearly to the tail and cut the tail off. The head, skin, guts, and tail were in one piece and looked much like a whole fish. Malik heaved it into the river. With his thumb he popped the air bladder in the piece he still held. "Now it's ready."

"That was quick," Sue said. "And you ain't even got to scale it."

"No."

"It's a good way," she added after an awkward silence.

"Now you," Malik said and handed her another perch.

Though Sue lacked Malik's quick skill, she soon had the offal separated from the edible flesh.

"That's a lot quicker 'n my old way," she said.

"Too slow still," Malik said. "You must practice many times. Now we will race. For every one you do, I do three. Begin."

Sue watched the quick, thin fingers reach for a perch; the two effortless slashes and the dorsal fin seemingly falling out of its own accord. Malik saw her watching and stopped his work.

"Begin. Begin."

He put a perch down in front of her and gestured with one hand and his knife until she had begun cutting into the fish. Then he set back to work. Sue worked as quickly as she could and stuck herself painfully several times with the sharp dorsal fin. She worked the skin loose and cut off the head and the tail. When at last she had finished cleaning the perch, Malik had indeed cleaned three fish in the same time. She began on another.

Sue thought she improved with each fish she cleaned. Malik kept up his quick, steady pace. The two of them worked together in silence. When Sue set down her last cleaned perch, Malik had just finished cleaning the pickerel.

"Now count," he said.

They matched their fish in lots of four — three from Malik and one from Sue. He had, in fact, cleaned more than three times as many fish.

"You work so quick," Sue said.

"Quick when I was young," Malik said keeping his eyes on the small mound of cleaned fish. "Now I am slow. An old man."

"Quicker 'n me. From now on I'll clean 'em the way you showed me."

Malik nodded without saying anything and without looking up from the fish.

"There's too many for just Pa and me," Sue continued. "You take some of 'em, won't you?"

Malik nodded.

"I'll take what we can eat for supper and breakfast," Sue said.

She began putting some of the cleaned fish into the sack she had carried her dinner in. When she guessed she had enough, she set the sack aside.

"The rest are yours," she said, rising to go. "Thank you for showin' me how to clean 'em your way."

Malik nodded again. Sue picked up her pole and the sack and set out walking along the shore of the bay so she could collect a little firewood to take home with the fish.

IX

Malik awoke early in the morning with a pounding ache in his head and a great thirst. He lay on his back, staring at the bark roof of his tiny shelter as the stupor of sleep slowly ebbed from him.

Vestiges of dreams lingered in his thoughts, all of them of the far better time when he had been a young man. The dreams had brought back to life the wife and the children he had once had and had resurrected the time when salmon had been abundant in the Connecticut River, when hunters could still find moose and deer in the valley, and when a skilled trapper could take the pelts of beaver, otter, sable, fisher, mink, lynx, bobcat, and wolf.

Consciousness brought with it the bitterness of reality. Malik again found himself an old man and realized how alone he was. His people were all gone. White settlers now covered the land. Their dams kept salmon from ascending the river. The thoroughness with which they had cleared land, hunted, and trapped had caused the creatures of the forest to disappear with little chance that they would ever return. A man could no longer find a good living from the river and the forest. The way of life Malik had followed as a young man — the way of his ancestors for centuries — was gone forever.

Half sitting, Malik reached for his bottle wrapped with woven black-ash splits, unstoppered it, and drank. He shuddered slightly, lowered the bottle for a moment, and then drank again. As he replaced the corncob stopper, a warming numbness spread through him. He was glad to see that the bottle was still more than half full; that there was more than enough rum to ease the bitterness throughout the day. He rolled out from beneath his blanket and set the bottle outside, took down his fishing basket from where it hung beside the low entryway, and then crawled out into the morning.

He yawned and stretched and gazed down the slope at the tannery. In an hour or two men would be working there, but for the time being it was quiet. Malik wrinkled his nose at the smell of decay from green hides soaking in vats down beside the building. Then he turned towards the rattling croak of a raven and looked up behind his shelter and past a huge, mostly white boulder. His eyes searched the cliffs on the side of Barston Hill until he spotted the bird. The raven pumped its wings as it wheeled around the side of the hill, catching fully the sunshine which had yet to reach Malik's shelter.

Hunger made Malik think of the girl who had given him food the day before. Her bread and cheese had been all he'd eaten that day. As he'd been trading the fish he'd caught and the others she had given him, he had thought about saving some to eat. However, his thirst had been too strong. He had filled his rum bottle and had had no fish left over for himself. Drinking in the evening had made him forget about food. The girl had been good to him, giving him that bread and cheese and then the fish. Something about her reminded him of the daughter he had once had. She had died of smallpox many years earlier while he had been off hunting and trapping at Umbagog with his life-long friend, Nabatis. Nabatis, too, was now dead. That girl the day before had been kind to him. So few other people ever were. Old Sam Barston was, but Old Sam always made him uncomfortable by trying to give him too much — something more every day without ever giving him a chance to repay the gifts. Eli Parker, while he'd been alive and living up the river in North Barston, had been a good friend, but

Eli Parker was dead. Some people in the village greeted Malik whenever they saw him and were glad to trade with him; some stepped to the other side of the street and ignored him; some, like Benjie Barston and his two friends, plagued him with cruel tricks. That big girl was the only one who had given him anything — besides Old Sam — for a long time. He would remember her. In fact, he would give her a gift. He thought for a moment what he might have to give her. Then he crawled back into his shelter, took a basket of herbs down from its hanging place, and dumped the herbs onto his blanket. With the basket in hand, he backed out of the entryway. Then, taking up his fishing basket and his rum bottle, he walked southeast down towards the village. Before he had reached the canal, the chill of the morning air had caused him to take several more drinks from his rum bottle. He was down at the river fishing by the point well before the sun came up over Rattlesnake Hill. It seemed colder to him down beside the river. He drank his rum freely.

* * * * *

Malik lay back in the heat of the mid day sun. He gave no thought to his fishing. It had been several hours since he had checked his line, but he didn't care. The sun was warm, and with enough rum in him he didn't feel hungry. He shifted his position a little and then fell back asleep. He awoke early in the afternoon, sat up, and yawned. The girl was there again, fishing where she had been the day before. He watched her for a while, wondering how many fish she might have caught. He wondered if she would give him fish that day so that he might trade for more rum. He watched her and then thought of the empty basket he had brought; thought that when he gave it to her she might give him more fish. Lurching to his feet, he took the basket in his hand and walked over to her.

She was startled; he could see that. She had been standing out knee deep in the water with her britches legs rolled up, but wet above where they were rolled so that she might just as well have left them unrolled in the first place. She'd been intent on the fishing, and he'd had to stand on the ledges for a long time. It hadn't been until she was pulling a perch in to shore that she had noticed him.

"Hello ... Malik," she said, and then she waded up out of the river. She stood barefoot with her cuffs dribbling a pair of dark spots onto a dry ledge and then two thin, dark lines down towards the river. "You slept a long time. Catchin' any fish today?" Her voice came to him as if from a great distance, though she stood right beside him. He didn't speak, and she began to look at him queerly. Then he held out the basket.

"For you. Carry fish in it." His own voice sounded strange to him.

Sue thanked him. She was embarrassed, but he didn't notice because already he had turned from her and headed back to where he'd been asleep. He pulled in his line and put a piece of cut mussel onto the bare hook. Then he heaved the line out into the Connecticut and forgot about it. He drank more rum and stilled the few thoughts in his head. The warmth of the sun and of the rum in his stomach together enveloped him and led him once again to sleep.

A long time later voices woke him, coming to him at first as if from dreams.

"What's it to you?" (a boy's voice)

"I ... I don't think you should." (the girl)

"We're just goin' to have some fun. He don't care." (another boy)

"It ain't right to pick on him like that." (the girl)

"So, are you goin' to stop us, or what?" (a third boy)

"None of your business anyways what we do."

"Careful Benjie. Don't get her mad or she might sit on you." (laughter)

Malik opened his eyes and saw the girl with Benjie Barston, Foss Richardson, and Tom Beasley. Benjie had a pot in one hand and a brush in the other. There was blue paint on the brush. The girl's face was red; her eyes downcast. Her hands fidgeted with each other.

"How about if we don't paint him all over, but just put a couple stripes on him?" Benjie said. "They don't even have to be on his skin. We could just kind of decorate his britches and shirt. How about if we ..."

"Now you went and done it, girl!" Foss Richardson said. "You went and woke him up — spoiled everythin'!"

The three boys drifted away from where the girl was standing and kept an eye on Malik. He stared at them stupidly for a moment, but then got to his feet with his fish knife in his hand.

"Well, we should get the paint back 'fore your pa misses it, Benjie," Tom said.

"No hurry," Benjie said.

"Scalps, Benjie Barston," Malik said in a quavering voice. "I want three scalps."

"You want scalps, Malik, you'll have to buy 'em," Benjie said without taking his eyes off the knife. "You couldn't even catch a drownded cat to scalp it. Couldn't even scalp a punkin on a vine."

"Couldn't even scalp yourself if you stood on a chair," Foss said, also staring at the knife.

Malik growled at the three boys, a sound meant to frighten them, but one whose impotence set them laughing instead. They started walking towards the lower warehouse, but kept throwing back words over their shoulders.

"One of these days you're goin' to wake up blue," Benjie said.

"You and your girl friend both," Tom Beasley said.

"Don't let her sit on your lap, or she'll flatten you into shoeleather," Foss said.

"Hey Benjie," Tom said. "Let's all have blue shoes some day."

"Sure," Benjie said. "Good idea. Drink plenty of rum, Malik, and don't starve your fat girl friend."

The three boys kept walking away, and their words passed out of hearing. Occasional bursts of laughter reached Malik, but then they, too, were gone. He put his knife away and shook his head. What otherwise might have been anger filtered through the rum haze as nothing more than a minor annoyance, a disturbance. The girl looked upset, however. She brushed at her eyes several times, but couldn't keep ahead of the tears, which soon streaked her face. Malik puzzled about her for a moment, then went up to stand right in front of her.

"What is your name?"

"Sue."

"I am Malik. Thank you, Sue."

She looked at him with watery eyes, nodding. She brushed her face again with the backs of both her hands and stopped the tears.

"They would of painted you blue — same as they put the woodchuck on your line. And they're goin' to do other things to you too and keep doin' 'em just so long as you keep drinkin' too much rum and keep fallin' asleep right out where you're a temptation. Is ... is that what you done with the fish yesterday? Traded 'em for rum?"

"Yes."

"Save any to eat?"

"No."

Sue looked at him hard, few traces of her tears remaining.

"You had anythin' to eat since yesterday?"

"No."

"Well, what do you usually eat?"

"Fish sometimes or what I trap. When I have rum, I don't need food."

"Course you need food. Everybody needs food. Now what 'll you eat today?"

"I have rum left. Maybe I can catch fish today too."

"But nothin' else?"

"No."

"No wonder you're so thin. Well, have this."

Sue took bread out of a sack at her feet and gave it to Malik. She looked at him closely as he ate.

"You can't even take care of yourself," she said. "It don't matter to you if you eat or not. And it's all on account of drinkin' rum. If you didn't trade everythin' for rum, you could have plenty of food. I wouldn't of given you the fish yesterday if I'd of known you'd get just rum with 'em and no food."

Malik continued to eat, not saying anything. He was aware of Sue staring at him as he ate.

"Listen to me, Malik," she said. "I cook for my pa, and we always have plenty to eat. He works on the canal and in the lower warehouse, so he can buy all the food we need. I can cook food for you too, Malik. It's food you need and not rum."

"Too much giving," Malik said. "It is not good. I cannot give back enough until winter, when I can trap furs."

"No. It's tradin', Malik. It won't be givin'. Ever since I caught so many fish yesterday I been thinkin'. Pa works all day long, and there ain't much for me to do. I was thinkin' I could fish every day and trade fish the way you do. We could fish together, and I could take some of the fish you catch and give you cooked food for 'em. It'd be a good trade for me and a good one for you. And you could show me some things about fishin' here that maybe I don't know and help me with tradin' 'em. If we fish together, I bet those boys won't bother us. I need somethin' to do, and you need good food."

"Yes," Malik said between mouthfuls of bread. "I can teach you. One time I knew how to fish well."

"I ... I don't want you to drink rum all the time when we're fishin' together. I want to catch fish. I want to learn how to get the biggest ones. If we're goin' to fish together, I want to catch fish every day so I can get money or trade for things me and Pa need."

"All right," Malik said. "We will fish together. I will give you fish and you will give me food and I will not drink so much rum when we are fishing. Tomorrow in the morning we will begin. Today I drink rum."

Malik went back to his fishline, drank rum, and slept for the rest of the afternoon. He was still sleeping when Sue left to cook supper for her father. As far as she could tell, Malik hadn't caught any fish during the whole day.

X

Upstairs in Jared Barston's house the earliest light of dawn crept into Benjie's room; across the bed in which the boy was still asleep, over a blanket chest, and onto a wall of shelves.

The shelves and all four corners of the room were filled with an impressive array of carved sticks, rocks, bones, snake skins, old iron, a cow skull, feathers, Indian artifacts, broken toys, leather scraps, hats, ox shoes, horse shoes, paper wasp nests, animal skins, single deer and moose antlers collected decades earlier when moose and deer could still be found in the area, scraps of birch bark mostly curled into tight scrolls but a few still spread out enough to show crudely scratched scenes or writing, a huge bracket fungus, a bear skull, cow horns in various stages of being converted into powder horns, a derelict gun with an exploded barrel, home-made bows and arrows and quivers — all of the clutter blocking views of additional trophies behind or beneath. An unfortunate series of events in past years had caused Benjie's mother to lay down strict rules for what could not be kept in the room: no fish he had just caught and was meaning to clean right away, ever; no dead animals or parts of animals with any flesh clinging to them (including untanned hides); no paper wasp nests until they had been left in a back shed for most of the summer without any sign of wasps using them; none of those wasp nests brought into the house at any time during the winter, ever, even if Benjie had kept an eye on them for months before and was certain there were no wasps living in them; no frogs, toads, snakes, bugs, turtles, or furry animals, ever;

no fish in buckets even if they didn't smell at all while they were still alive and swimming around; no bows to be strung in the house, ever; no fish spears, hatchets, axes, or throwing knives; no food unless it was in his hand and he was in the process of eating it, all of it; no birthday packages from his friends to be stored there unopened, ever, as he waited for his birthday to arrive. Still, in spite of all the burdensome conditions Benjie's mother had imposed on the room, he was comfortable in it and very pleased not to have to share it with his two brothers and three sisters, all of whom also had their own rooms.

A clatter at his window caused Benjie to stir, but didn't wake him. Then a hail of small pebbles against the window glass and a series of hissing sounds — slowly escalating to a level which it was hoped might wake Benjie, but leave others in the house sleeping — pulled Benjie quickly from bed and sent him to the window. Foss Richardson and Tom Beasley were down below at the foot of the big ash tree, crude bows in hand and arrows in shoulder quivers made from leather scraps given to them by Benjie's great-great uncle, Old Sam, who owned the tannery.

"If you want to shoot any, you can't sleep right through the day," Foss said.

"I'll be right down. Don't make so much noise," Benjie said.

Benjie's nightshirt fell in a heap on the floor. He pulled on his britches and shirt in an instant, took his best bow and a quiver full of arrows down from one of the shelves, and set out barefoot to sneak through the upstairs hallway, down the stairs, and out to join his friends. However, the creaking floor of the hallway betrayed him, or perhaps it had been his friends' loudness. At any rate before he had reached the head of the stairway, an apparition at the doorway of his parents' bedroom startled him badly.

"Benjamin Barston," his mother said. "What on earth are you doin'?"

"There's woodchucks to shoot, Ma. We got to get at 'em early while they're still out eatin'."

"And of course it's more important for you to get an early start on killin' woodchucks than to eat a decent breakfast."

"But Ma ..."

"Not another word about it, young man, and none of your tricks. We'll march right down to the kitchen together and get some food into you, and you won't set foot outside of this house 'til I'm sure you won't faint away from hunger before dinner time."

Benjie was disgusted at the bad luck of his capture. He hung his head, resigned to his fate. He could have escaped, but knew from experience that whatever he might gain at the moment by running away from his mother would not be worth the attention his father would give him later in the day. When his mother returned from the bedroom wearing a robe and went down the stairs, he followed her meekly. Then he endured her tortures in the kitchen: the intolerable slowness of firing the stove, the oatmeal which took an age to cook, the unending chewing and swallowing, the new torture of eggs and ham just as he was nearing the end of the oatmeal, and finally the two heavy pieces of toasted and buttered bread she thrust upon him as soon as he had finished the eggs and ham. He ate them and satisfied his mother. There was nothing else she would force upon him. He mumbled thanks to her for the food, though he felt anything but thankful.

"You come in for dinner too, Benjie. I won't have you missin' meals. You hear me?"

"Yes, Ma. Can I be goin' now?"

"Yes Benjie. Run on out and play."

She watched him go, pleased that once again she had

done her duty as a mother. Then she heard someone else coming down the stairs and turned her thoughts away from Benjie.

Bow and quiver in hand, Benjie made directly for Tannery Brook. His mother's last words rankled in him. Mothers just didn't understand that hunting was not play. Hunting was serious work. Play was for babies. He and Foss and Tom were hunters; young men.

Before he got to the alders growing along the sides of Tannery Brook, Benjie strung his bow and nocked an arrow. He held the arrow on the bowstring with his middle three fingers ready to draw and shoot at the first hint of a target. Slightly crouched over and with his eyes roving this way and that, he sneaked down into the alders, waded across the brook (choosing on purpose a spot where the water was waist-deep even though he could have crossed on rocks a few yards downstream or on the bridge a short distance above), and then hunted carefully as he kept on towards the old brickyard. As he sneaked along, he was one of Rogers' Rangers alone and surrounded by Indians and couldn't use his gun because of the noise it would make. An Indian lay dead back behind him, killed with Benjie's own knife. Benjie now carried the Indian's bow and was stalking his enemies to kill them silently even as they were hunting for him.

The shrill whistle of a woodchuck froze Benjie and made his heart leap. He saw the woodchuck up on its rear legs looking directly at him. Instantly the bow was drawn; the feathers of the arrow at Benjie's cheek. The woodchuck scurried. The arrow flew. It stuck into the ground well behind the woodchuck, which quickly disappeared down its hole. Benjie walked up to retrieve the arrow.

"A man can't miss a woodchuck by much less than that," he lied to himself. "That was wicked close."

He found Foss and Tom ranging slowly around the old

brickyard with their arrows nocked. They were both wet up to their waists. The three boys converged by a pile of broken bricks.

"She catch you again?" Foss asked.

"She was waitin' for me," Benjie said. "You two must of made too much noise."

"We could of whispered at you for a week and not woke her up, but you'd still be sleepin' too," Tom said.

"Any woodchucks?" Benjie asked.

"Saw a couple, but didn't get any shots," Foss said.

"I just had a shot at one that was runnin'," Benjie said. "A wicked lucky woodchuck. I think I might of creased it with my arrow. If I'd of had a little better shot, there'd be a dead woodchuck right now."

"Well, let's see if we can't get one this mornin'," Tom said. "Let's hunt here for an hour or two and then go check our snares. We might find one someplace. Got to or else old Malik 'll starve to death."

The three boys laughed.

"That was the best ever," Benjie said. "Remember that look on his face when he found our old woodchuck on his hook? Best part was we got so disappointed when we couldn't wake him up the first time, but then when he finally did wake up, there we all was to see him get his surprise."

"And he ate the thing — that old woodchuck," Foss said. "Cleaned it and ate it. I bet it was close to half maggots. Think maggots leave a body when it's under water? Anybody know?"

"But that was a fresh ..." Tom began.

"No sir," Benjie interrupted. "No maggots. Too rotten even for them. Don't know as I'd even think about eatin' somethin' that the maggots and the crawfish left alone. No takers on land or under water — not 'til Malik found it. A little too rich for my taste. That's for sure."

"If we could only of painted him blue," Foss said. "That would of been even better 'n the woodchuck on his hook, but that big girl messed it all up."

"Who is she anyways?" Tom asked.

"Somebody that moved in a month or so back," Benjie said. "Her pa rents one of Grampy Tom's brick houses and works on the canal — the one that works with Mark Hosmer."

"Oh him," Foss said. "Now there's a couple men with meat on their bones — him and Mark. Don't know as I'd want to tangle with either of them in a fight."

"That girl's got a lot of meat on her bones too," Tom said. "Wonder how big she'll be when she gets her full growth. She could be a real chair-flattener."

"Turn sideways to squeeze through a door," Benjie said.

"Put a wick in her mouth and burn her for a candle," Tom said.

"Thrash the wheat just by walkin' through the field," Foss added.

"Raise and lower the water in the canal just by gettin' in and out of the locks," Benjie said.

"Eats a horse for breakfast every mornin'," Foss said.

The three lapsed into silence trying to think of more words about the girl. Tom gave up first.

"That wasn't very nice of her to keep us from paintin' Malik yesterday," he said. "He would of looked good all blue, and that paint would of come off after a while."

"Just our bad luck she was there," Benjie said. "Well, never mind. She won't always be there when he's drunk and asleep. We'll have a blue Injun in town 'fore the end of summer. Count on it. She's just delayed us is all."

"I s'pose we should wander by and have a look at him sometime today," Foss said. "Maybe this afternoon after he's had some time for drinkin'. Might as well."

"All right, men," Benjie said. "Let's see if we can't get

him another woodchuck, too. We'll hunt hard here for a couple hours and then go check our snares. A woodchuck won't shoot itself. Let's go."

The three boys separated and wandered off into the early morning, bows and arrows ready; searching hard for woodchucks.

* * * * *

At noontime Benjie bounded onto the loose planks of the upper bridge across the canal trying to make as much racket as he could. Halfway across he found a particularly warped plank that rocked under his feet. He set down his bow and quiver and for several minutes jumped back and forth from one end to the other, well satisfied with the crash the plank made each time he landed on it. Then, sweating hard, he sat down on the edge of the bridge, dangled his feet over the canal, thought about the morning he'd just had, and wondered what the afternoon might bring once he got the chore of dinner out of the way. His britches were pretty dirty, he noticed.

They had gotten no woodchucks either with their arrows or with the snares they had set in several entryways of woodchuck burrows. He had shot at a woodchuck at mid morning; Tom at a different one. Neither shot had even come close. Some of their snares hadn't been touched. Three had been sprung; a fourth bitten through. They would have to change the way they set their snares, he thought. Maybe they should try to figure out how to rig deadfalls. Perhaps they would be better than the snares. A woodchuck under a deadfall was dead, for one thing, and wouldn't gnaw its way out.

"Well, Benjie."

The voice startled him. It was his father, Jared Barston, coming from the village. Benjie was surprised to see him.

Usually Jared went home by the most direct route from the lower warehouse: up on the road west of the canal and parallel to it until he came to Tannery Road, then a left turn up to the six brick homes they and various relatives lived in. That day, however, he was returning for dinner by way of the blacksmith's shop, which was on the north end of the village square. He carried a wooden runner for a sleigh, newly sheathed in iron. The old iron on the runner had broken on a rock right at the end of the winter, and Jared had finally gotten around to having it repaired by the blacksmith.

"Hello Pa."

"Must be providence, boy, that sat you down here on the bridge for me to find 'fore you got home to your ma. What on earth you been up to this mornin'?"

"Huntin' woodchucks with our bows and checkin' our snares," Benjie said.

"More 'n that, unless you burrowed down the woodchuck holes after 'em. You could be plowed and planted the way you are now, son."

"Well we did get a little dusty."

"Ha! 'Wallowin'" is the word."

"We been diggin' secret caves, Pa. Big holes with trenches connectin' 'em. Then we cover 'em over with old plankin' and put back the sods. We made a hidden trap door to get in. Add more tunnels and rooms whenever we can. It's nice and cool in there."

"Sounds like fun, boy. And of course you can't tell me where they are. Sworn to secrecy, I hope."

"Yes Pa."

"Well good. Now it's over into the canal with you — clothes and all. You scrub, and I'll be the judge of when you're clean enough to see your ma. In you go, Benjie."

Benjie leapt off the bridge, making as big a splash as he could. He rubbed his britches and shirt wherever he could reach, turned onto his stomach and back for his father's scrutiny, gave more attention to scrubbing where he was told, and at last passed inspection. Climbing out of the canal on the ladder underneath the bridge, he took up his bow and quiver and walked with his father up Tannery Road towards the six brick houses they and some of their relatives lived in. The dust in his tracks was caked and darkened with dribbles of water from his clothes, which were far cleaner than they had been a few minutes earlier. Only his feet, which hadn't felt shoes for weeks now, would spark comments from his mother.

* * * * *

After dinner Benjie stepped out into the woodshed beside the house and took down his fish spear from where it hung. He carried it as he would a tall cane and poked the ground with the spear butt at every fourth step. Easing around the corner of the house, he then walked right out into the middle of Tannery Road and stopped, facing down towards the canal. He shook his head, trying to clear from it the dullness which comes from eating too much. He needed to get down to the village and start doing something with Tom and Foss, he thought, or he would fall asleep.

Three brick houses stood on each side of Tannery Road where Benjie stood. All six houses were large and had been expensive to build. He lived in the one behind him on his left, furthest up the road towards the tannery. Grampy Sam (not Benjie's grandfather at all but a great-great uncle who was called "Grampy" by everyone in the six houses except for his nephew Tom and his nieces — Tom's sisters — Rebecca and Sally) lived in the house directly across the road from Benjie's. Uncle Seth's house, next to Grampy Sam's, managed quite well the challenge of being an expensive brick house and looking shabby. It needed only new paint on its wooden trim to replace the bare and flaking remnants of the last painting effort and an hour's axe and scythe work to reduce the tangles of vines, saplings, and coarse weeds out in front, but even that small amount of work was beyond Seth's inclinations and strengthened considerably his reputation as a lazy man. Tom Barston's house, the largest but not the best kept in the village, lay third in line. On the other side of the road Benjie's great-aunt Rebecca Kimball — a widow — lived in the house next to his father's; her sister, Sally Parker — also a widow — lived in the sixth house.

There were other Barstons in the village and more scattered elsewhere through the township of Barston and through Wheelock across the river, but not nearly as many as there might have been. All of Tom's, Sally's, and Rebecca's cousins and most of their nieces, nephews, sons, and daughters had headed west into New York state and the Ohio Valley — Barstons, Parkers, and Kimballs who had felt restless and stifled by having so many relatives surrounding them. A series of cold winters, culminating with the strange year of 1816 — in which there had been frost and snow every month — had driven many out of Barston and Wheelock. Grampy Sam often spoke to Benjie of 1816 as "the year when we had some weather that would catch a man's attention and hold his interest." Benjie had been seven then and remembered well snowstorms during the summer months, the barren garden at mid summer, and the great dependence on oatmeal for food. The unusual weather of 1816 hadn't impressed him fully until after the next few normal, hot summers with good crops, swimming, dust, and not so much oatmeal. He was impressed too by the numbers of Barstons, Parkers, and Kimballs who had left for the west every year since 1816, saying that they refused ever again to wallow through a

Vermont snowdrift in July or to try to make a living plowing up boulderfields. ("There's no flesh on this land. It's all bone," Grampy Sam's own son had said the week before he went to Ohio.) Grampy Sam laughed when he argued for relatives to stay and reminded them that New York and Ohio had gotten at least as much summer snow in 1816 as Vermont, but that there just hadn't been enough people out there to do a decent job of complaining about it. He had no comments to make about plowing boulderfields nor any answer that would change the minds of those who spoke of restlessness, overcrowding, or the need to strike out on their own into unsettled land. They had left in droves. Some, on the point of departure, had quite unkindly commented that in a few years only the lazy and shiftless would be left behind in Vermont or New Hampshire; that anyone with energy, ambition, or intelligence would go west. Benjie remembered those words and sometimes wondered if he would want to move out west when he got older. For the time being he was having too much fun right in Barston Falls. If he wanted adventure, then there were many places up and down the Connecticut to explore before he would give much thought to going west.

Benjie yawned and stretched and then headed down towards the lower bridge across the canal, where he was to meet Foss and Tom.

XI

The three boys stood on the west side of the canal next to the first lock and stared out over the bay as far as they could see downriver.

"Nope," Tom said. "Nothin' comin' up."

"And Pa won't have 'em bring down a box unless there's a flatboat to send up the canal first," Benjie said. "At least not 'til he catches up on some other work."

"Don't s'pose we'll need our spears," Foss said.

"Let's put 'em in the warehouse," Benjie said, "and go see if Malik's asleep. A flatboat might come up later in the afternoon. There's no tellin'."

"Blue paint?" Tom asked.

"If he's asleep, we'll go back for it," Benjie said. "Pa might get after me if we keep takin' paint every time we think there's a chance to do up Malik."

The three put their spears into the warehouse and then walked to the lower end of the canal. They could have crossed on the bridge up at the second lock or on top of the closed gates between the first and second locks, but they never even mentioned the possibility. Instead they plunged into the water right at the mouth of the canal, swam across, and waded up onto the broken rock and ledges on the other side. Then they marched over toward the point to find Malik.

Three boyish oaths rent the air. Malik was wide awake. He and the girl were fishing side-by-side, knee deep in the water. They talked constantly and didn't even notice the boys. Malik gestured up the river and then swept his arm and the girl's attention out towards the eddy and the bay.

"Look at him," Tom said. "He don't look drunk at all. No blue paint today, I guess."

"Guess not," Foss said. "Well, we could go up and see what George is poundin' on this afternoon — hold a horse for him if he's shoein' it maybe. It's always good if you're there when Annie brings over somethin'. My ma's food tastes like sawdust compared to what Annie cooks."

"Can't say I'm any too hungry," Benjie said, "but let's go up anyways. Nothin' here for us and won't be 'til Malik and that fat girl stop jabberin' and he gets to drinkin' again."

"Sure," Tom said. "Let's go."

* * * * *

George Ballard, the only blacksmith in Barston Falls, ran his shop at the north end of the village square. George was a coarse-featured man in his late twenties. Red hair poked out around his head in unmanageable clumps and would have looked better cut short if it hadn't been for his ears, which stuck out almost as far as his hair. A thick spray of freckles covered his face and concentrated into a pale-red birthmark the size of a man's hand on the right side of his neck and upper chest. His fingernails were chewed short, yet always managed to have thin lines of dirt under them from his work. A decade of constant blacksmithing had left him with an upper right arm which gave Annie difficulty when she made his shirts and with a right shoulder so limbered from work that it seemed half a foot lower than his left. People noticed George's teeth more than his other features, for they were large, white, crooked, and always on display. George was a favorite in the village because of his ready smile and because of his evenness: a nature seemingly never subject to anger or despair. Men liked him for his steady and unruffled approach to doing high-quality work and for the low prices he charged. Children

liked him because he never ignored them; treated them as if they were the same age as he himself. Occasionally he would caution them about getting too close when he was working with hot iron, but if there were any other limits on children wandering in and out of his blacksmith shop whenever they wanted to, it was because the parents of those children had imposed them. Women liked him because of his slightly bashful regard for them, because he was always good to the children, and because the effect of his cheerful nature lingered with the men of the village after they'd been visiting him for blacksmithing work or otherwise.

George pumped the bellows until the red coals burning around a piece of iron in his forge had turned white. He was making a froe; had already formed the eye and with his pounding had nearly finished drawing out a blade edge on the flat metal slab. He turned the froe in the coals with tongs, pumped the bellows anew, and then took up his two-pound hammer. He snatched the glowing froe up onto his anvil and continued drawing out the edge.

Three boys stood watching the sparks fly from the anvil with the first half-dozen hard blows of the hammer, quietly worshipping the strength of the blacksmith.

"Be with you soon, men," George said. "I'm nearly done with this."

George hammered with the rhythm he had always used: one hard blow followed by two light taps and then the three strokes repeated until either the metal needed reheating or else the work was done. George worked quickly, evening the splitting edge of the froe along its full length. At last he turned the froe repeatedly with the tongs to inspect it, gave a nod of approval, and plunged the hot metal into the tub of water behind him. After the violent hiss and boil George lifted the froe steaming from the tub and dropped it into a box of sand.

"There," George said, smiling his wide smile as he set

aside the tongs. "If it's a froe you men need today, you're in luck. It's ready to hang and sharpen."

"We don't need a froe today, George," Benjie said. "Just wanted to see if you might need a horse held or if we could help some other way."

"Well, I don't have shoein' to do unless somebody just shows up — nothin' arranged, I mean. But I tell you what. There's a load of charcoal comin' sometime this afternoon, and I can use a few good men to help me unload. This mornin' your pa said it'd be here today, Benjie."

"Be glad to help, George," Tom said.

"Sure would," Foss added.

"Well thanks. Now how's the fishin and huntin' business with you men?"

"It's slow, George," Benjie said.

"Well it's a hard way for a man to make a livin' these days, but I s'pose if anyone can, it's the three of you," George said.

"If we had salmon like in the old days, things 'd be different," Foss said. "But we don't. And they say you could practically catch 'em with your hands."

"They never should of went and put in the dams," Tom said. "Didn't need 'em, for one thing. They got by fine when they just had the carries. Didn't need all the canals and dams, just carry roads and freight wagons. Should of left the salmon alone."

"That's the truth, Tom," George said. "But a lot of men can't let well enough alone; think they can make their own work a little easier, so they go ahead and do it and don't care what happens on account of it. It ain't right, but it happens. I sure wouldn't mind if we still had salmon in the river."

"Me neither, George," Benjie said. "How's work with you?"

"Busy enough. Fact is I got three other jobs to start and

finish 'fore I can shut down the forge tonight. So you men make yourselves at home. I can use your help with the charcoal if you're here when it comes, but I don't know when that might be, so if you get tired of waitin', don't feel like you got to stay here all afternoon."

George got back to work. The three boys loafed both inside and outside the shop talking among themselves about fishing and hunting, with George, and with customers coming into the shop. The boys felt quite proud to have George Ballard as a friend.

In the middle of the afternoon the three boys' faces broke into wide smiles when Annie Ballard entered the blacksmith shop. They liked Annie at least as much as they liked George and at that moment liked her even more because of the covered basket she carried.

"They're right out of the oven, George, and I was afraid you might be wastin' away before supper. You'll have to share 'em now, but I think I made enough."

Annie smiled at the boys. All three of them compared her to their own mothers and silently bemoaned their bad luck. If anyone had then commented to them that she was over-large and plain-featured, they would have argued the point — with their small fists if necessary.

"The men are here to help me unload charcoal, just as soon as it comes," George said. "Might as well feed 'em, Annie, if I'm goin' to get any work out of 'em."

It was pie and cookies both in the basket. The pie was too hot to eat. Annie set it on top of the anvil to cool and helped George and the boys make two dozen cookies disappear. While Annie was checking the pie, Joe Reckford came in. He stood before them; huge, awkward, ill-at-ease.

"Help you?" George asked.

"Your charcoal's out in the wagon in barrels and sacks, Mr. Ballard. They need the barrels and sacks back, so I'll

78

have to take 'em with me. Tell me where to unload it, and I'll get right to work."

"Fine, but call me George. There's a bin where I keep it over there on the side. I'll give a hand, and we got three more men to keep us from overworkin'. Then after we're done there's a pie that needs eatin'. Should be cool enough by then."

"Don't mean to put you to any trouble," Joe said, fidgeting from foot to foot with his eyes downcast. "Can be dirty work carryin' charcoal."

"So little trouble," George said, "that it ain't worth mentionin'."

The two men and three boys set to work. The men managed the barrels and sacks of charcoal, carrying them from the wagon and dumping them into the bin. George told Joe to let the boys carry the empty barrels and sacks back to the wagon, so he did. Annie set the pie outside to get it away from the cloud of charcoal dust by the bin and watched. When she noticed that only two of the boys had anything to take back to the wagon each time the men carried in charcoal, she spoke up.

"I'll help carry in to even things up," she announced.

She promptly slung a sack of charcoal over her shoulder, carried it in to the bin, dumped it out, and handed the empty sack to Foss. She went back out and tried to lift a barrel, but finding it too awkward or heavy, carried only sacks of charcoal after that. Each time she passed by Joe walking between the wagon and the charcoal bin, she was surprised at how nervous he was; how quickly he averted his eyes when she saw him looking at her.

The work, which might have taken Joe half an hour by himself, was soon finished. The six people — all sweating hard and dusted to varying degrees with charcoal — stood together outside the blacksmith shop catching their breaths. Annie's shoulder was well-darkened with dust from the sacks. Streaks of black ran across her face where she had wiped off the sweat. George laughed at her, wet a rag, and took off the worst of the black. He brushed at her shoulder, but the sweat there had fixed the charcoal dust.

"You're a good man to have around, Annie," George said.

All of them laughed.

"I thank you for your help," Joe said. "Now Mr. Barston 'll be wantin' me to ..."

"No you don't," George said. "We helped you unload, so now you got to help us with a pie. Can't go 'til it's all gone. Can he, Annie?"

Annie took a long look at Joe Reckford, puzzled at why he should be so obviously ill-at-ease; so unwilling to meet her glance.

"No. George is right," she said. "You got to eat pie with us 'fore you go, but first tell me your name."

"It's Reckford, ma'am. Joe Reckford." He paused, as if he were done speaking, but then blurted out more words. "I'm sorry you got charcoal on your dress. I thank you for your help, but I wish you hadn't of got your dress dirty for the trouble you took."

"It ain't anythin' that won't wash right out," she said. "And my name is Annie Ballard, Joe. That's what you should call me: 'Annie'. And don't you go callin' George anythin' but 'George' or he'll start gettin' unreasonable ideas about how important he is and be impossible to live with. That agreed?"

"Yes ... Annie."

"That's better. And these boys are Benjie Barston, Foss Richardson, and Tom Beasley. Now you sit right down there and rest and help us get rid of that pie."

The six of them sat outside the blacksmith shop, gathered around the pie. They all laughed as Annie cut it with the brand new froe, George claiming that it was probably the only dried-apple pie in the history of Barston or perhaps the whole state of Vermont that had ever required a froe to split off a piece. He joked about "shingle pie" and "clapboard pie." Annie served it into their hands, and it was soon gone. Joe rose to go and wiped his hands on the seat of his pants.

"I thank you for unloadin' the wagon, and I thank you for the pie. That was the best one I've ate for ten years. I mean it. Glad to meet you, George and Annie Ballard, and you boys too. Now I got to go see what Mr. Barston wants me workin' at next."

"Come back any time you want," George said.

"Thanks," Joe said. He untied the horses from the hitching post, climbed up onto the wagon, and drove it away through the village square on his way down to the lower bridge.

"There goes the shyest man in Barston," George said.

"Sure is," Annie said. "Know anythin' about him?"

"Nothin' more 'n what Mark Hosmer tells me," George said. "Mark's worked with him for a month and a half now and hardly knows him. A widower with a daughter to care for. They rent one of those little brick houses from Tom Barston. Mark says he's as quiet now as he was six weeks ago and that he won't say much more 'n about a dozen words a day. He's the quietest man in Barston, and I tell you he's the strongest man in Barston too."

"No!" Benjie said. "Stronger 'n you, George? Stronger 'n Mark Hosmer?"

"That's right. Mark's a good deal stronger 'n I am. We found that out some time back. And Mark says he can't hold a candle to Joe Reckford. The two of 'em carry a lot of things down at the warehouse, and Mark told me that when there are things he can't hardly budge, Joe just picks 'em up and strolls away with 'em like they was a basket of flowers. That's how strong he is."

"Sure is a big man," Annie said. "But how come he's so nervous around people? Somebody that big and strong you'd think 'd just boom words out and walk where he pleased, leavin' it to others to get out of his way. But that Joe Reckford looks like a puppy's shadow 'd make him jump. I wonder why."

"Careful Annie," George said. "You pay too much attention to him, and I might get jealous. I expect you like him better 'n me already on account of what he said about your pie. Next thing you'll be claimin' he's better lookin' than me. A man could get wicked jealous, even if I am ..."

"Ha! Who could be better lookin' than you, George?" she said, reaching up and running her fingers through his hair. "Hair a mad porcupine 'd envy, and red too! Ears there ready for anybody drowndin' to grab hold of. A big birthspot and more freckles than anybody can count and handsome skin around 'em just the color of a frog belly. What could be better lookin' than that?"

George smiled. The boys laughed.

"But don't just take my word on it, George," Annie continued. "We'll put it out to a jury. You boys ain't seen many better lookin' men in town than George, have you? 'Cept for yourselves I mean. Wouldn't you say he's just about the best lookin' blacksmith in the village?"

"Sure Annie," Benjie said. "Just about."

"There, Annie," George said. "You heard it. Now I want you to appreciate me more."

"All right, George," Annie said as she put the pie plate back into the basket. "I'll think about you the whole time I'm cookin' your supper. I won't even think about lookin' at another man."

Annie left George and the boys behind and walked down through the village square to see what she could get for supper. As she walked, in spite of her words to George, she couldn't help puzzling over Joe Reckford.

XII

Sue knelt beside Malik, occasionally glancing at the quick, sure movements of his hands as he cleaned fish. Six days earlier, when they had begun fishing together, he had seemed such a frail, old man, but each day since then he had strengthened by eating the food she had given him. His astonishing appetite had made her wonder how long it had been since he'd eaten decent food regularly. Each day his face lost some of its drawn and haggard look, his shoulders weren't so hunched over the thinness of his chest, and he looked better rested.

Sue had caught many fish with Malik every day. On the first day of their partnership Malik had taken their catch up to the village square to show Sue where to trade, calling out loudly to passers-by and seeking as actively as a man could to sell fish. Sue had sat by him silently then. Toward the end of each afternoon on the following days, she had gone to the square by herself with her fish basket and had left him to fish.

Each day she had sat and waited at the spot where people had been used to buying fish from Malik. Reluctant to call attention to herself by urging people to buy from her, she had set a few fish from her basket out onto a cloth, had waited for customers to come, and had sold fish that way. She had settled sales awkwardly. Too embarrassed to set a price for the fish, she had told people to pay her what they usually paid Malik. Some customers, she thought, took advantage of her because she didn't want to haggle.

Occasionally, she was certain, people stared at the hugeness of her hands and feet and gazed in wonder at her height and bulk, as if she were a freak of nature to have such a young face on so large a body. That had caused her to wear a perpetual blush and to stay sitting most of the time so that people couldn't see as easily how large she was.

Sue took goods-in-trade for the fish and a few — very few — coins. Each day after the fish were gone she took the goods to the store on the east side of the square and exchanged them there for things she and her father could better use. Then she would return to Malik and divide with him whatever fish he had caught in her absence. Finally Sue would go home and cook her father's supper. Malik always stayed and fished after she had gone home, making a supper of food Sue had left with him and, she supposed, eating fish for breakfast.

For six days they had fished together, eaten together, and talked. That had been Sue's biggest surprise: how much Malik had talked. He had spoken of his childhood, of his friends, of hunting and trapping, and of fishing in the Connecticut in the early years. Sue mourned with him the loss of salmon from the river. He had surprised her with his accounts of driving sawlogs and masts down the Connecticut for a man named Parker, who had lived in North Barston — working in those years with Old Sam Barston. He told her of the Great Falls down the river, of how treacherous the water had been there in the days when the river was higher and before the canal had been dug, of how good the salmon and shad fishing had been, and of the difficulties in getting masts and sawlogs past the Falls. He described how he and others used to fish at Barston Falls when the salmon had still been in the river. As nearly as Sue could tell from his accounts, the salmon had been gone for about thirty years.

On the second day of their partnership, while they had been eating, Malik had suddenly pulled at a leather thong around his neck and had drawn out an old medallion from his shirt. He lifted the thong over his head and handed the medallion to her. It was a disk about three inches across, black with tarnish. Sue thought it might be silver, but she couldn't be certain. On one side there was a curious design: the heads of three cats underneath a strange-looking horse that seemed to have wings sprouted out of its back. Beneath the cats were four words which made no sense to Sue, but she thought it was because of her poor reading skills: *"En Dieu Est Tout."* She had better luck with the inscription on the other side. Malik's name was there and words of thanks and friendship for something he had done in 1768 and in 1773. At the bottom of that inscription was the name "John Wentworth."

"Governor," Malik had said and after a while had made her understand that it was the old British governor for New Hampshire before the Revolution. Malik claimed he had shown the governor many places in the upper Connecticut River Valley, over by the headwaters of the Androscoggin River, and north of Lake Umbagog. Sue wondered at Malik's pride for having gotten a medallion from the hated old Governor Wentworth. She remembered having heard from her father about Governor Wentworth's greed: granting vast areas of land to himself and making thousands and thousands of pounds by selling ship masts.

The day after Malik had shown her the medallion, he had made her stop fishing for an hour in the middle of the morning, saying that he had something to show her. He had then taken her along the west bank of the river up by the head of the falls and had pointed out carvings on the rocks: crude outlines of heads for the most part, some with representations of feathers decorating the tops in Indian fashion. Malik said that the carvings were from the ancient times; that they had been there long before any of the oldest men he'd known as a boy could remember. Sue had admired them, and then they had gone back down to fish at the point.

During the six days they'd been fishing together, Malik had had no rum as far as Sue could tell, for he'd had nothing to trade but a few fish he had caught at the end of each day. She assumed he had eaten those fish in addition to the food she had left him, but if he had traded them, they wouldn't have brought him much rum. When Sue had traded, it had been mostly for other food, part of which she had cooked and given to Malik. The third day, however, she had been increasingly conscious that the value of Malik's share of the fish was greater than the value of the food she'd been giving him. She had suggested that he allow her to trade for new clothes, but he didn't want new clothes. He wanted rum. The following two days he had told her the same thing. Reluctantly she had gotten rum the day before — filling an old bottle from her house with it. However, she hadn't given the rum to him then. It had sat at the bottom of her fish basket the whole time. Now with the fish cleaned and ready to rinse and be put into her basket so she could carry them to the village square, she had to decide whether to put them in on top of the bottle or not.

"Here, Malik," she said at last. "Here's rum I got for your share of the fish. The bottle belongs to Pa, so I'll need it back when you're done with it."

He took the rum greedily from her as she began rinsing off the cleaned fish and loading them into her basket. He unstoppered his empty bottle with the woven wrapping on it. Then, even before he'd begun to fill it, he took a long drink from the bottle she had given him. When she left with the basket of fish, he was drinking from his own bottle, the other resting empty on the ground. He hadn't changed a bit she thought. She wondered how drunk he would be when she got back from trading the fish; whether he would be any help at all the following day. She thought about Malik all the way up to the village square, as she had thought about him — and prayed for him — each of the nights since they had begun fishing together.

* * * * *

Foss Richardson yawned and ran the fingers of one hand through his red hair. He, Benjie, and Tom were riding on a box of lumber down through the canal. Foss glanced at Benjie and Tom standing on the end of the box with their spears ready and scanning the water closely as the middle lock began to drain. The two of them by themselves could certainly spear whatever fish might appear. They didn't need him. Before the water in the lock had dropped more than a few inches, he set down his spear and hopped from the lumber box over onto the east side of the canal. Benjie looked at him for a moment, but then quickly turned his gaze back to the water at the end of the box.

"Be back in a little," Foss said. "Take care of my spear." He jumped over the sluiceway and disappeared as he walked between two of the mills.

Foss returned when the box of lumber was in the lower lock; stepped down onto it and then peered over the shoulders of the other two boys.

"Any fish?" he asked.

"Not yet," Benjie said. "Might not get a thing this time."

Foss looked around to see where Joe Reckford and Mark Hosmer were; then spoke in a low voice.

"Malik's there alone, and he's drinkin'. Maybe we'll get him today."

"Alone? That fat girl finally gone?" Benjie asked.

"Well, she ain't there now. He's got rum, and he's pourin' it right down. If he keeps it up like that, he'll have a long sleep sometime today."

"We don't want to miss it if he takes a nap," Tom said.

"A nice, long nap," Benjie said. "A nice, long, blue nap."

"He'll be awake for a while yet," Foss said. "There ain't any hurry to get over there."

The three boys stayed on the box of lumber as Mark, Joe, and the horses moved it from the lower lock over to the wharf by the warehouse. The boys hadn't speared any fish, but weren't disappointed. The thought of Malik alone and drinking again took their minds off the fishing. They wandered into the warehouse long enough to drop off their spears and to make sure that the blue paint was still where they could get it quickly. Then they swam across the mouth of the canal and strolled over towards Malik's fishing point. They sat up on the ledges about as far as they could be from Malik and yet still keep an eye on him as he sat down by the water's edge. They sprawled out after a while, talking and laughing in low voices; watching and waiting.

"Hey Benjie," Tom said after what the three boys thought had been a long time. "He's asleep!"

Benjie sat up abruptly and stared down towards Malik.

"Looks like it from here. You two wait while I go down and check."

Benjie went down the hill quickly, stood over Malik for a brief moment, then grabbed one of the Indian's feet and gave it a shake. He shook it several times, but couldn't rouse Malik. With a great grin on his face he returned to Tom and Foss.

"Blue Injun day! Let's go!"

The three boys bounded over to the canal, swam it, and then raced one another to the lower warehouse.

* * * * *

With her basket of fish next to her Sue sat on the ground at the southeast corner of the village square. She leaned against a large stump. Beneath growths of fungus the stump still bore charred marks from the fire which had killed the tree eighteen years before. Out across the square Sue noticed that all the trees were small. Though she didn't know it, those trees she saw — all elms — were ones Israel Barston had planted after the great fire of 1804 had destroyed the earlier village. He had laid out the public park in the middle of the village square, intending it as a place for villagers to meet or to sit and relax and hoping to live long enough himself to enjoy the shade of the elms on hot summer days. Israel had placed the four rows of buildings surrounding the square so that each was five rods from his park, thus leaving ample space for people in carriages to get by standing horses and wagons and go about their business.

As Sue waited for customers to come buy her fish, she was lost in reverie. She played a game she had often played before: watching women one at a time and trying to decide if she would like to be the particular woman she was studying.

An old woman ... small ... harsh eyes ... tight-lipped ... *No, I wouldn't like to be her.* A young mother carrying a year-old infant ... *Yes, she's happy and small ... little hands ... a nice shape to her and pretty in that blue dress* ... three girls about fourteen years old, all small and giggling; two with brown hair and one with straw-colored ... *Yes it'd be nice to be one of those three* ... A wiry, forty-year-old woman with gray hair and obvious toughness in the way she walked ... an average height ... face browned from many hours in the sun ... harsh, red hands probably from a great deal of work in a washtub ... *Yes* ... A short, fat woman waddling through the square ... likely not more than twenty years old ... stubby fingers ... round shapelessness ... *No, but at least she's not too tall* ... A tall and husky woman carrying a basket ... firm stride ... smiling and greeting people ... stopping for a moment to talk with a shopkeeper ... not quite young, perhaps twenty-five years old ... brown hair ... plain face ... a nice way of smiling ... strong looking ... big ... *big as me. No, she's too big. Best one's that little woman with the baby. The brown-haired woman has a nice smile, but she's half a foot too tall and too husky ... but she's comin' here ... she's comin' right to me.*

"You still fishin' with Malik these days?" the brown-haired woman asked.

Sue stood up. She didn't feel awkward standing in front of a woman as tall as she was herself, but still she was bashful speaking; her words came quietly, and her gaze couldn't fix on the dark eyes of the brown-haired woman for more than a moment before it dropped towards the ground again.

"Yes, ma'am. He stays down fishin' while I'm up here."

"Got any fish left today?"

"Yes, ma'am." Sue uncovered the basket and showed the remaining perch to the woman.

"George liked the last ones I got. Guess I'll take all of those. That man eats like a horse. Works like one and eats like one. Wait. Here's a cloth to wrap 'em in."

Sue dumped the fish onto the cloth, spread them out, and counted them.

"Price the same as last time?" the woman asked.

"Yes, ma'am."

"Well I have coins again — George gets 'em at the black-smith shop. If coins ain't what you want, I can go trade for somethin' else at the store."

"I can do that, ma'am," Sue said. "Coins are fine."

"Well thanks for the fish," the woman said, counting out a few coins and handing them to Sue.

"You're welcome, ma'am."

"Now you call me 'Annie' the way everybody else does, for I'm uncomfortable if you call me anythin' else. I'm Annie Ballard. What's your name?"

"Sue. Sue Reckford."

"Oh ... Reckford. Then that was your father drivin' the

wagon the other day, deliverin' charcoal at the blacksmith shop. Pleased to meet you, Sue."

Sue's downcast eyes for a moment kept her from seeing Annie's outstretched hand. When she did notice, she made an awkward lunge for it. Her face burned in embarrassment at her clumsiness, but the woman seemed not to notice. She took Sue's hand briefly in her own strong, large-boned grip and looked evenly at her with dark brown eyes.

"He ... he works at the lower warehouse and takes boats through the canal too," Sue said.

"And where do you live, Sue?"

"Pa rents a little brick house from Tom Barston," Sue said. "Over the lower bridge, straight across the old carry road. We're on the left, three houses past the carry road."

"Well, George and I live up north of the square right across from where Tannery Road begins. We both like fish, so if you ever have trouble tradin', think about haulin' your fish on up to us. We'll likely buy some."

"Thank you," Sue said. The blush wouldn't leave her cheeks. She continued to stare at the ground.

"You had a chance to meet many people in the village yet, Sue?"

"Pa and I are mostly too busy to meet people," Sue said.

"And how old are you now?"

"Twelve. Be thirteen in September."

Annie laughed and looked hard at Sue.

"I remember how it was for me when I was your age. I had your size when I was eleven, and my brothers teased me awful about it. I used to slouch down so folks wouldn't think I was so big. Then I stopped growin' all of a sudden, and every one of my brothers got bigger 'n me. But you ain't got any brothers?"

"No. It's just my pa and me. Ma died when I was two."

"Well enough of my pesterin' questions, Sue, but I just

wanted to know a little about you. Come see me if there's fish you can't sell here, or just come up and see me for no special reason."

Annie Ballard turned to go, but then stopped abruptly.

"No, Sue. Before I go I'll hear you call me 'Annie.' You ain't done that yet."

"Annie."

"Good. Now you call me 'Annie' again the next time you see me. That understood? 'Annie' and nothin' else. None of this 'ma'am' any more. Don't forget. All right?"

Annie put her hand on Sue's shoulder and gave it a squeeze.

"All right, Annie."

"That's better. Good-by, Sue."

Sue watched Annie walk through the square and disappear up towards where she and George Ballard lived. As Sue set out to rejoin Malik, she wondered further about what it would be like to be Annie Ballard.

* * * * *

Sue leaned over Malik, dabbing at the wet paint on his face with a handful of grass. She threw away the grass and stripped off a handful of leaves from a yellow birch sapling, this time wiping clean a small patch of skin on one cheek except where the blue had settled into the deep wrinkles. Soon she had used up all the grass and leaves within reach and had to move over to get more from plants rooted in another wide crack in the ledges.

"Malik. Malik, wake up," she kept saying between stints of trying to get the paint off the old man's skin. He groaned when she shook him hard, but would not wake up. Shaking him, slapping him, and talking loudly to him wouldn't pull him from his stupor. Her efforts quickly fouled her own hands with blue paint.

Sue had shed several tears of pity when she'd discovered Malik, but they had disappeared quickly. Anger had abruptly replaced all other feelings. She was furious with the three boys. No one else would have painted him blue: his face, hair, hands, bare feet, shirt, and britches. Not having the boys there to vent her rage on, she directed it instead at Malik.

"You got no sense at all," she muttered. "Useless, old drunken fool. Swill down the rum first chance you get. Let people do whatever they want to you. Well there's nobody to blame but yourself. Don't know why I should even bother with you."

And yet for over an hour she did what she could to clean his face and hands and feet. She didn't bother with his clothes; nor was there any way to clean the paint out of his hair. While she was working, she saw the three boys briefly looking down at her from up on the ledges. She grew more angry thinking about them and half-made up her mind to confront all three of them, but they left while she was still thinking.

Her anger gradually cooled. In its place she felt disgust for Malik and his drunkenness. He still hadn't awakened when she finally decided that she had done all she would for him. Before she left to go home, she emptied Malik's rum bottle into her father's bottle, which had held the same rum earlier. There would be no more rum for Malik when he awoke, she decided. She would give it all to her father, who would enjoy it over a number of days and who had sense enough not to besot himself. Malik would wear his blue badge of shame for a long time, she thought. Well, he deserved it. As she left, she decided that since Malik would be useless on the following day, she would fish just for herself then. Malik would get no more food from her until he could catch fish again.

XIII

Sue fished alone the next morning, trying to decide on the words she would use when Malik appeared. For certain, she would give him food only after he'd earned it. Never again would she get rum for him. The image of the thin, old man lying on his back in a stupor and covered with blue paint kept throwing Sue into alternate moods of rage and disgust. She felt no pity any more for the old Indian, having decided the night before that he'd been as much to blame as the three boys for getting himself painted. From time to time as she fished, she glanced over at spots of blue on the rocks, in the dirt between ledges, and on twisted wads of grass and leaves. She divided her anger evenly between Malik and the gang of boys.

Malik hadn't appeared by mid day. Sue's anger towards him slowly gave way to concern, which nagged at her until mid afternoon. Then she decided to find Malik. Of course he wasn't to have food from her. He needed a lesson, in fact. Though Sue wasn't hungry, she ate what remained of her food so there'd be none left even if Malik begged her for it. After that she put the fish she had caught into the shade and went in search of the old Indian.

Sue didn't know where Malik lived — only that Old Sam Barston let him live somewhere on land he owned.

"Very well," she thought. "I'll find Old Sam Barston and ask him."

She got directions in the village square, crossed the upper bridge, and went up Tannery Road to the six brick houses. Old Sam Barston, according to her directions, lived in the third brick house on the left. She gazed at the six buildings as her steps slowed, thinking that any of them would have made four or six houses the size of the one she and her father lived in. Nervous and embarrassed, Sue went up Old Sam's brick walkway, mounted the three quarried stone steps to the huge doorstep, and knocked on the door as loudly as she dared. There was no answer. She knocked again three or four times, more loudly and with less embarrassment each time.

"What do you want?" someone bellowed from the house next door. The abrupt loudness of the voice startled several pigs in a pen off the side of that house. Their brief squeals trailed off into nervous grunts as they milled around. Sue lifted her gaze from them to a man leaning out of an upstairs window. He was probably in his early thirties, fat, mostly bald, and looking as if he'd been asleep.

"I'm tryin' to find Old Sam Barston," Sue said.

"Not home. Prob'ly at the tannery."

Sue stood unmoving for a moment. The man spoke again with a wave of his hand.

"Straight up the road on the right. The tannery. You can't miss it."

The man yawned and ducked his head back inside the window. Sue continued on up Tannery Road.

She smelled the tannery before she saw it, wrinkling her nose at the clinging and all-pervading stench of rotting flesh. Then she saw the tannery itself: a long, narrow, brick building standing low to the ground between the road and Tannery Brook. As Sue approached the building, she saw many large, coopered vats scattered around outside. Each stood two feet tall and might have been ten feet across. The staves of each vat were banded with iron hoops. About half the vats had covers of planks, held down with rocks. Looking into several empty and uncovered ones, Sue saw that they were sunk into the ground four or five feet. Just east of the vats stood several huge stacks of hemlock bark.

There was only one man inside the building. He was busy sorting through tanned hides and stacking them into half a dozen different piles. Sue approached him, hesitating before she spoke.

"A man said I might find Old Sam Barston here."

"Well you might if you was earlier or later, but Old Sam don't like to spend much time with the hides these days. You'll find him down back fishin' in the brook."

"Well, thank you," Sue said.

The man nodded and waved in the general direction of the brook. Sue walked back out the door she had entered and circled around to the back of the brick building. There she passed a series of wooden sheds which sheltered piles of burned lime and ground hemlock bark. Beyond them was a dumping ground for old hair — cords and cords of it flung out to rot. She continued on down to the brook.

Sue soon spotted Old Sam fishing in a pool upstream. He was a heavy, round-faced man with white hair and a white stubble of beard and with deep wrinkles around his eyes and on the lower contours of his cheeks. He was intent on his fishing and didn't notice her as she approached; was talking loudly even though there was no one Sue could see for him to talk to.

"Come on you worthless runts. Run home and find your grandpa and send him up to Old Sam. There's a good meal down there for anybody that's more 'n just a sawed-off runt. Take it. Take it. That's it ... hit it again ... again ... There!"

The old man straightened his stooped shoulders and pulled at his bending pole. He hoisted a trout out of the water and swung it over to where he could grab it. Then with the fish in hand — a trout of about ten inches — he began lecturing to it as he worked the hook free.

"Ha! You call yourself a trout, I s'pose. You puff up and swagger like you're somethin' special, but the truth is that you ain't but a runt like everythin' else in this brook. In the old days we would of thought twice about usin' somethin' so puny even for bait. Not but about half a mouthful for the trout I used to get here. Well you run on home and see if there ain't some old folks around that might want to meet Old Sam, and send 'em back to me. Go home and grow up and stop pesterin' an old man like me 'cause I got just so much time left and can't waste it fussin' with minnows!"

He threw the fish back into the water with an awkward twitch of his arm, wiped his hands on his britches, and hunched over a small firkin, which evidently contained some sort of bait. He was muttering to himself when Sue walked up beside him.

"Well hello! Hello! Company I see. Up to buy a hide for shoe-leather?"

"No. I don't need ..."

"Well then. Up to throw scripture at me and prime my soul?"

"No, not that either. I ..."

"Of course not. Not with that look in your eye, young lady. You're up to court me. Out huntin' for a husband, found the best lookin' man around, and hope I'll marry you. But where's the pie? Where's the cake? You can't expect to marry me if you didn't bring so much as a cookie. If you're only a pretty young creature and forget the food when you come courtin' me, then you're wastin' your time. Go right home and bake. Bake!"

The outrageous bluster of the old man melted away Sue's nervousness. A smile spread over her face at his accusation that she had come to court him — a wrinkled, fat, lump of a man close to eighty years old if he were a day.

"I want to know if you can tell me where Malik lives. You are Old Sam Barston, ain't you?"

"That I am. And that old woodchuck, Malik, lives in a shelter up by the big boulder. If you go up and stand on the road by the tannery, you can look up the slope and see the white boulder with the cliffs on Barston Hill up behind it. His shelter's in a straight line between the tannery and the boulder and practically right up to the boulder. Fact is, if the boulder ever started to roll, it'd likely squash down the old Injun to about two inches thick; no tellin' how wide. Now what on earth would you ...? Course! You're the one he's fishin' with. Partners. Every day the two of you fish together, he says. Wanted me to come down and be a partner too, but I got too many creaks in my joints for that. And fishin' for what — perch and maybe eels? Not when I got trout right here in Tannery Brook. Malik's got no shame. Grown man fishin' for perch!"

"Yes. We fish together, but he didn't come this mornin' and I thought ..."

"Think the old goat's went and died on us?"

"He had rum yesterday afternoon and he ..."

"Oh, just drunk again then. Well he does that from time to time. Gets drunk and stays drunk 'til the rum or whiskey's gone. Eli and me and Nabatis and a few others — well you wouldn't know any of his old friends — tried to talk him out of his ways once, but that was a waste of time. We gave up on him and his drinkin' years ago. Best thing to do when Malik's got rum is to be right there helpin' him drink it. Help him as much as you can by drinkin' rum that otherwise would of wound up inside his stomach. Don't let him get so far down in his drink, and it ain't so far for him to crawl back up out of it when the rum's gone. He have a bit yesterday?"

"I couldn't wake him. And while he was asleep somebody painted him all blue."

"What? All blue! All blue like that on your hand?"

"Yes. I tried to clean him off, but I couldn't do a very good ..."

Old Sam's laughter interrupted her. "Blue all over?"

"They painted over his britches and shirt, but got him

everyplace else. I got a little of it off his face and hands and feet, but that was about all."

"Well, well, well. I was goin' to just point you up to Malik's shelter and let you find your own way, but I can see right now that even if my joints creak 'til I'm deaf, I'll take you up there myself. I don't get to see a blue Injun every day. And Malik too! Yes indeed. I'll remind him of this for some time to come and see if I can't make him blush right through all that blue."

Old Sam put a lid onto his bait firkin and sank the hook into the butt of the pole. With a shaky, tottering step he went with Sue up to the back of the tannery, put the firkin into the shade, hung his pole on some pegs, and grabbed a huge old walking stick. Then he led Sue across the road and onto the cleared slopes rising up towards Barston Hill. Sue saw the boulder quickly, but couldn't see the shelter Old Sam said was in front of it. Though they walked slowly, the old man was soon red-faced and out of breath and had to stop. Sue waited beside him as he leaned heavily on his cane. Gradually he regained his breath.

"Fat, old, and worthless," he said. "As you can see. But it wasn't always so. Fact is, back in my youth not only was I the handsomest man in the world, but I was the strongest too. When I found the spot to build my tannery on, I'll be cursed if there wasn't a great big rock right in the way. Well, you know what I did with that rock?'

"What?"

"Had fourteen friends help me put it on my shoulder, and I carried it up the hill. That's it right up there." He gestured up the hill. "That old white boulder with the dark stripes runnin' through it."

"But that's big as a house!" Sue said.

"Course it is! Don't you s'pose I know that better 'n anybody else? And now, fat and old, I don't know as I could carry it even half that far."

Sue laughed at Old Sam. They resumed their walking, but more slowly.

"Now I s'pose I better get to know you better," Old Sam said. "If you're goin' to come 'round courtin' me and laugh at my jokes too, I ain't one to let you slip away — not without puttin' up a pretty good fight, I ain't. And I like a woman with some size to her, too. Some men are drawn to those skinny, scrawny pullets that can lift just about a handful of potatoes before they wreck their backs and that get blown away every time there's a light breeze. Not me. I like a woman that casts a shadow. What's your name?"

"Sue Reckford."

"Sue. Good. Well, let me tell you, Sue, that this past week Malik has been better 'n I've seen him for years. You've helped him along somehow."

"You known him very long?"

"Close on to sixty years now," Old Sam said.

Old Sam's breathing got too fast for him to talk further. Sue asked if he wanted to rest again, but he shook his head and kept going. Sue walked in silence, slowing her steps. Suddenly she felt happy, as if a heavy deadness had been cast away from her. She liked Old Sam Barston and his teasing and joking.

As they got up closer to the boulder, Sue smelled smoke. She looked more closely and saw a low shelter: a three-foot-tall archway of limbs and hemlock bark perhaps four feet wide at the bottom and eight feet long. Smoke came from a pit out in front of the shelter.

"Where he lives," Old Sam said, sweating and breathing hard.

They waited for a few moments as Old Sam regained his breath. Sue looked out at the view from the slope of Barston Hill, admiring what she saw. Old Sam pointed out to her Eagle Hill, Moose Pond, Catamount Ridge and Hackmatack Ridge — both leading up to the top of Mount

Wheelock, and Rattlesnake Hill and Mount Moosilauke in the distance.

"I s'pose I'll sleep tonight," Old Sam said as they turned away from the view. "Now let's see if we can't find the old Injun."

Malik wasn't in his shelter, but Old Sam hadn't expected him to be.

"Just sleeps in it," he said. "Not big enough to do anythin' else. But look at the rocks in his firepit there. Those two are on top of the coals. That means he's got a sweat house here someplace for us to find. Likely the old goat is tryin' to sweat the blue paint out of his hide. Look around with me. Must be close. He won't want to haul the hot rocks very far."

Sue looked and didn't see a thing. Old Sam looked for a moment, then went back to the firepit.

"Here," he said. "He's draggin' the rocks, and there's his drag trail."

Sue went to Old Sam's side and looked at the scrapings in the dirt where he was pointing. Then she followed Old Sam a few rods. He stopped suddenly.

"There it is," he said, pointing at a bark-roofed structure rising scarcely a foot above the ground and surrounded by low bushes. "Dug in just like a woodchuck. What did I tell you?"

Old Sam went up to the entryway of the structure, slapped the roof several times, and screamed out a series of wild whoops. An answering whoop came from inside the sweat house. Malik's head poked out around the deer hide hanging in the entryway. There was a faded blueness to his hair and a blueness around his eyes and ears, but otherwise his sweating head was nearly clean.

"Hey you old goat," Old Sam said. "I brought my girlfriend, Sue, up here to see you, and I came myself to see what a blue Injun looks like. You all right?"

Malik glanced at Sue and looked hard back at Old Sam.

"Yes. You fat, old toad. Fat, old, white toad. Come in and sweat and melt away the fat that makes you carry two men on your back, Sam Barston."

"Always after my fat, you skinny old bas ... skinny old heron. Always jealous that I'm twice the man you'll ever be again. Well eat more, you old skeleton, and get your own fat. Now look here, you blue-haired Injun. I stole your woman. She's tired of squinchin' down her eyes every time she wants to see you and has decided to chase after a man who's easier to find."

"No, Sam Barston. Sue will leave you. She will see that all food near you goes down your throat and that only crumbs and bones remain for anyone trying to eat with Sam Barston. If I put salt on the great boulder, Sam Barston will eat it. Sue's hunger will soon drive her from Sam Barston to someone with skill to find food and without the great belly to fill that keeps all food from her mouth."

"Never. Why would she go back to a man who fishes for perch and eels when she could have one who fishes for trout and would fish only for salmon if we still had salmon in the river?"

"She is lost to you already, Sam Barston. She herself fishes for perch. Your trout are small jokes. Your salmon are only memories. Eat only your memories of salmon, Sam Barston, and soon you will be a proper size for an old man of your age. The perch are not salmon or trout, but they are there to catch in great numbers. She will stay with me, Sam Barston. You will see."

"What I'll see, you old goat, is that no woman wants a man with blue hair. Makes 'em nervous, it does. She'll go to a man with proper white hair — hair the color of winter snow — not the color of winter sky in the middle of the day when there ain't any clouds."

"Is the blue still in my hair?"

"Course it is, Malik. Sue ran screamin' away from that very same blue. She can't stand it. I don't know if you tried cleanin' it off yet or not, but I have to say that's the brightest blue I ever saw in my life — especially right there on top where you can't see."

Malik fingered the hair on top of his head, and Old Sam burst into laughter.

"Wait down by my shelter, Old Sam and Sue. Soon I will finish here."

"We'll wait down there, Malik, but there won't be anythin' to see even if you do forget your clothes — too skinny for that. You'll have to speak to us and jump up and down before we decide you ain't a cat-tail or a pickpole."

"Yes, Sam Barston. And some people are so fat that in their shadow the bats come out and the birds roost for the night."

"Well, I don't s'pose you know anybody like that, Malik," Old Sam said. "We'll be down at your shelter whenever you come."

Sue and Old Sam lingered by the shelter, glancing at Malik's meager possessions and gazing out over the views of Barston, of Wheelock across the river, and of the Connecticut Valley beyond the two townships. As they waited for Malik, Sue asked Old Sam questions that had been troubling her.

"How come Malik has to live up here in somethin' no bigger 'n a bear den? How come he eats old woodchucks or other things that anybody else 'd throw away?"

"He's a proud old Injun is why. It's the way he wants to live for one thing. Lord knows I've talked to him enough about it, but that man won't listen to common sense. I wanted him to come live in my house years ago, but he wouldn't hear of it. Always shows up here in the spring, builds his summer shelter, and leaves to spend his winters in the north country. He'll take a meal with me now and again, but when I try to give him a mound of food to use over a period of time or to carry north with him to help him through the winter, he just won't take it. Rather eat what he traps or hauls out of the river. He brings furs and baskets down with him every spring to trade. There's a pretty good demand for 'em around here, but before I found that out, I wound up with most of my attic full of baskets and furs. Used to have other folks buy 'em for me so Malik wouldn't know. Finally I traded 'em away downriver one winter when he was gone. If he thinks he's earned somethin', he'll use it. If he gets the idea that someone's tryin' to give him charity, he'll turn his back on it every time."

"How come he drinks so much rum?"

"Ha! S'pose I ain't asked him that a time or two?" Old Sam said, shaking his head. "Well to begin with everybody years ago used to drink two or three times more 'n they drink now. Rum, cider — everythin' is down to nothin' compared to what it used to be. We always said strong men needed strong spirits so they could do strong work. Drank a good deal in hayin' and ploughin', barn raisin's, and everythin' else. Now Malik, he just kept right on. Drank as much as he ever did, and then more, even though he didn't have any hard work. It's a pretty deep habit with him now."

"When he traded his fish, I think he always got rum," Sue said. "Rather have rum than food, and when he's got rum, he thinks he's got to drink it all right then. He pours it down his throat 'til he's so drunk nobody can wake him up."

"I know," Old Sam said. "He's done that a lot. That's why it surprised me to see him changed so after he started fishin' with you. He looked better 'n I've seen him for five years."

"Just no rum and eatin' good food for a change. He ate a lot. That's all the difference, I think. When he's tradin', he needs to get more food and less rum. Ain't there some way you can help him? Get him to change for his own good?"

"I thought about that for some time and ain't come up with anythin' yet. A few years back he fell into the river when he was drunk and nearly died on account of it, but even that didn't make him change. Only thing I can tell you is that when there's nothin' special to take up his time, he drinks more. No. Another thing I can tell you is that you'll never get him to stop drinkin'. You'll help him most if somehow you can make him drink less and eat more — just the way you said. If you keep givin' him food here and can get him to start thinkin' about layin' up a supply for the winter, that'd ease my mind quite a bit. He won't let me do much for him, but you've had better luck. He surely needs the food. Last summer he was so thin that I expected to see him fall over dead. When he left to winter in the north country, I didn't s'pose I'd see him again, but somehow he lived through the winter and showed up here again this spring. Well here he comes now."

"If you come fishin' with us, I bet he won't drink so much," Sue said. "You like fishin', so why don't you fish with us?"

"He'd drink just as much, and I'd drink more. I know how that works. Look at him now. He's quite a sight."

Malik approached them. He walked slowly with his head bent down and was picking at something in one hand with his fingernails. His clothes were still a deep blue. From a distance his hands and feet and face looked clean to Sue, but his wet hair was still an unnatural, faded indigo. When he stopped and stood with them, Sue saw that his fingernails and toenails still had a good deal of blue on them and under them, that several of the wrinkles on his face still held lines of blue, and that there were still tinges of color around his eyes and ears. He continued to pick at the medallion he had shown her, trying to remove paint spots.

"Well you old, blue Injun," Old Sam said. "That blue makes you look kind of drownded or strangled. Don't know as I like it all that much. Next time you take to decoratin' yourself, why don't you think about yellow or green? Maybe yellow skin and green hair; maybe green skin and yellow hair. I won't know which I'll like better 'til I see 'em on you. Keep the clothes blue. They look good, but get ev-.ery spot of paint off the governor's medal."

"Old Sam Barston," Malik said. "Humph." He kept picking at the medallion.

"And now Sue's after me to fish with the two of you, so I think you need to explain to her a little better that Old Sam won't fish for perch and eels. He's a grown man and won't fish for perch and eels like a boy. He'll tolerate fishin' for trout even if they are wicked small because he's got some good memories of trout when folks could still find a few decent ones around. But not perch and other little minnows down in the river."

"No," Malik said. "But Sam Barston will fish for trout and other little minnows in the brook. Sam Barston's mother won't let him go near the deep water in the river, but makes him stay by the brook with other boys who can't swim and who might be pulled into the water by any fish bigger than a smile."

"Ha!" Old Sam said. "That shows how much you know, you ignorant, blue Injun. The trout in the brook are every bit as big as any fish in the river. Your old age makes you forget that the salmon are gone. There are no big fish left in the Connecticut any more."

"Sam Barston is wrong again," Malik said. "It is a habit with the old man. Last year I caught an eel that was ..."

"Ignorant savage!" Old Sam interrupted. "I'm talkin' about fish, in case you've forgot. Eels ain't fish. They're snakes covered with slime. I don't go braggin' about how big a blacksnake I caught last year, so spare me any talk of eels. I'm waitin' to hear about fish you've caught lately, Malik. Fish! Any fish from the Connecticut that's bigger than your nose!"

Malik smiled and shook his head.

"I knew it," Old Sam continued. "You can't do it. Can't tell me about any big fish because there ain't any — nothin' but perch and pickerel and suckers and horned pout and chubs and other trash. And there you are, a man old enough to know better, out fishin' for 'em. Now you listen to me, you old blue Injun with no shame. Listen to what I'll give you if you can find a decent fish in the Connecticut. I have got a silver dollar at home that I will give you if you can catch a fish bigger than ... let's say ten pounds. Yes! You catch a fish bigger than ten pounds out of the Connecticut, and I'll give you that silver dollar. A fish, mind you. Nothin' with feathers or hair on it. Nothin' that gnaws down trees. Nothin' with legs on it or that looks like a snake. A fish over ten pounds and that dollar is yours. And I tell you right now that you'll never get that dollar just because there's nothin' left in the Connecticut that's much over half as big as ten pounds.

"Now are you goin' to come down to the house and have supper with me or not?"

"Not today, Sam Barston. I must rest today for the fishing tomorrow. Tomorrow we will eat supper at your house. We will eat a big fish, and you will give me your silver dollar."

"Ha! Ain't likely," Old Sam said. "But you come anyways even if you don't have a big fish."

"Yes, Sam Barston, but I will have the fish."

"I'll save arguments for tomorrow at supper, but right now I better get my old carcass started down the hill if I'm to get home before dark. I'm a little slower than I used to be — not like you, Malik."

The two men nodded to each other. Sue said good-by

to Malik. Then Old Sam led her down the slope, not towards the tannery, but rather in a straighter line towards his house. He tottered down the slope, complaining that his knees no longer had any strength. It seemed to Sue that they went more slowly down the slope than they'd gone up it. However, she didn't mind, for she enjoyed being with Old Sam and talking with him.

"Why's he so proud of that old medal?" she asked Old Sam. "From what my pa says, the governor wasn't much better 'n a pirate — givin' himself land in every town and makin' fortunes on his masts. Why is Malik ..."

"Hold it right there, young lady!" Old Sam roared. He stopped walking, straightened his stooped shoulders, and glared at her with such intensity that she was quite startled. "You're goin' to learn one thing today, and I don't want you ever to forget it! Listen hard! Benning Wentworth was the greedy pirate. His nephew, John Wentworth, was governor after Benning. John Wentworth was the best man I ever knew, not a lazy or greedy or selfish bone in his body. He loved New Hampshire and the Grants and did more for us than any other ten men before or since. Malik led him around showin' him the north country two different summers, and the governor appreciated it. Malik wouldn't take money for guidin' him, so John Wentworth sent him the medal instead. Silver it is. If it was me the governor had sent it to, I would of sewed it to my forehead and not just hung it around my neck. I would of been that proud. That was the kind of man John Wentworth was, and now nobody remembers him. Now, what have you learned today? Quick! Out with it!"

Sue stuttered through a false start before she answered.

"Benning Wentworth was a pirate. John Wentworth was the best man in the world."

"Good," Old Sam said quietly, winking at her. "Remember I didn't say 'handsomest' or 'strongest.' Only 'best'."

"Yes," Sue said and smiled. "Somebody else you told me about today was the handsomest and the strongest."

Old Sam laughed as they continued down the hill.

"Oh I would of made a good teacher," he said.

XIV

When Sue approached the point early the next morning, she found Malik already there. She stayed up on the ledges for a while to watch him fish.

He turned as he swung his bait and weight; released them and arched the fishline straight out across the current. Sue saw scarcely any paint on the back of his shirt or the back of his britches, but the front and sides of his clothes were still covered. His hair bore the same shade of blue as the day before. Sue waved at him, but he appeared not to notice. All his attention seemed to be on his handline as the fast-moving current pulled the bait down the river and swung it into the eddy. Retrieving the line in short jerks, he carefully coiled it at his feet until the bait and weight were back in his hand. He checked the bait, then swung it around, and cast. Sue approached him as he was retrieving the line again.

"Any luck this mornin'?" Sue asked.

"No."

"Out there in the current's the best place to catch a big fish, ain't it? You really want that dollar from Old Sam."

"Sam Barston can keep his dollar, or you can have it," Malik said. "It is enough for me if I show that Sam Barston is wrong about the fish in the river. Then I will have that to keep and remind him of."

"Should I fish the way we usually do or help you try and catch a big fish?"

"Do as you want, Sue," Malik said. He raised his hand to caution her about getting too close, then swung his bait and weight, and cast again.

"I'll try for a big fish then," Sue said. "At least for a while."

Sue set down her fish basket and pole. She took a mussel from Malik's supply and moved back out of his bait-swinging radius. Kneeling, she smashed the mussel with a rock, picked the flesh out of the broken shell, and baited her hook. Ready to fish, she sat instead and watched Malik. There was a strangeness to him — an intensity and abruptness of manner — which made her uneasy. She was used to thinking of Malik as a placid old man who talked a great deal, who often sat when he fished, and who gave the impression that nothing mattered much. Now he seemed changed. Sue watched him as she began fishing again. They stood two rods apart, and both cast out into the fast water, she with a pole; he without one.

Sue soon found that fishing out in the current was far more work than she'd been used to in her previous fishing. The bait moved too quickly, she thought. Almost as soon as she had cast it out, it would be down in the slack water at the edge of the eddy, right in the spot where she and Malik usually fished. Malik's line was longer and swung through a wider arc than hers, but even so it drifted so quickly down out of the current that he kept casting almost as frequently as she did.

"We need a way to keep the bait out in the current," Sue called over to him. "It gets pulled down too quick."

Malik nodded, but didn't say anything. He kept casting and retrieving. He could throw his bait out nearly three times as far as Sue could throw hers — out into the current, where he thought a big fish would most likely be. Still the current was so strong that he found himself wondering how deep the weight actually carried the bait before it settled down to the bottom in the slack water. His thoughts roamed for some way to keep the bait out in the current and down near the bottom. Sue interrupted his reverie after a while.

She had stopped fishing and had come over to stand right beside him.

"You feelin' all right, Malik? You're so quiet today, and you seem different."

"Yes. It is because of the fish for Sam Barston."

"I ... I hope you know that Old Sam cares about you. He is a good friend."

"Sam Barston does not always understand what it is to be a good friend," Malik said, letting his bait lie in the slack water down below.

"But he wants to help you," Sue said. "He'll give you a place to live in his house, if you let him, and food too. You'll need food to get you through the winter, Malik. You should be thinkin' about that now. Old Sam'd be glad to give it to you."

"That is what he does not understand — the giving. He was a good friend many years ago, but now he tries to give too much when I have nothing to give him. When a man takes too much and has nothing to give back, soon he is no longer a man. He becomes a child. But Sam Barston does not understand the insult of giving too much. He does not know that taking gifts all the time kills the spirit in a man. He does not know that a man with his spirit dying soon hates himself and then hates the man who tries to give too much. Sam Barston must learn to take from me what I can offer and accept the gift in friendship, but he does not. Always he says he must pay me for what I give him — fish, a basket, some furs. He does not understand any more how to take a gift from me, but wishes only to give and to drown my spirit with his giving."

"If you tell him about the gifts, maybe he'll understand."

"No. He must learn in his own heart how to take a gift from me. He must learn too that he cannot be right all the time. I will teach him that he is wrong about the fish in the river, and I will surprise him when I do not keep the dollar he tries to give. We will eat the fish in his home, and he will learn to take it as a gift. That is why I must catch the fish."

"You think there's a fish bigger 'n ten pounds here?"

"What I think does not matter. I will catch the fish first and then think."

"Well good luck, Malik," Sue said. "I hope you do. And I want you to know how much I like the fish basket you gave me."

Malik nodded. Then he laughed a short laugh as Sue went back to her pole and resumed fishing.

She is a good girl, he thought. *She would be a good granddaughter for a man to have.*

He turned back to his fishing, casting and retrieving his bait time after time. As he fished, he looked at the water out beyond his casting range. No one had ever fished there, he was certain. If a fish over ten pounds still lived in the river, it would likely be out where no one had yet fished. He gave more thought to discovering a way to fish out further; thought about it all through the morning.

* * * * *

The day wore hard on Sue. She caught a few perch, but missed many more fish because people kept distracting her. Word had spread through the village about the blue paint on Malik, and the curious found time to have a look at him. Though many people in the village did not, in fact, come to see Malik, it seemed to Sue that everyone had. They chattered together and pointed at him, laughing at the novelty of a man with blue hair and clothes, but Malik paid no attention to them. He continued with his fishing. People would stare, talk, and laugh. After directing some of their attention to Sue as Malik's fishing partner, they would finally leave, but only to be replaced quickly by others. Sue hated the attention; hated the laughter at Malik. The three boys came to stare and smirk. They shouted out a number of things to Malik, but he ignored them. They muttered comments among themselves about Malik and Sue — many of which she overheard — and laughed together. At last the three of them left.

In the early afternoon Malik stopped fishing and told Sue he wanted to borrow her fishline.

"What for?" Sue asked.

"To tie to my line. Then I can cast out further and catch a big fish."

A while later Malik began casting with the two lines tied together. He succeeded in heaving his bait further out into the river. However, just as before, the current kept swinging it in quickly out of the fast water — likely before the weight had carried it down very far beneath the surface.

"It still comes down too quick," Sue said. "Hard for a big fish to see it."

Malik nodded, but didn't say anything. He kept swinging the weight and bait, casting out the line, holding tension on it expectantly as it swung through its arc in the current, retrieving the line, and casting again. Sue watched him for half an hour. Then he told her to try casting it herself as he'd been doing. After half a dozen attempts Sue succeeded in heaving the bait out nearly as far as Malik had. She kept fishing. Malik watched, thinking.

After Sue had been casting and retrieving the handline for an hour, Malik stopped her.

"Come," he said. "This is wasting our time. I have thought of a way to keep the bait out in the deep and swift water. We will try it and see. But first we must catch many small fish together and trade them so we may get more line. We will need more line to fish in the new way."

Sue asked Malik questions about the new way to fish, but he wouldn't explain. He told her to wait and see. Sue retied her line to her pole and commenced fishing. Malik stood knee-deep in the water beside her and paid close attention to his own fishing.

It was early evening before they had finished cleaning the fish they had caught. Together they went to the village square to trade, but found scarcely anybody there and nobody who wanted fish from them.

* * * * *

Annie Ballard peeled potatoes at her dry sink and sliced them thin. They were early potatoes, dug while the potato vines had still been growing. George had brought them to her the day before from the blacksmith shop, where a customer had given them to him as partial payment for some work George had done. Ordinarily she didn't peel potatoes, but these had green skins from being left out in the sun, and she'd always heard it was poison to eat potatoes with green skins.

George and Annie lived in a small house north of the village square, right where the road out of the square met Tannery Road. It was an easy walk for George down to his blacksmith shop at the north end of the square. Usually when he got up in the morning, he went to the shop, started a fire in his forge, and went back home for breakfast. When he returned after breakfast, his forge was ready, and he could get right to work. He thought it a most convenient arrangement, particularly on winter mornings, when thick ice lay in his plunge tub beside the forge.

George had come home a quarter hour earlier at the end of what he said had been a long and hard work-day. His hands and most of his face had been black with soot and charcoal, but Annie was used to seeing him return home every day at least that dirty. She had joked with him a little as he had grabbed the kettle of hot water from the top of the cook stove. He had taken it with a bucket of cold water into the woodshed, where he washed at the end of every day. He had stripped, poured hot and cold water into a large basin, and had soaked himself with a wet cloth. Then he had soaped himself well from the firkin of soft soap that was kept in the woodshed. He paid particular attention to his hands, rubbing soap into them hard to get out all but the worst of the blackness. George splashed and rinsed and felt good. He blotted himself with a cloth, stood naked and drank long swallows from the water bucket as if it had been a giant drinking mug, and finally put on his other set of clothes when the last of the dampness had left his skin. He hung up his work clothes, pulled on an old pair of moccasins, and took the kettle back to Annie in the kitchen.

"Well, that certainly looks better 'n what walked in here a while back," Annie said.

"Feels better, too. What's for supper besides potatoes?"

"Ha! Too much rust and charcoal up your nose to smell it? Well then, it's a chunk of old, dead pig I found in a barrel downstairs, soaked the salt out of durin' the day, and then boiled for a while with some onions and other things. Interested?"

"Course I am and interested too why you didn't boil the potatoes along with the meat. They taste so good that way."

"Oh, I'm glad you asked me that, George! It's on account of a certain young businessman that can't learn to look close enough at things he's tradin' for. It's on account of a certain young businessman that took potatoes just about as green as a pine tree. When I went to put 'em in the pot, the green blazed right out at me. It was either peel the potatoes or poison us both. I already started cookin' everythin' else and then got distracted, so it was mostly cooked before I got around to thinkin' about the potatoes again. That's why I'm cookin' 'em separate."

"Oh."

"Don't take potatoes so green again."

"I won't."

George slumped down in a chair, stretched, and yawned. He flexed the tired muscles in his hands and arms and thought about closing his eyes for a few moments before supper was ready.

"Did somebody really paint old Malik blue?" Annie asked.

"That's what I heard at the shop. Didn't see him myself."

"What a thing to do!"

"He must of been drunk — only way I can explain it. Drunk and asleep."

"They know who done it?"

"There's a pretty fair chance a certain three boys we know might of had a hand in it. Don't know for certain, but that'd be my guess."

"I'll speak to 'em then and find out if they ever want cookies or pie from me again. They just can't go around treatin' poor old men like that. They can't ..."

"Well, hold on, Annie 'til you know for certain it was them. Don't be too hasty. You can ... Hold it. Somebody's at the door."

Annie opened the door. Sue and Malik stood in front of her, both carrying baskets. She was startled for a moment by the color of Malik's hair and by the blue lines still in the creases of his face, but recovered quickly enough not to stare at him.

"Come in. Come in," Annie said. "What can we do for you?"

The two entered the house, Sue in front of Malik. Sue stood quietly looking at her feet and lifting her eyes in short glances at Annie and George and their house. She expected Malik to speak, but he didn't. Embarrassed, she began.

"Well we was down in the square tryin' to sell our fish, but we ... There was nobody down there but a few people, none of 'em stoppin' ..."

"Hold it right there," Annie said. "You was to call me by my given name the next time you saw me, Sue."

"Yes. Annie."

"That's better. Now smile and look at me for my floor's none too clean and ain't been since George got back from work. And tell me what's on your mind."

Sue's face eased into a bashful smile. She looked into Annie's eyes and pulled her gaze back up quickly when it settled towards the floor.

"We got some fish we took to the square too late to trade. You said I should bring fish to you sometime if I had trouble tradin' 'em. But you've got your supper ready, so we shouldn't of come."

Annie looked hard at Sue, quite aware of the effort it took the girl to look directly at her; hearing the awkwardness and embarrassment in her voice.

"That's true, but I might well hold it over 'til tomorrow if we got fish tonight, or George might want fish for his breakfast. We could ... we could prob'ly take fish from you, if you ain't got too many. But why don't you two stay and have somethin' to eat while we talk about it? If George don't eat like a complete pig tonight, I think there might be enough for four people."

"Thank you, Annie," Sue said. "But you're just bein' nice. We ... we shouldn't of come."

"Nonsense. I'm glad you did. I'd like it if you two 'd eat with us."

"I can't," Sue said. "I got to get supper for Pa. Should be there now 'cause he'll be wonderin' where I am."

"I will stay," Malik announced. He threw back his shoulders and smiled. "Leave your basket with me, Sue, and I will give it back tomorrow."

George sat back, smiling a little at his own momentary consternation and then good-naturedly looking forward to the novelty of sharing his supper with a blue-haired Indian, who would attempt to trade fish after the meal was finished. It seemed a good joke to him and would be something to tease Annie about for a long time to come. He watched Annie's losing struggle to keep Sue in their house. The girl clearly wanted to go home, but Annie was reluctant to let her go. Then, after Sue had left, he found Annie's attempts to talk with Malik equally entertaining. The Indian spoke to her a syllable or two at a time, leaving her scarcely a chance to catch her breath between questions. Then, finally, supper was ready, and the three of them sat down together. Malik ate a surprising amount for so frail-looking an old man.

George's sudden leap into conversation with Malik after being quiet for so long startled Annie. Then she sat back in amusement and watched him. He had realized, she was certain, how much the old Indian might eat and how little he himself might get if Malik didn't start talking more. And yet, while he was asking questions to get Malik talking, he himself couldn't eat. George tried short questions which might yield long answers from Malik. ("How good was the fishin' in the Connecticut when you was a boy? ... I don't s'pose you got any good bear stories, do you? ... Ever kill a catamount?") Malik gave short answers and kept eating. When all the food was gone, George had lost. Annie was laughing to herself. Malik talked for some time about how the fishing in the Connecticut had been when he was a boy, about particularly huge bears he had encountered, and about the habits of catamounts and why he believed it was bad luck for anybody to kill one. Annie lighted candles as he talked. It was quite late when he finally rose to go.

"There is fishing again in the morning," he said. "I thank you for the supper, Annie and George. You may call me your friend. I will not forget this supper. Now where do I put the fish from Sue's basket?"

"In that I guess," Annie said, gesturing towards a wooden bowl. "Please tell me what I should give you for 'em."

"There is nothing," Malik said, as he put the fish into the bowl. "The fish are a gift from a friend. You will not insult a friend by paying him for what he means as a gift. I do not insult friends with talk of what I might pay for the supper, which was a gift. I do not insult friends with the talk, 'Here are fish I trade for the supper.' We do not trade. There are two gifts given — no trading. There was a gift of supper. Here is a gift of fish."

"But the supper wasn't worth nearly so much as the fish," Annie said.

"It is not the way for friends to think in such a way. I am an old man. No one in the village but Sam Barston and you take the trouble to have me sit at your table and eat supper. It is a gift I value. Now you will take these fish, and there will be no talk about them except the talk of friends."

"Well, thank you then, Malik," Annie said. "We will think of our friendship when we eat the fish. Thank you."

Malik nodded and went out into the night, carrying a basket in each hand. Annie stared at the blackness for a moment before she shut the door.

"Well George," she said. "A different kind of an evenin'. What a lonely old man he must be. We scarcely know him, and he counts us as his only friends aside from Old Sam — and Sue, of course. Hope I never feel that lonely."

"I hope you never feel that hungry," George said. "Did you see how much food he rammed down his throat? Amazin'."

Annie laughed.

"What I saw was a great big, jug-eared, red-headed man scared to death that a little old man would eat him into starvation. And those questions you asked him so you could eat and he couldn't. You should be ashamed of yourself. A good thing for him that he knew what you was doin'. 'Ever kill a catamount,' George?"

"No, but if one wandered by, I would right now just so's to have somethin' to eat. That old hog ate twice as much as I did. At least I can have some of those fish in the mornin', I guess."

"Have some right now if you want, George, and spare the night-rovin' catamounts. How many?"

"It won't be too much trouble?"

"Of course it will be, but only about half as much trouble as listenin' to you rave about starvin' to death. How many?"

"Six or eight might save me 'til mornin'."

"All right."

Annie fired up the cook stove again and before long was frying eight perch in a pan. As she was tending to them, she thought about Sue Reckford.

"That Sue is a girl scared of her own shadow, and she must be just as lonely as Malik. Good for the both of them to fish together."

"Takes after her pa," George said.

"She does," Annie said. "But it's more than that too. Never had a mother since before she was three years old. Movin' around so that she never gets to know much of anybody 'fore she moves away again. What could ail that father of hers do you s'pose?"

"No wife to plague him out of his loneliness?"

"Oh, you can stop that right now, George Ballard. Just think about Sue. Seems a shame to have her so lonely and unhappy when a little friendliness or attention might help her along. She must be miserable at times."

"Well, you'll make a fine mother some day. A fine mother, Annie. Only don't give away a poor child's food to the first blue-haired Injun that comes along. Have a care that you don't starve the poor thing to death. Speakin' of that ..."

"They're done now so you can stop your squawkin'."

"That's good news, but I wasn't thinkin' about the fish."

"I don't know what else you could be talkin' about, and I ain't even interested. Here are some perch to think about."

She set the hot pan on the table and lifted the fish onto a wooden platter with a thin, iron spatula George had made for her.

"There you go, George. Don't burn your mouth on 'em, and don't starve to death before mornin'. Dump the bones into the firebox so I won't have 'em starin' at me when I get up. I'm goin' to bed."

Annie leaned over and kissed George lightly on the cheek.

"Good night, George."

"Night Annie. Rest well."

Annie took a candle from the table and carried it up the stairs. She set it on a stand next to her bed, undressed quickly, got into bed, and blew out the flame. As she lay still and eased towards sleep, she thought of Malik with blue hair and of his gratitude for the supper she had given him, of George's consternation when he realized how much Malik was likely to eat, of Sue and her loneliness and her obvious need for a mother, and of Joe Reckford. He was such a large and strong man. What would he be like if he ever learned to relax around other people? What kind of a woman had his dead wife been? Would he settle in Barston Falls or move on again in a few months? Would he ever re-marry, for Sue's sake? The questions kept running around inside her head until she fell asleep.

Downstairs George finished eating the perch. He felt a great deal better with his stomach full and chuckled a little to himself at lingering images of Malik eating supper. He yawned and stretched and rose from the table, dumping the fish bones on top of the coals in the firebox of the cook stove. As he carried a candle up the stairs, he walked on the left side of the tread to avoid creaking the steps and waking Annie. In the hallway, however, the groan of a floorboard halted him abruptly. He listened closely for a moment, but didn't hear Annie stir. Then he tiptoed off to bed, thinking about the work at the forge that would face him in the morning.

XV

Benjie Barston leaned out the window of his room, staring at the trunk of the big ash tree there and mourning the tragedy of a second wasted day. He had hoped for two days of rain, but both days had been sunny and warm with light breezes — days he would have loved to spend outdoors with Foss and Tom. The two had come around the morning before full of plans for the day and had been properly appalled at the severity of his punishment: two days' confinement in his room with another day in addition if he so much as set his little toe outside. The chamber pot deprived him of even the slight diversion of a walk to the outhouse. Prison. His father had beaten him. It still hurt to sit down. Then the pain and humiliation of the beating had been followed by imprisonment. His mother had done her best to be cheerful when she brought food to him and talked about many things other than his punishment, but that had not changed the fact of the long hours of confinement he had endured and would continue to endure until daylight the next morning.

Benjie remained confused about his crime. He didn't know which had roused his father's anger: stealing the paint or painting Malik. Did his punishment mean that all pranks involving stolen paint were to end? Or did it mean that all pranks involving Malik were to end? It was irritating not to know. Perhaps he would ask his father after his imprisonment was over. He gazed down at the spots of blue paint which still remained on his hands in spite of his best efforts to get them off and wished he had been more careful while he'd been painting Malik. It had been stupid of him to advertise his involvement in the incident that way. With blue paint on his hands, denial had been unthinkable. He shook his head and knew he would be a good deal more careful the next time. He would think more clearly and not leave such obvious traces.

The day was beautiful, but there was nothing in it for Benjie to enjoy. He sighed, turned from the window, and sat on his bed. Sitting didn't feel very good. He lay back and looked at the ceiling and wondered if it would ever get dark.

* * * * *

Foss, Benjie, and Tom looked down towards the river.

"There they are," Tom said. "Hard at it again. Old Malik and his girl friend. They been like that two days now: Malik on his feet and fishin' hard with her. Both of 'em catchin' fish and takin' 'em up to the square to trade. They say Malik ain't had a drop of rum since he woke up blue."

"That's what Pa says, Benjie," Foss said. "Claims it was a public service curin' the old drunk like that. And Ma says if we feel like paintin' some more, there's half a dozen others in the village she'll buy us the paint for if it'll get 'em to stop drinkin'. She says to watch what happens to Malik after the blue wears off 'cause we might have to do him up again."

"Not me," Benjie said. "Not unless somebody has quite a good talk with Pa. My paintin' days are done, even if Malik does start drinkin' again."

"Those two catchin' anythin' good size?"

"No, mostly just perch," Foss said. "A lot of 'em though. Yesterday they filled a basket with cleaned fish."

"I'd get tired of that pretty fast," Benjie said, "if I had to catch and clean little fish all the time day after day. Just about like bein' in jail."

Foss and Tom nodded. The three boys watched Sue and Malik for a few moments more and then headed over to the canal.

* * * * *

The next day Benjie, Tom, and Foss were back at the same spot watching Sue and Malik with great curiosity.

"Now what do you s'pose they're up to with that plank?" Foss asked. "Tie it to a tree and float it. That don't make a lot of sense."

One end of a rope was tied to a tree near the riverbank roughly a dozen rods above where Sue and Malik stood; the other end to a short plank floating in the river. Malik kept prodding the plank out into the current with Sue's fishpole and then watching it swing right back in against the bank.

"What's that old dummy think he's tryin' to do?" Tom asked. "Course the plank's goin' to float back in. Why's he keep tryin' to push it out all the time?"

"Likely he's drunk again," Benjie said.

They watched Malik push the floating plank out into the current repeatedly. Finally he gave up and sat down beside where it had washed in. The three boys saw him speaking to Sue. Then they both went down to the point and started fishing. Soon they were catching small fish, probably perch, the boys thought. The three watched Sue and Malik fish for a while, talked among themselves about what possible purpose Malik had intended for a plank tethered to a tree with a long rope, and then left.

* * * * *

In the middle of the afternoon the three boys wandered by again. This time they were astounded when they looked down at the river. Malik's plank with a second plank trailing behind it was a good five or six rods out in the fast water. The two planks wavered a few feet from side to side in the force of the current, but otherwise held their positions. The same long rope tethered the planks to the same tree up along the riverbank, slashing a diagonal scar across the current.

"Now how on earth does that thing work?" Benjie said. "Why don't the planks swing right in? If it didn't work with one plank, why does it work with two?"

"What's it for?" Foss said. "That's what I'm wonderin'."

"That's about the strangest rig I ever saw," Tom said. "Let's go down and have a look."

They started down towards the river, glancing over to where Malik and Sue were fishing.

"Malik sees us, Benjie," Foss said.

The three boys stopped.

"And we see him too," Benjie said, waving at Malik. "Ain't much he can do to us, is there? He won't catch us. I know that."

Malik waved at the three boys. He extended an index finger horizontally and slowly drew it across his throat. Then with the same finger, pointed down and touching his own head, he traced a circle all the way around his crown.

"Ha!" Benjie said. "That ain't very friendly. Sometimes I think the old cuss didn't appreciate all the trouble we took to make him blue. If he keeps that up, we just might not paint him again. Serve him right. Never even thanked us."

Foss and Tom laughed.

"Come on," Benjie said. "I want to go up and see where the rope's tied."

The three of them angled over the ledges to where the rope was knotted around a red maple about as thick as one of their legs. They looked at the rope and down towards the planks floating out in the current and knew no more than they had before.

"Let's go down and get a closer look at those planks," Tom said.

The boys made their way down along the riverbank. Looking out at the floating planks, they nearly tripped over a fishing line tied around the trunk of a six-inch-thick yellow birch twenty yards back from the river's edge. The line disappeared straight out, perpendicular to the current. The three boys puzzled over it for a moment and puzzled further about a tripod of sticks standing beside the river a short distance further down.

"Well that's what this is," Benjie said suddenly. "The line goes right out to the planks. It's some kind of a rig so he can fish out in the current."

"That still don't tell us how the thing works," Tom said, "or what those sticks are for."

"Malik's starin' at us, Benjie," Foss said.

"That's all right," Benjie said. "Stare right back if you want. We ain't goin' to hurt his rig. I only want to know how the thing works."

Benjie tugged at the fishline. He pulled it in about a rod. It came easily, not disturbing the planks out in the current at all. He let the few coils in his hands go, and the line pulled out quickly until once again it was taut against the knots tied on the yellow birch trunk.

"It's all in the rope and the planks," Benjie announced. "The planks keep themselves out there, but cuss me if I know how. It's just a way to hold a bait out by the middle of the river."

"It'd take quite a weight to get the bait down out in that current," Tom said.

"I'd love to know how the thing works," Foss said. "What kind of old Injun trick do you s'pose he's usin'? Planks don't just float like that out in the current on a rope."

"Some day maybe we'll ask Malik about the thing," Benjie said, "but I think I'll wait 'til he don't have scalpin' on his mind quite so much."

"Think there's any fish out there, Benjie?" Foss asked.

"Not unless they're holdin' on to the bottom so hard that they don't have time to go after any bait. Otherwise they'd get washed right down the river. But you never can tell about what old Injuns know and what they don't. Maybe we'll stop by now and again to see if he's caught anythin', but I know I've wasted enough time here for one day. Let's go over and get some trout out of the brook. We can stop by on the way and have a look at our deadfalls."

Malik watched the boys leave. After they were gone, he walked up close enough to the fishline out to his plank-rig to see that they had not cut it. Then he went back down and started fishing again with Sue.

* * * * *

Towards the end of the afternoon Malik announced that it was time to stop fishing. They needed to clean their fish and get them up to the square to trade while people who might want them would still be there.

"What should we do with the big fishline and the planks?" Sue asked.

"You take them in, Sue, while I clean the fish. Coil the line and the rope and hide the planks. We will not leave them out where the boys might work their mischief. Then come back and help me finish the fish. We will take them together to trade."

Sue went up along the riverbank to the fishline and began pulling it in hand-over-hand. It came easily at first. She coiled it at her feet. Then, when most of the line was in, it caught against the resistance of the planks out in the current. She pulled hard on the fishline and with a great effort moved the planks toward her. Then, abruptly, the resistance on the line ended; the planks returned to where they'd been before. Sue kept coiling the fishline until she came to the cloth-wrapped stone — as big as her fist — Malik had used as a weight. Six feet beyond the weight the large, skinned perch they had used for bait looked just the same as it had that morning when they had threaded it onto the big hook they had bought at Steve Danforth's store. It would have to be a huge fish, Sue thought to take so large a bait and to free the line from the plank-rig. She took the perch off the hook, tossed it into the river, wiped her hands on her britches, wound the weight and hook into the coil of fishline, and hung the coil on the tripod. Finally she walked up to the end of the fishline and untied it from the small yellow birch.

Sue continued on up to the red maple where the rope to the plank-rig was tied. Without untying the rope from the tree she began pulling it in, surprised at what hard work it was and surprised at the behavior of the planks. Rather than come straight towards her as she pulled, they angled up into the current; traveled a long arc before she had them next to the bank.

Sue grabbed the first plank and turned it over. Three short, parallel boards were set on their edges diagonally into the plank, rising up about eight inches; each of them with a small, cloth bag hanging from it. She picked at some flotsam caught in the joints where the boards fit into the plank and marveled at Malik's ingenuity. She had understood quickly Malik's explanation that as the plank floated in the current, the water pushing against the diagonal boards would force it further out into the river. However, after Malik had built the plank-rig, he discovered that it didn't work. Then he had shown his real ingenuity. At first the buoyancy of the boards set into the plank had caused the rig to roll over in the current. To solve that problem

Malik had made weights by wrapping pebbles and sand in cloth and, with notches and lashings, had attached them to the bottoms of the three parallel boards. Thereafter, though the plank-rig stayed upright in the water, it still didn't work. No matter how any times Malik had pushed it out, it had kept drifting right back in to shore. Malik had puzzled about that problem for several hours as the two of them had fished down at the point. His solution had been to add another plank, trailing from the end of the first plank on a short rope. The tug of the second plank kept the first straight in the current and allowed the water to push against the board-fins underneath. With the second plank added, the rig had worked perfectly.

Sue ran her fingers over the smoothness of a peeled willow twig lashed to the lower end of the plank with the boards set into it and decided to leave it as it was for the night. The peeled twig had been Malik's solution for freeing the fishline from the plank-rig when a big fish jerked on the line anchored to the yellow birch. He had wanted to make certain that the fishline wouldn't tangle with the plank-rig while he and Sue were pulling in Old Sam's fish. Malik had lashed both ends of the twig so that the twig bowed out from the lower end of the plank. The twig and the plank together had formed a loop for the fishline to slide through. The lashing had been tight enough so that the force of the current against the bait and the weight wouldn't pull it free. That was the reason Sue had had to pull so hard on the fishline before one end of the twig had come out of its lashing.

There were many things about Malik's plank-rig that impressed Sue. The willow-twig loop was far enough from the board-fins to keep the fishline from tangling in them. The heavy weight kept the fishline well below the trailing plank so that it wouldn't tangle there either. The bait was large enough so that their hook wouldn't be picked clean by small, bait-stealing fish. Malik had even set up a tripod of sticks on the shore just below the fishline, telling Sue that when the big fish for Sam Barston pulled the fishline free from the plank-rig, they would know it because the line would knock over the tripod.

About the only drawbacks, as far as Sue could see, were the difficulty of pulling the planks in on the rope and the necessity, because of the boys, of taking the rig apart every evening and setting it up anew each morning. Still it was a good arrangement, she thought as she untied the rope from the planks and hid them; untied the rope from the red maple and began coiling it. The plank-rig allowed them to fish out in the current, where a big fish would most likely be. Once it had been set up each morning, they could go about their regular fishing. Glancing up at the tripod every now and then to see if it still stood upright wouldn't take any time at all. They would catch just as many perch as they usually did and have a chance to catch a huge fish as well.

However, as Sue finished coiling the rope, she wondered if perhaps Old Sam were right. Perhaps there were no more big fish in the Connecticut. Perhaps they were just wasting their time. She returned to Malik with the rope and the fishline. They finished cleaning their fish and together took them up to the village square.

* * * * *

For four days without attracting much attention Sue and Malik set their plank-rig every morning and took it apart every afternoon. They caught nothing with it. On their third day of using it they tied on another hundred feet of fishline and were able to fish further down the river in an area where the current began to slacken. They added more rocks to their cloth-wrapped weight to get the bait down deeper. Still they caught nothing.

Benjie, Foss, and Tom were quite interested in the plank-rig. Malik and Sue watched them closely every time when they came to look. The boys would wave from a distance and often mock Malik with throat-cutting and scalping gestures, but they never came down to talk.

Malik managed to avoid Old Sam Barston during those first four days of using the plank-rig. Each night he dreamed of catching a big fish and carrying it on a cord over his shoulder to Old Sam's house. Each day he began fishing again with the hope that he would catch a big fish that day, but he didn't. He and Sue caught only perch and an occasional pickerel or horned pout.

Malik grew increasingly silent and sullen and began to develop quite a yearning for rum.

XVI

Deep wrinkles creased Joe Reckford's forehead as he paced back and forth in the single downstairs room of his home. He passed a ball of crumpled paper from one hand to the other, mumbling to himself. For a moment he paused at a window and looked down towards the lower warehouse. Then he resumed his pacing. He stopped over by the cook stove. His fingers carefully pulled the ball of paper out into a wrinkled sheet. Once again he read over the words of the note.

"Now what in the world is that woman up to?" he muttered. "It just ain't right. What am I goin' to do?"

He tore the paper twice and then crumpled it again. Lifting a lid on the cold stove, he dropped the note into the firebox.

"Ha!" he mumbled to himself. "Get the basket back to her 'when I can.' She'd have it right now if I was here when she stopped by — the basket and the cookies both. Course she knew I was workin'. Planned it that way. Well she'll be a plague to her husband and her own ruination some day, but it won't be on account of me. What ails that woman?"

He strode back across the room, feeling better for having put the note into the stove. The basket of cookies sat on the table. Absentmindedly he ate a cookie and then a second.

Sue would be back from her fishing soon. For a moment he thought about eating all the cookies and hiding the basket so she wouldn't know about them and who had given them, but there were simply too many cookies for him to eat quickly. Sue would surely be back before he had finished. Better just to take it as a matter-of-fact gift to both Sue and him, thank the woman, and get the basket back to her without making any fuss over it. Go together with Sue when they returned the basket and make sure to go when her husband was at home. That would be the best way to do it.

The problem, he knew, was that he was attracted to the woman. That was what had made life so difficult for him ever since he had delivered that wagonload of charcoal and had eaten some of her pie. Otherwise he could simply have ignored her when, what had grown to be three or four times a day, she sauntered by where he was working. The more embarrassed he was at her presence — the more he blushed and the more he twisted his words — the more she teased him with her eyes and looked at him in a way which wrenched his insides into turmoil. It was obvious that she was throwing herself at him. He had seen little or nothing of her before he had delivered the charcoal, and then suddenly several times a day she had begun happening by wherever he was.

He reached up for his Bible in the cupboard and then sat down at the table with both of his hands resting on it. Though he had meant to open it and read some verses in Exodus, he left it shut on the table. He lifted one of his hands from it and took another cookie. Then he took three. God's will or the woman's, it was certainly temptation that was being thrown at him to see how weak or strong he was. It was a trial. If it had been a scrawny little mouse of a woman who had left a basket of cookies, he wouldn't have felt so uneasy. Even if she had been married, he wouldn't have felt uneasy. He would have thanked the woman by himself and returned the basket by himself, and wouldn't have had any difficulty. But it had had to be Annie Ballard — one of the two women in the village he thought warranted more than a glance. Annie Ballard: strong and solid and healthy, a fine example of a woman. He thought of her helping to carry the charcoal and of how unconcerned she had been when she had blackened her dress with it; thought of how firm and pleasant she had been when she had made him stay and eat the pie with the others after they had all unloaded the charcoal. Yes indeed, George Ballard was a lucky man, Joe thought. Annie Ballard. Perhaps he was attracted to her because she reminded him a little of Betsy, his dead wife. Of course there were a few similarities. Then perhaps his own loneliness made him confuse the two women in his mind. Yes, that was all there was to it: his own loneliness and reminders of the past. It was good to realize that and not to fall into some foolishness or other about Annie Ballard. He would bury whatever feelings he thought he had about her. If he got to know her husband better and made a friend of him, that might be a way to avoid the temptation as well. He wondered if he would be strong enough. He took another handful of cookies and thumbed through Exodus until he found the verses he was looking for. He had known them all by heart years ago, but it comforted him to read them over again. He gave a deep sigh and shut the book.

He stared at the wall and thought about Sue. He wished she were happier. He wished she had friends her own age, like a normal girl. However, it was better for her to fish with that old Indian than to stay at home and brood in her own loneliness, as she had in other places where they had lived. The Indian had seemed harmless enough, except for his drinking. That had worried Joe for a while, but then the old Indian — either because of being painted blue or because of Sue — had stopped drinking, at least for the time being. Sue still needed young friends, but having the old Indian was better than not having any friends at all. Every day when Sue returned from her fishing she would have something to tell him about the old Indian: some story from his past, some Indian way of doing a task, some information about the early days in the upper valley. He was harmless in a grandfatherly way, and Joe was glad Sue spent time with him. At first Joe had objected to having her take food to him, thinking of it as a charity that would never end, but had quickly discovered that it wasn't charity, but business. He had been proud of her for that. He had never eaten so many fish in his life (though, to tell the truth, he was sick of them). Nearly every evening they ate them and often the following morning as well. Some days he had taken cold, cooked perch with him for his dinner. He had been proud of her too when she had brought home flour, eggs, cloth, tobacco for his pipe, rum, and even some hard coin — all from fish she had traded. With Sue bringing all those things into the house, they would surely be able to save money if they stayed in Barston Falls.

The thought of rum pulled him to his feet. He took the jug from the cupboard and poured some rum into a mug. Then he put the jug back and set the Bible next to it. When he sat back down at the table to eat cookies and drink rum, Annie Ballard was again on his mind. She seemed stronger than ever in his thoughts, and it frightened him that she could have such power over him. By the time he had finished his rum, he felt afraid. The temptation of Annie Ballard bore down on him. He ate her cookies and thought about her.

Suddenly he knew it was no good. The temptation was too strong. He wanted Annie Ballard, married or not. No amount of reading the Bible, making George Ballard into a good friend, or pretending to ignore her would change that. There was no way to lie to himself about her. He didn't even feel weak in admitting how he felt. She was a strong, attractive woman, and he wanted her. It was as simple as that. He laughed at himself for his honesty.

"Ha!" he thought. "Upriver or down? Don't matter much to me, but when you can't beat temptation, the next best thing is to run away from it. Up or down?"

Joe ate more cookies and wondered where Sue was. He let his thoughts go to Annie Ballard again. Five minutes later Sue came through the door carrying her fish basket and holding a headless, plucked chicken by the legs. Joe stared at the chicken as he spoke to his daughter.

"So, you and the old Injun get that big fish today?"

"No, but you should of seen all the perch we got, Pa. Got a chicken each for 'em and more besides."

She set the chicken and her fish basket down on the table.

"Where'd the cookies come from?" Sue asked.

"Annie Ballard left 'em for us. Nice of her. Have some. Got to take her basket back sometime."

Sue took a cookie and started eating it.

"They're good, Pa. Hope you still got room left for chicken tonight."

"Never yet turned down chicken just 'cause I was full," Joe said. "Ain't goin' to start now."

"Supper 'll be late on account of the chicken might take quite a while. I got potatoes and flour and eggs today too. Guess I should get the chicken right on to cook."

"Well I'll start the fire in the stove," Joe said, leaping to his feet. "You go on out and chop the feet off of that chicken so that when we're eatin' we don't have to think about where they been walkin'. I'll get the fire goin'. While you're out there, spend some time with your hands and face in the wash bucket. "

"All right, Pa."

Joe scraped at the ashes in the fireplace as his daughter went outside. With a small shovel he pulled out a coal from the covered, smoldering wood, carried it to the cook stove, and put it into the firebox. Then using the note from Annie

Ballard and some birch bark for tinder, he got a fire going. The stove top was hot when Sue returned. She put the chicken into a pot, put some potatoes on top, dumped in some water, and went to sit at the table with her father. They sat with the basket of cookies between them. Joe looked at his daughter, not bothering with the cookies.

"You ain't made any friends here your own age, Sue, have you?'

"No, Pa."

"No one at all really but for the old Injun."

"Malik. Yes, he's my friend. Old Sam Barston and Annie Ballard are nice, but I don't know 'em much. I'm just shy with new people — like you, Pa."

"Yes, Sue. And Barston Falls is like a lot of other places we been to. People pretty much leave us alone. Don't go much out of their way on account of us, do they?"

"No, but we don't go much out of our way either."

"You happy here, Sue?"

"As happy here as anyplace else," she said. She felt tears starting to build and struggled to keep them back. There were so many things she couldn't talk to her father about.

"But no more 'n that?"

"A little happier, I s'pose. Why are you askin', Pa?"

"No special reason. It's just that I ... well, I'm startin' to get a little restless here. Thinkin' a little — just thinkin', mind you — about movin' along after a while. Might want to go upriver a ways or maybe down. I don't know. That's why I was wonderin' ... well now I went and done it."

Sue brushed at the tears on her cheeks and commenced sniffling. Joe rose, walked around the table to her, and put a hand on her shoulder.

"I was just thinkin', Sue. That's all. Nothin' to cry about. If you want to stay here, we'll find a way. It's just that some-times I get tired of workin' on the canal and in the warehouse. I was just thinkin' out loud. Ain't made any plans or anythin', Sue. No need to cry."

Joe patted Sue on the back trying to comfort her, gave that up, and then stood awkwardly beside her. After a while Sue got her voice back.

"It's just that no matter where we move, it's always the same. I ain't like other girls, and the boys are either afraid of me or else they laugh and say mean things. It's so hard for me to make friends. Malik's the only one, but that's more 'n I had before we came. If we stay, I might get to know Old Sam Barston and Annie Ballard better, and there might be some others too, but if we move away, I won't know anybody, and I'll have to start all over. I got fishin' with Malik to do here, for one thing. If we go away, I won't have that any more. And Malik 'll just drink all the time the way he used to, and I know he won't get good food."

Joe put his hand on Sue's shoulder. She wiped away the last traces of her tears.

"You all right now, Sue?"

"Yes, Pa, but sometimes I wish there wasn't so many things we never talk about."

"Well there's some things better that way. When your ma died, that was the worst hurt I ever was — the kind of hurt that would of bled forever if I'd of let it. If you leave it alone, it scars over and don't hurt so much. Other people — friends, relatives — kept tryin' to comfort me after she died — kept openin' the wound again when I didn't want 'em to touch it. Finally I just had to get away from 'em all. Didn't matter much where I went so long as it was someplace I was a stranger, and where people wouldn't keep remindin' me about your ma. I might of left you with her sister before I went away — she made the offer — but I couldn't bear the thought. So I dragged you along. I struggled. We struggled. I never was the same after your ma died, but I left that wound alone, and finally it scarred over enough so it didn't hurt so bad. Even now there's things I don't tell you — don't need to and don't want to on account of I don't want to open up old wounds — same as there's prob'ly things you don't tell me."

"Yes, Pa."

"There's such a thing as the need to be left alone," Joe said.

"Yes, but if there's somethin' that maybe we can help each other with, then maybe we should just speak our minds."

Joe looked long and hard at his daughter. He had always thought of her as a big child, who would take her time growing up. That time wasn't so far off, however, when she would be a young woman. He wondered where the years had gone.

"That might be true," Joe said. "Tell me now if there's anythin' you want to talk about."

"Just about movin' again. Sometime we should just stay in a place. If it takes us a long time to get to know people, then maybe we should just stay however long it takes. I want to belong someplace; don't want to keep movin' on all the time to places that ain't goin' to be any better 'n right here. I want to stay here for a while, Pa."

"Well if that's how you feel, I guess I can put up with the work a while longer," Joe said. "We'll see how you feel a month from now. All right? Anythin' else botherin' you that you think we should talk about?"

There were five things that kept her from being happy, Sue thought. There were five things ...

"Anythin' else, Sue?"

"No, Pa. Anythin' you want to talk about?"

"No, Sue."

The cookies were gone long before supper was ready. Joe and Sue ate all the potatoes that had been cooked with the chicken and about half of the chicken, saving the rest for the next day. Neither spoke much during the meal or afterwards as Sue cleaned up and Joe smoked his pipe. They mentioned the weather and fishing a few times. Then they went upstairs to their bedrooms.

Sue lay awake guessing how much longer she might be in Barston Falls. She wanted to know Old Sam Barston and Annie Ballard a lot better than she did and worried about what would happen to Malik after she left. She wondered where she and her father might move to next; whether they would ever stop wandering. When she fell asleep, vestiges of tears were still on her cheeks.

Joe turned in his bed, worrying. He muttered faint curses at himself for being so poor a father. If Sue had been younger or if she hadn't surprised him by wanting to stay in Barston Falls at least a while longer, they might very well have been off and traveling to a new future the next day. However, he had as much as promised her that they would stay at least another month. Another month! And after that month he had said they'd see how Sue felt then. She might even have the idea that they would stay in Barston Falls forever. Oh how had he gotten himself into such a fix? In another month he would likely feel ten times the panic he felt at the moment. He was weak. That Annie Ballard would keep after him. How would he avoid her for a whole month? It didn't seem possible. He wanted to run away, but he couldn't because of Sue.

Joe finally got to sleep, but he slept fitfully. Towards morning he awoke in a sweat. He had been dreaming that he was walking arm-in-arm with Annie Ballard down by the Connecticut. He shuddered at what he remembered they had been saying to each other.

In the morning Joe sent Sue alone to take the basket back to the Ballards.

XVII

Each morning Sue and Malik would arrive at the point with their lines, ropes, and fish baskets and would immediately begin fishing for perch. Then with the first big perch of the day they would go up along the west bank, retrieve their hidden planks, and set up the plank-rig. It became a routine: tying the rope to the same red maple, tying the long fishline to the same yellow birch, baiting the hook with the freshly skinned perch, lashing a willow twig underneath the upper plank, wishing luck to the rig as they launched it out into the current, and carefully letting out all the fishline so it wouldn't kink or tangle. Then they would return to their usual fishing down at the point, regularly glancing back up at their tripod of sticks during the day to see if it had been knocked flat. The tripod continued to stand. When at the end of each afternoon they took apart their plank-rig, they hoped that perhaps the next day it would catch a big fish for them.

On the fifth day the plank-rig had been in operation Old Sam Barston came down to have a look at it. Thereafter he started visiting the point towards the middle of every afternoon to tease Malik. Sometimes he had a trout with him. If Malik remained sullen and ignored him, it didn't seem to bother Old Sam a bit, nor inhibit his needling monologues. The crowds of gawkers, who, days earlier, had gone down to the point in response to the rumor that Malik had been painted blue, had seen all there was to see and came no more. However, to Malik's way of thinking, Old Sam was more of a plague to him than all of the gawkers put together.

"Any fish in the Connecticut bigger than this trout?" Old Sam would ask on the days when he had brought along a trout. "Think there's a chance you can find any? ... No, you crazy old blue-hair. How many times have I got to tell you that eels ain't fish? Fish! Any of those perch measure up to this trout I caught? No, I didn't think so. Now I wonder what I ought to spend that dollar at home on. Seems a shame to have it just sit there all the time. It's snow in July if you ever earn it by catchin' a fish over ten pounds out of the Connecticut."

"And fat Sam Barston does not remember even from when I reminded him yesterday of the snow in July six years ago?" Malik would counter, briefly breaking out of his silence. "There will be a fish some day, Sam Barston."

"Well you can talk today after all, Malik. I was afraid you might be dead. You looked dead and acted dead, but come to think of it you didn't smell dead. And you think you might catch a fish here some day big enough to earn that dollar? Ha! Well I know you won't, but if it'll make you feel better, I won't spend my dollar today."

Old Sam would tease Malik for an hour or so and then apologize profusely to him for having to leave. Malik was always glad to see him go.

After the eighth day of using the plank-rig with still no sign of a big fish, Malik refused to speak even a few words to Old Sam, who then began appearing at the point several times a day. Whenever Malik saw Old Sam coming, he would wade out to his knees and stay fishing with his back to him. Old Sam, not in the least disturbed at Malik's behavior, would stand on the shore and keep talking at the Abenaki's back. Whenever Malik came in to unhook a perch or to re-bait his hook and the teasing intensified, Malik would refuse to so much as look at Old Sam. ("Well your toes don't look all that blue, Malik. Don't see why you think you have to soak 'em so much, but if you think you have to then I won't stand in your way. But the thing that really needs soakin' is your hair. That's all I can see of you that's still summer-sky blue ... Ha! That ain't a very big perch, but my eyes might just be playin' tricks on me. Might be that it's awful heavy for its length. Want to take it over to the flour scales and see if it'll go ten pounds? ... Back out again so soon? Well, maybe there is some blue left down there under your toenails where I can't see it. You know best of course. But really, Malik, think about doin' somethin' with that blue hair. Even a big hat would be an improvement. Right up there on top — right where you can't see — that's where it's the brightest ... Another perch as quick as that? Well, maybe this one 'll go ten pounds. Want to weigh this one?")

Sue did not ignore Old Sam. She enjoyed his company, but felt uneasy because, as she dodged his teasing, Malik would so pointedly ignore both of them. After Old Sam left each day, Malik generally stayed sullen for an hour or two before he would speak readily with Sue again. Sometimes he wouldn't break out of his moodiness even by the end of the afternoon. He would quietly clean the fish as Sue dismantled the plank-rig. Then he would send her up to the village square to trade. Often he fished until dark.

During the afternoon of the tenth day they had used the plank-rig, Malik seemed particularly sullen. After he had finished cleaning the fish, he announced to Sue that henceforth they would each take half the fish to eat, trade, or do with as they wished. Sue didn't have to cook food for him any more either, he said.

The next day he was drunk and worthless. He didn't show up at the river until late in the morning, and Sue had to set up the plank-rig by herself that day. He spent much of the afternoon sleeping in the sun; drinking constantly from his rum bottle when he was awake. He cursed Old Sam when he came by and told him to go away. Old Sam began teasing him, but soon left off when Malik's curses continued. He spoke to Sue for a while about Malik and then went home. Sue caught all the fish that day, cleaned them, and took them up to the village square to trade at the end of the afternoon. After she had finished her trading, she returned to find Malik unconscious. She was very angry with him. Spitefully she took his bottle and poured what rum remained in it out onto the ground. After she had taken apart the plank-rig, she went home and got an old quilt. It was nearly dark when she dragged Malik onto more comfortable ground and covered him with the quilt. Then she went back home and, though she wanted to have a long talk with her father about Malik's drunkenness, she never quite got around to it.

Old Sam came the next afternoon to check on Malik. He didn't once tease him. Malik sat on the old quilt, red-eyed and haggard. Before long he fell asleep. Old Sam talked to Sue about him.

"We got to take care of the old Injun, Sue, the two of us. There's no one else to look after him. He just ain't got a bit of sense when it comes to rum. He won't take a thing from me any more so it's mostly up to you. Make sure, at least, that he gets good food. I'll pay you for it, but don't tell him that.

"Any idea why he started drinkin' again? Ain't been drunk like this since he got painted."

"All I know," Sue said, "is that he don't want you to be right about the size of the fish in the Connecticut. And he don't like it when you give him things all the time and he can't give you anythin' back."

"Always was a proud old cuss," Old Sam said. "I was hopin' he might get over all that some day. Known him since ... let's see. I've known him since 1767 — well over half a century if you can believe it — and a friendship that old shouldn't have some silly little thing like pride get in the way now, should it? Course not. But there it is anyways. Might even be nice if I was wrong about the fish in the Connecticut, but there ain't much chance I am. The dams took care of all that. The salmon have been gone for years, and there's nothin' else that ever had any size. But you keep that rig out there goin'. Hear me? At least give me a chance to be wrong. Who knows? I might even enjoy givin' Malik that silver dollar."

"Some day I hope he realizes what a good friend you are," Sue said.

"Ha! No danger of that. Not from that stuck-up, blue-headed, old Injun. No reason the old cuss should realize anythin' more 'n he does right now. Pig-headed is what he is, and I don't know as I'd recognize him any other way."

The two of them talked about Malik for a long time.

Old Sam told Sue of a bad dream he kept having that Malik, because of his pride, would either freeze or starve to death up in the north country to plague Old Sam's conscience for the rest of his days for not having forced Malik to winter with him in Barston Falls. He said he always worried about Malik every fall when he went upriver for the winter and that the worries kept nagging at him until he saw Malik again in the spring. He told her more about Malik's near drowning at Barston Falls a few years before, when he had stumbled into the river after he'd been drinking.

Sue started to tell Old Sam about Malik's latest drunkenness after a fortnight without any rum. She got as far as recounting how she had poured out the remainder of the rum. Old Sam's explosive interruption startled her badly.

"Don't you ever do that again, Sue! That's about the biggest sin there is! A sin and a waste! If you need to pour out rum ever again, you come up to my house and pour it out into one of my jugs. But never, never, never pour it out on the ground! Hear me?"

Sue promised not to waste rum again. Then Old Sam quieted down, and they continued speaking about Malik.

As they were talking, the three boys appeared. They had heard about Malik's drunkenness, Sue thought, and had come to see what they could do to him. They stayed up on the ledges for a while looking things over, but then Old Sam shouted and waved for Benjie to come down and see him. Tom and Foss followed, the three boys shuffling as unconcernedly as they could manage down to where Sue and Old Sam stood. As the boys took long looks at the unconscious Malik, Sue wondered what mischief might be on their minds.

The three boys stood there without looking Sue in the eye. She towered a full head over any of them. How easy it would be, she thought, to grab one of the boys by the front of his shirt and give him a good shaking.

"Well, Benjie," Old Sam began. "Jared tells me you're stayin' out of mischief. I like to hear that, but I find it hard to believe for a boy of your talents. He says that the two days of prayer you had in your room evidently did you a world of good. Prayer's good for guidance that way, ain't it Benjie?"

"Yes sir, Grampy Sam," Benjie said, shifting from foot to foot.

"I wanted to talk to you and Foss and Tom about a very good friend I have there sleepin'. He's such a good friend, and I've known him for so long, that the thought of havin' anythin' happen to him disturbs me greatly. I hope you understand that. Here now. Ain't that a lot of dust there on your britches?"

Benjie looked down at his britches, which didn't seem especially dusty.

"Well, no sir. I can't see it."

"Not there. On the seat. Ain't it in need of a dustin'?"

Benjie, who had been facing Old Sam the whole time,

couldn't understand how the old man could see the seat of his britches. He twisted, looking over his shoulder.

"No. They look clean to me. I can't see it."

"Maybe not. Maybe I was wrong, but they might need dustin' sometime, mightn't they? A great deal of hard dustin'? Very hard dustin'?"

"No sir. I don't think so."

"Good. I hope I'm wrong. But understand that what happens to my old friend Malik is of great concern to me. Great concern. If he is left alone, then perhaps there'll be no more need for hard dustin' or for days of prayer. I want you to protect him, Benjie. Keep an eye on him to make sure there's no bad luck in his life, just as a favor to me. Dustin' and days of prayer — now can't you think of much better ways to spend your days?"

"Yes sir. I s'pose I can," Benjie said.

"You might get to know Malik too," Old Sam said. "There ain't much he don't know when it comes to fishin' or huntin' or trappin'. Ain't much at all. You might learn a lot — you and Foss and Tom. Now what are you up to to-day?"

"Nothin' much, Grampy Sam. Just wanderin' mostly."

"Well wander on now, but make sure you wander back here often to keep an eye on old Malik so you can protect him from any bad luck. You understand what I'm sayin'? Benjamin?"

"Yes sir."

"Good. Well, run along now."

The boys left. Sue watched them with a smile and wished that Malik could have been awake to hear.

Old Sam announced that it was time for him to think about heading home, but he lingered nonetheless. He spent more time with Sue talking about Malik and about rum.

"You won't get him to stop drinkin', Sue, so don't waste your time tryin'. But there is such a time after a man has drunk a certain amount of rum when havin' more on top of it is as much of a sin as pourin' rum out onto the ground — and a time after that when it's less of a sin to pour rum out onto the ground than it is to pour it into a man. That's what jugs got invented for — so a man wouldn't have to drink up all his rum at once, but could save some for another day."

"Yes," Sue said. "That's about what Pa says. He's got a mug he fills and drinks from, and he won't have any more rum than that in a day."

"Good," Old Sam said. "Maybe he can explain that to Malik sometime."

After Old Sam left, Sue fished for the rest of the afternoon. Often she glanced up at where Malik was sleeping. She wanted to tell him about Old Sam's words to Benjie and the likelihood that the three boys wouldn't plague him any more. She thought about Malik as she fished and about Old Sam. Never once did she think about her own unhappiness.

When Malik awoke at last, Sue took food to him. His mouth hung open as he stared at her. At first he shook his head at the food, but she forced it upon him. He ate slowly, nodding at her every now and then, and saying a syllable or two in response to her questions. He didn't pay much attention to what she was saying, but did understand that she would be giving him rum every day from then on, though she would decide how much he was to have. He would have all the food he could eat, too. She said something about the three boys as well, but he didn't understand that. When she left to trade the fish she had caught that day, he fell asleep again. Later, right at the end of the afternoon, she returned and gave him more food. He felt much better then and asked her about the plank-rig.

"No, we didn't catch anythin' on it today."

"We must take it in for the night," Malik said.

"No. You ain't listened to me, Malik. Old Sam was here. Benjie and the other boys too. He told Benjie to protect you. They don't dare do anythin' bad to you again. It means that we don't have to haul in the planks any more and hide 'em; don't have to haul away the rope and the fishline with us to keep 'em safe. We can just leave 'em set up and maybe check the bait every day or two. That'll be enough. If the boys play tricks with the rig or take it, they'll be in bad trouble with Old Sam."

"Ha! Old Sam. He should leave me alone, Sam Barston."

"Well, he ain't goin' to. He worries about you — says you was always stubborn and pig-headed. No, he ain't goin' to leave you alone. He's still your friend."

"Ha! Fat Old Sam Barston," Malik said.

He rose to his feet and thanked Sue for the food. Without saying anything else, he walked up to the village square and from there back up to his shelter by the great boulder.

Sue went home. At supper she told her father what Old Sam Barston had said about drinking rum and asked him how much he thought Malik should have every day. He showed her the mark on his own rum mug; said that was plenty for himself, but that since Malik was smaller, she could cut the amount down a little.

That evening as darkness came on, Malik's planks continued to float in the Connecticut, wavering slightly as the current caught the lower plank and the board-fins unevenly. The fishline ran through the loop of peeled willow lashed to the upriver plank and then kept going down deep below where the current slackened — over sunken ledges and broken rock. The rock-filled, cloth sack rested on the bottom right on the edge of a drop-off into the deepest hole up or down the Connecticut for many miles. There on the edge of the drop-off the skinned perch drifted here and there on the six feet of line between it and the stones in the cloth: slowly, back and forth, rising and settling.

In the middle of the night the planks lurched violently twenty feet towards the western bank of the Connecticut. Then the current caught them again and carried them back to their usual position. A lone tree thrashed horribly in the darkness.

In the morning Sue cooked breakfast for her father and packed food for his dinner. She put food to share with Malik into her fish basket. On her way towards the river she swung up north of the village square to return a basket and a pie tin to Annie Ballard. She stopped again at Steve Danforth's store on the east side of the square to get Malik's rum for the day. Then she went down towards the river to check on the plank-rig.

XVIII

Sue was angry as she stared at the tripod sticks, which had been knocked over, and at the place where, just the evening before, the fishline which had belonged to Malik and her had stretched out towards the floating planks. Now the fishline was gone.

"Old Sam told 'em to leave Malik alone, and they didn't," she muttered. "They saw that we left the line out overnight, and they stole it. If Benjie Barston was here right now, I'd shake him 'til he gave it back. I would!"

She waited by the tripod for Malik, imagining various punishments for the three boys. Then she grew impatient and went down to fish for perch. When Malik arrived, she told him of the theft and stamped angrily back up to the tripod to show him that the fishline was gone. They looked at the sticks of the tripod lying on the ground.

"It's got to be those boys," Sue began. "Old Sam told Benjie to leave you alone, and when he finds out that Benjie and the other two ..."

Malik silenced her with a quick motion of his hands: jerking them up by his shoulders with the palms facing her.

"What is it?" Sue whispered.

"Smell," Malik said.

Sue's nostrils dilated for a moment, and she recognized a faint, sweet smell of wintergreen.

"But why ..." she began, glancing around among the rocks and ledges for the small, wintergreen plants.

"The birch," Malik said, strangely excited. "Come."

He led her up to the yellow birch they had tied the

fishline to, a small tree sprung up from the ashes of the village fire eighteen years before; led her around to the back of the tree, gave a sharp cry, and pointed. Sue saw that the bark was missing in a strip four inches wide from near the ground all the way up as high as Malik could reach. Sap oozed from the bare, white wood. Tatters of bark lay on the ground and dangled from the top and edges of the wound. Malik laughed and ran his hand over the smoothness of the wet wood, smelled his hand, and then rubbed it across his face. He said something in his own language and turned to Sue.

"Benjie Barston did not do this," Malik said in great glee.

"Who did then?" Sue asked.

"A fish," Malik said. "A big fish for Sam Barston."

"No. That can't be."

"Yes. A big fish pulled the line hard into the bark and skinned the tree. The line caught where the branches come out, just there, and the big fish broke the line."

"But it couldn't," Sue said. "That line was much too thick for any fish to break. Somebody's playin' a trick on us."

"No," Malik said. "See how the tree bends toward the river. The big fish pulled hard and bent the tree and broke the line. Now we must get another line and another hook and catch the fish."

"Maybe it was just a log or a whole tree floatin' down the river, Malik. It drifted into our line and got tangled and was so big that it skinned the tree and bent it and then broke the line. I bet that's what it was."

Malik's face clouded. He had not thought of a tree or a great log drifting down into the line; didn't want to believe it had been anything but Old Sam Barston's fish.

"No. A big fish for Sam Barston. We must get another hook and another line. Come. We must catch many small fish to trade. Come, Sue."

Sue argued with Malik as they began fishing together.

He insisted that nothing but a big fish had broken their line; she that no fish in the river could be big enough to break the line they had been using. She knew she was right, but eased off on her arguments when she saw how intent he was on fishing for small fish. When he refused the day's ration of rum, saying he would trade it along with the fish so that they could get a new fishline more quickly, she ceased all arguments. She told him that, indeed, it must have been a fish which had broken their line.

Malik stopped fishing in the middle of the afternoon long enough to clean the fish they had caught by then. He sent Sue up to the village square alone with directions to trade the fish for whatever might be easily exchanged later towards a new fishline. While she was gone, he continued to fish. Early in the evening Malik gave Sue fish to take home to her father for their supper. He was still knee-deep in the river fishing while she was pulling in the rope for the plank-rig, hiding the planks, and coiling the rope; still there when she went home.

Early the next morning, when Sue arrived for another day of fishing, Malik was knee-deep in the river fishing intently. Already he had half a dozen perch in his fish basket.

* * * * *

Benjie, Foss, and Tom were close to ecstasy as they crouched over the two dead woodchucks. They felt vindicated for all their previously unsuccessful trapping efforts: the leather snares which, at best, held woodchucks only for the moment it took the creatures to chew through them; the poorly functioning boxes with the hinged doors and bait and trip pan inside; the deadfalls they had made with trigger sticks that would not work — either dropping the log at the slightest breeze on the bait or else holding it so strongly that nothing short of a good kick from one of the boys would work it. It had been the deadfalls which had finally succeeded. The boys had improvised and experimented enough to get them right. Their reward had been to find two dead woodchucks underneath their deadfalls on the same morning. In their euphoria they denied the possibility that anything other than their own trapping skill had gotten them the woodchucks; that luck had had anything to do with it. In their buoyant optimism they knew that they could reset their deadfalls and find at least two woodchucks beneath their logs every morning until the end of time.

"Old Malik or some other Injun couldn't of done any better 'n this," Benjie said. "Two woodchucks the same mornin' and nothin' to it but to get the deadfalls rigged right."

"Remember how much time we wasted with the bows and arrows tryin' to get the woodchucks?" Foss said.

"We did get one," Tom said. "Leastwise I got one."

"That was fun," Benjie said, "but it was a wicked hard way to go about it. Trappin' is so much better on account of the traps keep workin' while you're doin' somethin' else. Now that we got deadfalls figured out, I want to try 'em on muskrats and minks and raccoons. Might even go after otters or fishers. S'posed to be otters by Eagle Pond. There's bobcats too we could catch. If we go over to Mount Wheelock and rig a big enough deadfall, we might even get a bear or a catamount."

"Have to be wicked big," Tom said. "I'd be afraid we'd come by one mornin' and find somebody under it — some man I mean."

"They put up signs near 'em sometimes, " Foss said. "Or they build a fence around 'em to keep people out."

"Ha!" Benjie said. "That'd keep a bear or a catamount out too now, wouldn't it?"

"Pa says that's the way they used to do it," Foss said. "I don't s'pose they'd do it that way if it kept a bear or a catamount out. Be a waste of time if the fence kept out what you was tryin' to get."

"Bears can jump wicked high, Benjie," Tom said. "Hop right over a fence as tall as a man and never even touch it. And catamounts can jump even higher."

"Bears climb," Benjie said. "They can't jump over things like that."

"Can too," Tom said. "Pa says that ..."

"Well he don't know what he's talkin' about," Benjie began. "They're too fat and slow ..."

"Shows how much you know, Benjie Barston," Foss said. "Bears are wicked fast when they want to be. Run faster 'n a dog or a horse. Only they can't run down a hill, so if you ever ..."

"It's uphill they can't run," Tom said. "Course they can run down a hill. Anybody can run down a hill."

"You two can do me a favor and stop spreadin' stories," Benjie said. "Bears can't run and they can't jump neither. That's just lies you heard from people that don't know what they're talkin' about. You hear somethin' and you naturally believe everythin' right off without ..."

"But my pa says ..." Tom began.

"Your pa, the great trapper?" Benjie sneered. "He ever trap a bear or a catamount? Ever rig a deadfall? He prob'ly don't even know what a woodchuck looks like."

"He knows a lot more than you, Benjie Barston," Tom said. "He knows a lot of things like that, more prob'ly than anyone else in the village."

"Ha!" Benjie said. "More 'n Malik? More 'n Grampy Sam?"

"Well, not more 'n Malik," Tom said in a quieter voice. "And I guess that maybe Old Sam knows a lot too just because everybody from the old times used to know everythin' about fishin' and huntin' and trappin'. Malik both bein' from the old times and bein' an Injun, prob'ly knows more 'n anybody else now. But my pa ..."

"That's what Grampy Sam says," interrupted Benjie, forgetting the argument. "I guess that maybe old Malik knows more about such things than we ever will. Grampy Sam says we could learn a lot from him. You know, I wish we'd of got born a hundred years ago. Then we could of fought Injuns and hunted and trapped all we wanted and caught great big salmon out of the river. We could of gone out and killed everythin' we ate and starved to death if we didn't get anythin'. There's just no adventure to it now when you can go down to a root cellar and get food, or go out to the hen house or butcher a hog or a beef or a sheep. There ain't a chance you can starve to death any more, and that takes all the fun out of it."

"A hundred years ago would of been perfect," Foss said. "We got cheated — just born too late."

"That's for sure," Tom said. The three boys crouched in silence for a moment before he continued speaking. "Well, what do you s'pose we should do with these woodchucks now? Want to carry 'em down to the square and parade 'em around?"

"No," Benjie said. "Let's make hats out of 'em. Trappers' hats."

"But there's only two," Foss said.

"So what?" Benjie said. "We'll get another woodchuck tomorrow and make another hat. Then we can wear 'em around together, and everybody 'll know that we're trappers. It'd be fun to have a woodchuck hat."

"So how do we make one?" Tom asked. "I know we could hack the skins off these things and have somethin' to put on our heads, but how do we make decent lookin' hats out of 'em? How do we keep 'em from smellin' like rotten meat and crawlin' with maggots?"

"Just skin 'em and be careful," Benjie said. "What more can there be to it than that?"

"I don't want to ruin 'em," Foss said. "It took us a long time to get these woodchucks. I think we should find out the best way to skin 'em before we start on these. I know we'll get a lot more woodchucks now that we know how to rig the deadfalls, but we might waste a couple dozen skins hackin' away 'til we get the hang of it. I'd just as soon have those couple dozen woodchucks skinned right so we can trade 'em. Might get a gun for all that many skins."

"Well, maybe you're right," Benjie said. "Where do we find out how to skin 'em right though?"

"Let's go to Malik," Tom said. "He's the best one. Let's go to him and find out. And after we've got the skins, maybe Old Sam can show us a fast way to tan 'em."

"Think Malik 'll want to help us?" Foss asked.

"Course he will," Benjie said. "We'll give him the meat. It's good and fresh. We'll tell him if he shows us how to skin 'em, he can keep the meat. He'll be glad to have it. Besides, most of the blue is wore off of him by now — even his hair and clothes. He's prob'ly forgot all about it anyways. If we give him the meat, he'll do it — be glad to. We can watch him, and then we'll know how to skin the rest of the woodchucks ourselves. What do you say?"

"Let's go," Tom said. "We can ask him about bears and catamounts too, and maybe Benjie can learn a few things."

"Sure," said Foss. "Let's go."

Benjie lifted the two woodchucks by the cords around their necks. Carrying one in each hand, he led Foss and Tom down Tannery Road, across the bridge, through the village square, and down towards where Malik and Sue were fishing.

XIX

Malik stood knee-deep in the river, fishing below the point. His fingers kept a light touch on his line as he felt the tap of a fish going after the bait, another tap, a third. He jerked and then hand-over-hand hauled in the line as he backed up onto the ledges. Another perch. He ran his fingers down the perch's back carefully to flatten the sharp spines in the dorsal fin, grasped the fish firmly to keep it from raising them again, twisted out the hook, and tossed the fish in on top of the others in his basket. For a moment he paused to heft the basket, but then quickly re-baited his hook and waded back into the river.

"We must catch many more fish," he called out to Sue, who was herself standing in the water.

Malik swung the weight and bait three times over his head and then released the line. It arched out, pulling free the coils in his left hand, and sliced into the water. He kept the line taut, kept alert, and waited for the tap of another fish going after the bait. Sue caught a perch. On her way to putting it into Malik's basket, she spoke over her shoulder to the old man.

"Should we get a stronger fishline for the plank-rig this time, Malik, or one the same as before?"

"We will decide when we see the lines and hear the price," Malik said. "Maybe the line will be stronger, but we will see."

Sue dropped the perch into the basket with the others. As she was re-baiting her hook, a movement up above caught her eye. She glanced up to see the three boys walking towards her.

"Scalps, Malik," she announced. "Three scalps."

It was their private signal; their joke for when one of them sighted the boys. Sue was surprised to see them approaching. Ever since they had painted Malik blue, they had kept their distance — all except for the day when Old Sam had told Benjie to see that no mischief came to Malik. One of them had something he was carrying. She shaded her eyes to see better. It was Benjie, and he had two dead woodchucks.

Sue stood as tall as she could and waited. Benjie halted directly in front of her. The other two boys stopped behind him, flanking Benjie's small shoulders. Sue glared at them all and didn't say anything.

"We wanted to see Malik," Benjie said.

Sue nodded towards Malik in the river. Her silence confused Benjie for a moment. He seemed embarrassed. He shuffled past her down to the water's edge carrying his woodchucks.

"Say, Malik," Benjie called out.

Malik looked over his shoulder at Benjie and past him at Sue and the two other boys. Then he turned back to his fishing.

"Say, Malik," Benjie continued. "We got a couple woodchucks with our deadfalls. We was wonderin' if we could give you the meat, and you could show us the best way to skin 'em. Want to make some hats."

Malik kept at his fishing.

"They're fresh," Benjie said. "We just got 'em. Good, fresh woodchuck meat if you can show us the best way to skin 'em. What do you say to that, Malik?"

Malik turned slightly towards Benjie, but still kept his attention on fishing.

"Woodchuck meat?" Malik said.

"Yes, and it's yours if you can show us — tell us — the

best way to skin 'em so we can make hats. Can you do that, Malik?"

"Yes, Benjie Barston. I can tell you the best way to skin the woodchucks."

He turned his back on Benjie and went back to his fishing. Benjie stood shifting his weight from one foot to the other and watched Malik's back. The silence embarrassed him, finally growing to be more than he could stand.

"Well, what's the best way, Malik?" Benjie asked.

"With a knife, Benjie Barston. The best way is with a knife."

Malik kept fishing. He thought he would keep fishing with his back to Benjie until the boy went away. After a while he glanced over his shoulder. The boys were still there, but they were whispering among themselves; wondering what to do. Just then Malik caught another perch and had to take it in to his basket right by where the boys were standing. They scattered out of his way as he approached and regrouped around him as he stripped the fish from the hook and threw it into the basket. He knelt down by his supply of mussels.

"That's a lot of fish you caught," Foss said.

Malik looked up from baiting his hook. Benjie stepped forward with the woodchucks just then. He held them out in front of Malik's face.

"See, Malik. They're big, and we got 'em just this mornin'. You can have the meat. We just want to make some hats."

Malik left his hook on the ground. He reached out to one of the woodchucks and pulled out some hair. He held up the hair for Benjie and the other boys to see, then let it fall to the ground.

"It is a foolish boy, Benjie Barston, who takes skins in the summer, when they are at their worst. Foolish. He should wait until the fall just before the woodchucks go in

for their winter sleep. The hats made from the skins a foolish boy takes in the summer soon look like old, rotten moccasins. Only a fool wears such a hat."

"Oh," Foss said. "We didn't know."

Malik rose to his feet and glared down at the three boys.
It gave Sue pleasure to sense their discomfort. She tried to
scowl at them with the same intensity as Malik.

"They are foolish boys," Malik continued, "who kill
creatures and have no aim to eat what they kill, but only to
carry the dead creatures around to show so that many
people may know of their foolishness. An Abenaki boy eats
everything he kills and is not so foolish. End your foolishness. Use the meat, and throw away the skins. Now take
your woodchucks away. I do not wish to waste my time in
the company of foolish boys."

"But Malik, we only wanted to ..." Benjie began.

Malik's hand shot out and grabbed Benjie hard by the
forearm, making him drop one of the woodchucks. Foss
stumbled back to avoid the sweep of the other hand, which
brushed against him and then clenched onto Tom's wrist.
Benjie and Tom struggled, but couldn't free themselves.
Tom began to whimper.

"Ouch!" Benjie said. "Stop it, Malik! You're hurtin' my
arm!"

"Yes, Benjie Barston. And perhaps some day I will hurt
more than your arm. There will be a time when you three,
foolish boys will regret many things you do. Remember
what I say. Remember well. Now go."

Malik released his grips on Benjie and Tom. The three
boys stumbled as they retreated, backing away from Malik, who stooped for the woodchuck Benjie had dropped
and flung it after them. Foss picked it up without taking
his eyes off Malik. Sue glared at the three boys with hatred
and took a few steps towards them. Her heart beat quickly

in an urge to hurt them with her words, though when she opened her mouth, she didn't know what she would say.

"Malik hates you boys on account of what you done to him. If you hadn't of been so mean, he'd tell you things and help you, but all ... all he can talk about now is how some night he's goin' to sneak in where you're sleepin', bash in your head with a club, and cut off your scalp."

"You're a liar!" Benjie screamed as he continued to back up the slope. "A big, fat liar!"

Sue had an urge for a moment to catch Benjie and pound him with her fists, but she stayed where she was. She forced herself to smile hard at him and to calm her voice.

"Foolish boys," she called out to them. "Foolish, little boys. I don't care what you think. Just wait and see what happens to you. No. Wait and see what happens to the other two and think about when your turn is comin'. Foolish, little boys."

Unable to think of anything else to say, Sue turned away.

"Liar!" Benjie shouted at her back. "Big, fat liar! Big, fat, fat, fat, fat liar!"

Sue kept her back to the boys until they went away. She had never hated anyone as much as she hated Benjie Barston.

* * * * *

As evening settled over the village, George and Annie Ballard lingered in their chairs, the supper dishes long since pushed aside. George was hunched over, resting his forearms on the table as he spoke.

"... what Mark says. He's about the same with everybody: quiet and stays to himself. Mark claims he can get a smile out of him, but he never heard him laugh. He's a good worker, Mark says, but it's like pullin' teeth gettin' him to talk. Him and the girl both. He's got some religion, but he won't go to church. A strange one all right — a different kind of a man."

"Different for sure," Annie said. "When I go out of my way tryin' to make the both of 'em feel more at ease in the village, I don't have much luck. There's hope for Sue, but he's a trial. I left baked things at their house, but it makes him uncomfortable, I guess, rather than what I wanted. When there's a basket to return, he ain't once brought it back himself — always sends Sue. She says her pa thanks me too, but I ain't yet heard it straight from him. And when I happen across him in the village, he's about as relaxed as a barefooted man standin' in nettles. Sometimes I think I might have a rattlesnake crawlin' out of my ear from the way he looks at me."

George laughed.

"That's what Mark says. Claims Joe Reckford is scared to death of you. Says he could practically stumble standin' still when you're around. Joe prob'ly just ain't used to seein' so much womanhood crammed into one person. Or maybe he's just scared of all women."

"Oh stop your teasin'. Just look at the man. He was married once and had a daughter. I don't guess he was scared of his wife. He must of been different once."

"Hard to say," George said. "We never knew his wife and barely know him. The way the girl is, she got it all from him — grown up that way."

"Yes," Annie nodded. "Too bad she ain't better around strangers. But I guess he raised her to work hard at least — her fishin' I mean."

"That's the truth. That girl and Malik are down there all the daylight hours — most all of 'em anyways — and they get an awful lot of fish. Say, there's somethin' I heard today you might be interested in. You know how old Malik has generally got enough rum fumes in him so a man has to think twice about smokin' a pipe nearby? Well, today he went into Danforth's store and sold some rum back to Steve Danforth. Think of that! Steve said he was sober as a baby. That'd be somethin' if the girl could make him change like that."

"Her name is Sue," Annie said. "And it'd make her feel like she fit in better if you'd call her by name when you see her. It's tough for a girl to be that big when she's so young. Likely she's scared she'll be seven feet tall before she's through."

"Now I seem to recall a girl that was big and strong and awkward like that when she was twelve or thirteen. But she stopped growin', and it's a good thing she did or I might never get anythin' to eat."

Annie smiled.

"I recall that girl too," she said. "I worried a lot about growin' more and had a hard time then, but it was a good deal easier for me than it is for Sue. I grew up knowin' everybody in the village, for one thing, and had friends. I never felt alone. Sue's different. She's got a good start on bein' miserable and needs a few friends to help her out of it. That's why I'm tryin' to be friendly with her. She's still got a chance — more 'n I can say for her pa."

"Just goes back to what I been sayin' about you all along," George said.

"What's that?"

"Some day you'll make a good mother," he said with a slight tease in his voice.

Annie looked at him squarely.

"Well, maybe I will."

"Sue won't have a chance to be lonely and miserable in peace — not with you after her all the time. I can see that. I s'pose Joe Reckford's a harder case though."

"Seems so," Annie said. "I try to be friendly, and it just scares him. Maybe Sue can help him some day. I don't think anybody else ever could."

"He's prob'ly carryin' around a lot of scars inside him. They say it's awful rough on a man losin' a young wife. Some get over it, but a lot never do."

"I guess he's one that ain't goin' to. I'll give my cookies and pies to Sue from now on and leave her pa in peace. He'll be more comfortable if I just leave him alone."

Annie rose from the table and began clearing the dirty dishes.

* * * * *

Benjie crept silently on his hands and knees toward the window. The glow of moonlight filtering through the leaves of the ash tree outside his room broke the darkness just enough for him to see his surroundings. A floorboard creaked beneath his knee, and he stopped for a moment, listening to the sound of his own breathing.

If he comes, it will be by the window, Benjie thought. *Up the tree and in through the window.*

His stomach rumbled loudly, a sound as loud to Benjie's ears as a voice. He remembered the woodchucks with a faint wave of nausea. The taste was still in his mouth even though he had eaten his mother's food afterwards. He and Foss and Tom had cut the heads and paws and skins from the two woodchucks, had torn out the guts, and had flung all the offal into the river. Next they had rinsed the two bodies repeatedly. In spite of their efforts, however, a heavy musk had lingered on the woodchucks and on their hands. Then with feigned cheerfulness they had taken a coal from the fireplace in Foss's home, had built a fire up in the woods, and had roasted the two woodchucks. They had begun trying to roast them whole, but the meat had been cooking so slowly that finally they had cut the bodies up and had cooked the meat in small strips held over the fire on sticks. A musky, greasy smell mingled with the smoke all the time they were cooking the woodchucks. That smell had kept them from eating any of the meat until all of it had been cooked. Then, each under the gazes of the other two, they had sat down together for their "Injun feast." The meat had tasted as vile as it had smelled. Any of them alone would have spat out the first mouthful of woodchuck meat and flung the rest into the woods. Together, however, they sat and ate until it was all gone, each of them taking pains not to eat any more than was his proper share. Afterwards they had separated and had gone to their homes for supper. Benjie had eaten as much of his mother's food as he could, but it was so much less than what he usually ate that he attracted her notice. He told her that he and Foss and Tom hadn't been running around as much in the afternoon as they usually did and that he hadn't worked up his usual appetite. That explanation seemed to satisfy her enough so that she left him alone.

It will be by the window if he comes, Benjie thought.

He finished crawling to the window. Then, rising slowly to his feet at one side of the window frame, he peered out into the night. Scarcely breathing and with his mouth open, he stared hard at the tree and then surveyed the moonlit spaces on both sides of it. Nobody was in the tree. No one was near it on the ground. Nowhere was there any movement — just the quiet, night sounds of summer. Benjie continued to stare.

Maybe he's comin' right now. Maybe in a minute I'll see him sneakin' through the shadows and comin' up to the tree.

He tried to remember what the girl had said as they'd been leaving. He tried to remember Malik's words. He and Foss and Tom had laughed at them while they'd been cooking the woodchucks. How did they go? "... *you three boys will be very sorry ...*" No. "... *you'll regret many things ...*" Something like that. The woodchuck on the hook. Painting Malik blue when he was drunk and asleep. "*He hates you ... sneak in some night and bash you with a club ... scalps."* He couldn't remember the exact words she'd said. *Maybe he's comin' in a minute. Maybe he's after Foss and Tom now, and he's comin' for me soon.*

Benjie sighed and rubbed the bruise Malik's surprisingly strong grip had made on his arm. He remembered the mark Malik's fingers had left on Tom's wrist. He and Tom had both been astounded at the old Indian's strength. They had thought he was a feeble, old man, but his grip certainly hadn't been feeble. And Malik hated the three of them — had good reason to. No, the three of them hadn't been very nice to the old Indian. The woodchuck on his hook had been a good joke, but maybe they shouldn't have painted him blue. Maybe that had been a mistake. It might have made him stop drinking for a while the way some people claimed, but Malik didn't seem to appreciate that the way he should. He would just remember that three boys had painted him while he was asleep. He would remember them at least as long as the paint stayed on his clothes and in his hair. He would remember them and hate them, as the girl said, and would wait for a night when he could come and get them while they were asleep. Yes. They had certainly gone out of their way to make an enemy of Malik. He had every reason in the world to hate them.

Then there was what Grampy Sam had said about Malik's skills — all the knowledge of hunting and fishing and trapping that was just what three boys who had been born a hundred years too late needed: all the knowledge from the old days; all of the old Indian skills that no one but a few old Indian men knew about any more; all the knowledge that would be so easy for the boys to get if it could be taught to them and so difficult or impossible if they had to blunder around and discover it for themselves. That girl was learning those things from Malik. What a waste it would be if she wound up knowing more about hunting and fishing and trapping than he or Foss or Tom did! And Grampy Sam had told him that Malik knew more about medicines than any doctor in Vermont or New Hampshire. Doctors would find somebody sick and paw through their bags for some medicine that was always vile-tasting and which very seldom worked. Malik, Grampy Sam had told him, would take a look at someone who was sick and then go off into the woods for roots or berries or flowers or leaves or mushrooms, come back and make poultices or teas, and cure anybody of anything except for consumption and smallpox, provided that the sick person wasn't too far gone to begin with. Grampy Sam had seen Malik work his medicines for many years and had said that Malik knew more than any dozen doctors he'd ever seen. Malik was probably telling that girl some of those things about medicines along with the information on hunting and fishing and trapping. He'd seen the two of them talking a lot. They must have been talking about such things. What a waste! The girl probably wasn't even paying attention. No. They should have been a lot nicer to Malik. They should have given him presents instead of playing tricks on him. Then maybe he would have taught them some of the things he knew instead of calling them foolish boys as he pointed out their ignorance to them and instead of threatening them. Well, it was too late for that now. Malik hated them and might even be coming to get them.

Benjie looked down at the trunk of the ash tree. Could that old Indian climb up the tree? Could he climb up it with a club and make that little hop to get in through the window? No. That was ridiculous. That big girl had been lying to them. Malik was surely asleep, resting for his fishing the next day. There wasn't a chance in a hundred that Malik would come after them at night. Benjie shook his head in exaggerated disgust to convince himself of his foolishness in worrying about old Malik and strode back to his bed.

Still, wouldn't it be better to be safe? Malik was a lot stronger than he looked. He had raised bruises just with his grip. Even if there were only one chance in a thousand he would come, wasn't there still that one chance? Yes, there was. Benjie decided to be safe about it. Foss and Tom would never have to know. When he saw them in the morning, assuming that they were both safe, the three of them could repeat their jokes and mutual assurances that the girl had been lying. He would see how their stomachs felt, too, after eating the woodchuck meat.

Benjie stood beside his bed for a moment and looked at the lump in his bedclothes. He looked at it in the dim light just as somebody else would — somebody bothering to climb the ash tree with a club and come in through the window. Yes, the lump was convincing enough. It looked just like Benjie Barston sleeping. He smiled to himself and crawled back underneath the bed, wrapped himself in the blankets there on the floor, and, after being kept awake by his thoughts for a while, finally fell asleep.

XX

Sue and Malik sat beside the Connecticut on the upriver side of their new fishline. Their eyes followed the course of the line in from the two planks wavering slightly out in the current. From time to time they gazed back up at the yellow birch which anchored the line and down at the driftwood tripod, which the past two mornings they had found knocked flat.

"Shouldn't we go catch perch pretty soon, Malik?"

"There is no hurry now. We have the new line."

"I know, but we still got to catch 'em so we can trade for things."

"Yes," Malik said. "You are right. I will have my rum now. Then we will go back down and catch fish for our trading."

Sue rose and went over to her fish basket. She took out Malik's rum bottle and carried it back to him.

"Remember that's all there is for today."

"Yes. It is as you told me yesterday, Sue."

Malik unstoppered the bottle and took a very small sip, holding the rum in his mouth for a moment before he swallowed. It felt good, very good, going down his throat. He turned his face to the sun and closed his eyes until the taste of the rum faded.

"Tell me again what took the bait last night and the night before," Sue said. "I want to hear that again."

"The great fish," Malik said. "The great fish for Sam Barston. A fish as long as my leg, fat and heavy. It is big and very clever, for did it not steal the skinned perch from the hook two nights? The perch were too big for any little fish to eat. The fish for Sam Barston is big and old. But it is clever, for it knows of the hook."

"And tell me again why we're goin' to catch it today."

"It is because we take more care baiting the hook. This time all of the hook hides in the bait with the point just beneath the flesh. When the great fish swallows the bait, the point of the hook will come through, and we will catch the fish and carry it to Sam Barston to show him he was wrong."

Malik took another tiny sip of rum.

"And the line's stronger than the one we lost," Sue said. "It'll hold the fish if it takes the bait at night when we ain't here to pull it in. If we don't catch it today, then we'll get it tonight, and it'll be on the hook waitin' for us in the mornin'. Right, Malik?"

"Yes," said Malik.

He started to raise the bottle again, but lowered it abruptly without drinking. The rum must last, he thought. There would be no more for him that day than just what was left in the bottle; what might fill a wooden mug of medium size. Sue would give him that much rum every day, but no more than that. If he got as drunk again as he'd been when the boys had played their pranks on him, she wouldn't fish with him any more or give him food. He wanted more rum than what was in the bottle, but he wanted to keep fishing with Sue as well. For the time being his need to keep fishing with Sue and to catch a fish to fling down with laughter and scorn on Sam Barston's table or lap was stronger than his need for rum. He thought of the dream he'd had for the past several nights. In that dream he was sitting in the sun watching the plank-rig. A great salmon, as big as any from the old days, had taken the bait and had begun leaping high over the water. Malik had fought it hard and with great skill. After a long battle he had pulled it in to shallow water and had plunged one hand into its gills for a grip and with the other grabbed the base of its tail. Then with Sue trailing along behind exclaiming how big the salmon was, he had carried it, still flopping, up through the village square, where people had shouted in amazement at its size. Men had offered to buy it from him, offering many dollars, but he had told them it was not for sale. He had carried the fish across Tannery Bridge and right to Sam Barston's home. Striding in through the door, he had found Sam Barston: in one night's dream sitting at his table eating supper; in another night's lying in bed; in the third night's sitting in a chair in front of his fireplace. In each dream Malik had flung the fish down, onto the table or onto Sam Barston's lap, and had heard Sam Barston admit that Malik had been right about big fish in the Connecticut. Malik had simply nodded to him and had then gone back down to the village square. Many people had surrounded him there to ask questions about the fish he had caught. After a while Sam Barston had arrived at the square with the salmon — a fish so large that he had trouble carrying it, though Malik had managed it easily with one hand. Yes, they would catch the great salmon either that afternoon or that night.

While Malik was basking in a feeling of triumph from his reveries, a shadow passed over his thoughts: the realization that the dams kept the great salmon out of the Connecticut; that there hadn't been a big salmon in the river for many years. He took another sip of rum and brought back the image from a moment before of Sam Barston's surprise to see the great fish being carried through his door.

Sue watched Malik, wondering what thoughts had put such a smile onto his face and then what had caused the smile to fade so quickly. She studied his pleasure at drinking rum, knowing that he would have swallowed any amount she gave him. He had quickly finished his ration the day before and then all through the afternoon had yearned for more. Sue had been firmer than she had known she could be, telling him that if he drank more rum than she gave him, she would no longer fish with him or give him food. She was to keep his emptied bottle every night; had arranged to give Steve Danforth fish every afternoon in exchange for Malik's ration of rum the following morning. She would continue that arrangement of getting rum from Steve Danforth every morning, she thought. She wanted Malik to know that the bottle was empty when she took it home so that he wouldn't be tempted to pester her or her father at night if a thirst for more rum overwhelmed him. Sue thought about how sensible her father's example and Old Sam's advice had been: limiting Malik's rum rather than trying to make him stop drinking completely. She had prayed the night before that Malik would be satisfied with his ration.

For a moment as Sue looked at Malik, she regretted the ultimatum she had given him about drinking too much rum. Yet she had said it: if he got drunk, she would no longer fish with him. Perhaps she had been too harsh telling him that. A slight shudder of fear passed through her because she didn't ever want to stop fishing with Malik. In all the places where she and her father had lived, she had never found anything she liked nearly as much as fishing with the old Indian. He talked with her a great deal. He never said anything about her size or her coarse looks, and, in fact, seemed to admire her strength. He told her stories about the days when he had been young. He explained things to her patiently when she had questions. Nowhere else she had lived had she found anyone like Malik. And what would happen to him, she asked herself, if she stopped fishing with him? Who would keep him from trading every fish he caught for more rum? Who would see that he got good food to eat? No one would. Without her Malik would slide right back into his earlier way of life: catch fish, get rum, stay drunk as long as the rum lasted, and then recommence the cycle as soon as he felt up to fishing again. He would be an object of scorn to everyone in the village. The boys would play more tricks on him. No. He simply could not start his heavy drinking again. He needed her to look after him.

Malik brooded, looking troubled. Sue left him to his thoughts for a long time before she spoke.

"Is somethin' wrong, Malik?"

"I was thinking, Sue. In my dreams for three nights I catch a great salmon from the river and take it to Sam Barston. The dreams are clear that it is a salmon and yet when I awaken, I know again of the dams that the salmon cannot pass. I know that there are no more salmon in the river except for the ones up above the upper Co-os that are only the size of trout. It troubles me."

"Catch the big fish for Old Sam first, and then think about it," Sue said. "That's what you told me before."

"Yes. We try, but still we do not catch the big fish for Sam Barston. I dream of the fish, but when I am awake I wonder if there are big fish left to catch. When I am awake, I think that a tree heavy from lying many months in the water washed down and tangled in our line. The line skinned the birch before the force of the current against the tree broke the line where it was tied. Now at night perhaps it is not true that the large bait keeps the small fish away. Perhaps small eels or horned pout steal our bait from the hook and not a clever, big fish at all. Perhaps the hook is too large to catch the small fish while they strip away the bait. I want to catch a big fish to throw in Sam Barston's lap so he might remember he can be wrong, but perhaps there is no such fish left in the Connecticut for me to catch."

"We'll keep tryin'," Sue said. "You baited the hook a new way, and maybe tonight we'll catch somethin' on it — maybe even this afternoon."

"Yes. Perhaps there will be a big fish and not just the foolishness of an old man remembering when fish of great size swam in the river. An old man expecting that such fish still swim even though the dams have been up for many years. Such foolishness clouds an old man's eyes from the truth. It is a game only to keep him busy and away from long thoughts."

"What thoughts do you mean?" Sue asked.

"The look behind and the look ahead. The look behind tells me that once my life was not empty. There were many friends when I was a young man, but they are all gone now — all dead except Sam Barston. But Sam Barston forgets things about friendship. The look behind reminds me that once I was a man rich with a family. Once I was a man happy with a wife and with children."

"Where are they now?"

"Dead — all. Dead from the smallpox one winter when I was away hunting and trapping in the north with Nabatis. I was a rich man when I said my farewells. I promised I would return with many furs. When at last I came back with the furs, there was no man poorer in the world. I wanted the smallpox for myself then and a grave beside them."

"It must of been awful," Sue said. "Same as for Pa when my ma died. I was very young when we buried her and couldn't understand that she wasn't ever comin' back. And I remember Pa cryin' then and every time after that when he took me to sit by the grave. Then we moved away, and he didn't talk about her any more."

"He has a daughter to be a comfort to him as he grows old," Malik said. "When I think the long thoughts ahead, there are no children. Few years remain to me. I have no family to bring joy to me for that time. When I die, no children will care for my grave. Ahead I see only emptiness. The long journey to the north will be hard. And the winters there grow longer and bring more aches to my bones. Soon there will be no more trapping for me because my bones will be too old. I think of an old man I knew when I was a boy — an old man with no children: worthless and growing worse; waiting only to die because there was nothing else left for him. Nothing but sitting and waiting and thinking the long thoughts of an old man who is alone."

"Well, you ain't alone," Sue said. "We'll keep fishin' together, and neither one of us 'll be alone. And I think you and Old Sam should be friends again."

"I am still a friend to Sam Barston," Malik said. "He forgets what it means to be a friend to me. Yes, we will keep fishing together, Sue. Even if there is no big fish, we will fish together."

"I don't want you drinkin' too much rum ever again," Sue said. "It ain't good for you. You know that, don't you?"

Malik drank from his bottle and after a long moment nodded at Sue, but didn't say anything. He looked out over the planks floating end-to-end and let his thoughts drift back to the wife and the children he had once had. Sue left him alone for a long time before he realized she was speaking again.

"Listen to me, Malik," she said. "You hear what I said to you?"

"No."

"If it was just little fish that stole the bait from the hook, they couldn't of pulled hard enough to free the line from the planks and knock down the tripod — and two nights in a row too. There's a big fish down there, Malik, and we're goin' to catch it. Don't you think it has to be a big fish?"

"We will see," Malik said. "In my dreams there is a big fish. When I am awake, I am not sure. If there is a big fish, I do not know how it can pull hard on the line and not have the hook deep in its jaw. There are many things here I do not understand. We will keep fishing, and we will see."

They passed another hour by their new fishline before they dropped back down to the point to catch perch. They kept their eye on the tripod for the rest of the afternoon, but it remained standing. Sue traded fish up in the village square and afterwards returned to Malik. The two of them pulled in their fishline to check the bait and then reset the plank-rig for the night.

Again that night Malik dreamed of a big fish on their line.

* * * * *

After Joe Reckford left for work the next morning, Sue hurried over to Danforth's store to get Malik's rum and then walked quickly down to check the fishline. She found Malik sitting by the flattened tripod waiting for her.

"Did we catch it?" Sue asked. "Did we catch a big fish?"

"No," Malik said. "There is a fish, but we did not catch it. We need a new hook before we can catch the fish."

He held the end of the fishline out towards her.

"Look here, Sue," he said.

She looked at the hook on the end of the line. It had been bent out nearly straight.

"The hook was not strong enough for the big fish," Malik said. "We will trade for the biggest hook we can find, and then we will catch the big fish for Sam Barston."

In the middle of the afternoon Sue took perch to Danforth's store and got the biggest hook that Steve Danforth had.

XXI

Joe Reckford gazed out his window into the gray, early morning drizzle, wondering if it would break into hard rain and clear off in the afternoon or else continue throughout the day. Sue was busy setting food onto the table behind him.

"Hope there's plenty of work in the warehouse this mornin'," Joe said, "and no flatboats to take up through the canal. If it rains hard, Sue, don't stay out fishin' in it. No sense beggin' for sickness."

"Come and have breakfast before it gets cold, Pa," Sue said. "I'll just be a minute outside."

Joe sat and began eating the oatmeal in his bowl. He thought about Sue, and he thought about Annie Ballard.

Fishing occupied Sue's time better than anything else had for as long as he could remember. Sue got great satisfaction from trading the fish she and the old Indian caught and from bringing home tobacco and other presents for him in addition to food. Joe made a point of fussing over the gifts, and that always brought smiles to her face. For a while he'd been concerned about having her fish with the old Indian. In one of the few conversations he'd had with anyone, he'd asked Mark Hosmer about him and in a snort of laughter and scorn had heard him described as "a harmless, old drunk." Harmless or not, Joe's concerns had continued. He despised the weakness of drunkards nearly as much as he hated the meddlesome, self-appointed guardians and judges of people's private lives who thundered down pronouncements against rum from their pulpits on Sundays — as if the simple and natural act of taking a swallow of rum amounted to communing with the devil. He hadn't wanted Sue to keep fishing with a drunkard and was glad when she had asked his advice about a sensible amount of rum the old Indian might have every day. They had talked it over together during several evenings, and Joe had cut a wide notch into one of the woven, black-ash splits on the Indian's rum bottle. Sue could fill the bottle to that mark for the old Indian. That would be enough rum for him to have in a day. Every morning thereafter Sue had gotten rum at Danforth's store, and each evening Joe had asked Sue about the Indian's drinking. So far it seemed that the rum-rationing had worked, but Joe would continue to ask Sue about it.

Joe was still wary of Annie Ballard. Her shamelessness had pushed him to the verge of leaving Barston Falls, in spite of Sue's feelings. Suddenly, however, the woman's pursuit of him had slackened — perhaps even ended. One day she had wandered by three or four different times, as she had done during many previous days. The next day he didn't see her, nor on the day following that. Then he had seen her only as much as he might have expected to see anyone else in the village. The cookies and pies, which had kept coming in an avalanche with her notes to him, had kept him constantly nervous and feeling guilty about sending the baskets and firkins back with Sue when clearly Annie wanted Joe to return them himself. Now, however, the food came only about a third as often and — perhaps out of spite, he thought — the notes with it were for Sue and not for him. Perhaps it was a ruse to lull him off his guard before she came back at him again. Perhaps she had finally realized her duty as George's wife. He didn't know and didn't care as long as she didn't pursue him further. She was a fine woman, and George Ballard was a lucky man — or would be if she gave more attention to him. If she left Joe alone, he knew he would remain in Barston Falls.

If she came after him again, he would go. Sue would just have to get over the hurt of leaving. In the long run, he told himself, it might cause her more pain if they stayed.

Sue returned with an armload of wood, which she dumped into the woodbox near the stove. She put two sticks into the firebox and sat down next to her father to eat her own breakfast.

After Joe left for his work, Sue cleaned up the dishes from breakfast quickly and hurried out into the drizzle to get Malik's rum up in the square. After she had it, she went down to see if she and Malik had caught anything on their new hook during the night.

* * * * *

Malik sat cross-legged on the ground staring at the bare hook in his hand and doing his best to ignore the drizzle. He had been staring at the hook for several minutes lost in thought. The suddenness of Sue's appearance startled him.

"What happened, Malik?" she asked.

"Again the bait was taken," Malik said. "It did not make a difference how I baited the hook. The fish is too clever. We must think again and do something different this time, but I do not know what."

"Well let's reset the plank-rig and think about it," Sue said. "We don't have any perch, do we?"

"No."

"If you want to go down and catch one, I'll pull in the planks."

"All right, but while you work, Sue, think about what we can do so that we might catch Sam Barston's fish."

Sue went up to the red maple where the rope was tied and pulled the planks in, breathing hard from the effort when she at last had them by the riverbank. *A different bait?* she wondered. *Was a skinned perch good enough?* She tried to decide. *The bait we're usin' is fine. It's hookin' the fish that's the problem.* She carried the two planks down to the tripod. Malik hadn't returned. Sue relashed the willow twig to the upper plank, setting the fishline through the loop the twig formed with the plank. Finishing that, she sat and waited and tried to think of other changes they might make to catch whatever had been taking their bait. Finally Malik returned with a perch, skinned and ready for the hook.

"Do you think about how we can catch Sam Barston's fish?" Malik asked.

"I thought about usin' a different bait," Sue said, "but that ain't goin' to help us hook the fish any better. Then I thought that if we put two hooks in our bait, we'll have a better chance of hookin' whatever's been takin' it. Or maybe we could put two hooks and two baits on the same line. You think of anythin', Malik?"

Malik nodded.

"I think the hook and the bait are good. The fish gets away because we are not here to pull the line before the fish can feel the hook and spit it out. We must pull hard when the fish has the bait in his mouth."

"But the fish only took the bait at night," Sue said. "We'd have to be out here fishin' at night."

"Yes," Malik said. "Perhaps Sam Barston's fish does not eat during the day."

They talked further while Malik baited the hook and while he paid out line as the current swung the planks out towards the middle of the river. For half an hour they waited there, watched the line, and tried to guess about the fish that kept stealing the bait. The drizzle continued. Finally they both went down to catch perch. From time to time they glanced up to check the tripod, but it remained standing.

Towards the middle of the afternoon the sky darkened considerably, and the steady drizzle turned into a light rain.

Malik and Sue didn't mind the rain, which was warm and came with no wind, but the perch stopped biting. They fished for half an hour after the rain had begun and caught only horned pout.

"That is enough fish for us today," Malik said at last. "Let us clean what we have and take them to trade. I will have my rum while we clean them."

"All right," Sue said. "Let's take 'em up by the tripod. The rum's in my basket up there."

They knelt between the tripod and the river a few feet down from their fishline. Sue handed Malik his rum bottle, glanced out at the plank-rig, and began cleaning the fish. Malik sipped at his rum and looked out over the river for several minutes before he, too, began cleaning perch and horned pout with his knife. His practiced fingers worked far more quickly than hers. Sue paused to stretch when there were only half a dozen fish left.

"There ain't many perch today, Malik," Sue said. "Prob'ly not even half what we usually get. Wonder why that is. And we ain't ever caught but a few horned pout here before today."

"Perhaps it is the darkness," Malik said. "Perhaps the perch think that night comes early, and they do not eat at night. That is why we caught the horned pout this after-noon — because of the darkness."

"Oh. I didn't think of that."

Malik set down his knife and again sipped from his rum bottle, watching as Sue finished cleaning the fish. He drank more and thought about returning to his shelter and going to sleep early. Fishing in the rain made him sleepy, he de-cided. Sue at last rose to her feet, washed off her hands and her knife in the river, came back to stand beside Malik, and yawned loudly. She was sleepy too, Malik thought.

"Malik," Sue began. "I was meanin' to ask you. When you was a boy, did you ever ..."

Then as quickly as a gunshot Sue felt herself upended and in the air with pain across her ankle. The knife flew from her hand. She landed with a hard jolt just as the sticks of the tripod clattered to the ground. Dazed, she struggled for breath. Malik was shouting in his thin voice.

"Sue! Sue!"

In a momentary stupor she gazed at him straining against the fishline with his bony hands and arms. He called for her again and again. She stared at him numbly. Then, suddenly, her breathing returned.

Sue bounded to her feet and grabbed the line behind Malik. They heaved against it as hard as they could, but nonetheless the line pulled them sideways — further up the slope. They stumbled over the loose rock, broken ledges, and low bushes; barely able to keep their footing. Then the line stopped abruptly; bowstring-taut and ankle-high. Sue strained to lift it as Malik waved bloody hands and shouted for her to let go. The words meant nothing to her. Malik grabbed both her wrists and repeatedly tugged at them until finally she released her grip.

"But why ..." she began as she looked down at Malik's blood on her wrists and on his hands.

"Come!" he screamed and pulled her by one wrist in a staggering run which didn't end until they both stood at the point. Malik gasped for air.

"Look!" he shrieked. "Look! Look!"

His bleeding hands swept her attention down along the fishline and out past where it disappeared into the river. Her eyes searched the expanse of the eddy and found nothing. Abruptly her attention shot out to a sudden swirl followed immediately by another further over towards the entrance to the canal and then a third further over in the same line. Just beyond the third swirl something large and dark and looking like the end of a tapered plank poked upright out of the water, disappeared, then poked up again.

"What in the world ..." Sue began, but her words ended by themselves.

The strange object disappeared. Malik glanced behind him at the fishline dragging sideways across the ledges, then jolted his attention right back out to the eddy. For a moment there was nothing, but then another swirl appeared further out from the shore. Almost immediately the surface of the eddy broke again, but this time an enormous dark mass rolled up above the water, hung for a long moment, and then disappeared. Sue and Malik clutched each other's forearms hard; their heads turned towards the river.

"Did you see the size of that?" Sue whispered.

Malik didn't even nod. He let go of Sue's arms and scarcely breathed as he stood frozen in place and stared. The fishline, sweeping back out of the eddy and towards the east bank of the river, nearly tripped him. He stumbled, caught his balance, and stepped over the line. Turning towards Sue, he saw her stooped over and pulling against the fishline again.

"No Sue!" he shouted.

"But why ...?"

"It will burn through your fingers if it breaks above!"

Sue let go and stepped over the line. Just then there was an incredible commotion out in the river. She and Malik turned and watched a violent thrashing on the surface; stillness for a moment. Then, as if in a dream, they saw a monstrous, leaping body rise completely out of the water — a fish larger than they could ever imagine: seemingly as big as a canoe; as big as a sawlog. It crashed back down into the water and then immediately was in the air again, its head towards the western shore and thrashing so violently that the small sack of rocks they had used as a weight snapped back and forth like a squirrel caught by a large dog. The fish then bolted out into the eddy, leaped twice more over towards the canal entrance, turned, and swam back so rapidly that the line raised a froth where it cut through the smooth water of the eddy. Then the fish was in the current, headed up the river. It ran all the way to the end of the slack, turned, and surged down the river with the current. The line jerked taut, the fish leaped at the end of its surge, and suddenly the sack of rocks flew through the air back towards Malik and Sue further than a man could have thrown it. The fish was gone.

They didn't speak. In shock they pulled in the line. Their sack of rocks was intact. The fish hook was straightened.

Malik found his bottle and finished in one drink whatever rum hadn't spilled when he had dropped it. Then he went back to where Sue was sitting on the ground in the rain. Both of them were soaked thoroughly, but neither gave it a thought.

"*Kabassa*," Malik said at last. "The great fish for Sam Barston — *kabassa*."

"You think anybody else saw it, Malik?" Sue whispered.

They both peered out into the rain.

"No. We are the only ones out in the rain," he said.

"Then no one 'll believe us," Sue said.

"No," Malik said. "No one will believe we saw the *kabassa*, so we will not tell them."

"I saw it, but I can't hardly believe it," Sue said. Then with a look of wariness she continued, "How big was the fish you saw, Malik?"

Malik laughed at her.

"What you saw, Sue. The same. There was not rum enough in me to make it bigger. The fish was heavier than Sam Barston. You must believe your eyes."

"Yes, but it don't seem possible."

"It is as it is," Malik said. "You would not believe stories about such a fish, but you must believe your eyes. We will not be foolish and spread stories for people to scorn. They believe what they see and what they touch. We will catch the fish before we tell our stories. Then people will listen. I will tell no one. You will tell no one."

"All right, but how can we ever catch a fish like that? We couldn't even come close to holdin' it just then."

"We will find a way to catch the fish," Malik said. "You will see. But first we must think and talk to discover the best way, and we must have a bigger hook."

"But that was the biggest one Mr. Danforth had."

"Then we must find it elsewhere, for we will need a hook twice as large — four times as large. We must have a hook such as no one in the village has ever seen before."

"I don't know where we can find ..."

"We will need stronger line, too, and more line. We will need so much line that the fish can swim all through the eddy and up into the fast water and far down the river without running out of the line so that it can break off. Everything must be bigger."

"I don't see how we can ever hold the line," Sue said. "A fish like that could pull us right into the river. And look at your hands. I should wash 'em off for you, Malik."

"There are roots in the woods I will get to heal my hands," Malik said. "I will care for them later. But now we must sit and talk and think together. We must discover the way to catch the great fish."

During the rest of the afternoon Sue kept fingering the bruise which stretched across her ankle in a thin, straight line; reminding herself that she had not simply imagined the fish. That evening it was difficult for her not to tell her father about the fish and even more difficult to get to sleep. She kept remembering the fish leaping out of the water; kept wondering how she and Malik would ever catch such a monster.

XXII

George Ballard carried his sack up the steps of Steve Danforth's store and through the open door. He found Steve slouched against a counter and looking over a book of accounts.

"So what's new with you, George?" Steve asked.

"Not so much. Brought you a few more candlesticks. When things slow down some, I'll make the rest."

"Suit yourself. I ain't in a hurry for 'em."

"Still, I been meanin' to finish 'em for some time, but just one thing after another gets in the way. Keepin' me too busy. Ha! Strange one the other day. That's for sure."

"Well what's that?" Steve asked as he closed the book of accounts. He hiked himself up onto the counter and sat dangling his legs.

George looked around for a moment.

"Oh, sit on that counter there, George. It don't matter."

George clanked the sack onto the counter and sat beside it.

"Well," he began. "I just finished fittin' some iron to a pair of runners for Charlie Porter's pung when the girl come in — that big one fishin' with Malik."

"Oh sure," Steve said. "Comes in a lot. Her pa works with Mark."

"That's the one. Well she just stands back and waits, so I ask what does she want, and it turns out you ain't got fishhooks good enough for her, and she wants me to make her one. She ..."

"Course I got fishhooks!" Steve said. "And good ones too!"

"Not to suit her, you ain't. Way she looks at it, they're all too small."

"Well I don't know what she ..."

"Hush then and I'll tell you," George said. "Anyways, I joke along with her and tell her that I never made a fish-hook before, and it'd likely look pretty ragged by the time I got through with it on account of bein' so small. But she says she wants a big hook. I ask her how big and that stops her for a little, but she looks around and finally points to a horseshoe — a horseshoe! — and says if I made one for her out of it, that'd be just right.

"Well, I was laughin' to myself then and started teasin' her about what kind of fishin' she and Malik was up to, but she was serious — never even smiled. It was all I could do to keep from laughin' in her face, but then I thought 'why don't I?' and got to work. It was an old shoe that'd been around the shop for a while, the forge was good and hot, and I'd just finished with the runners for that pung. I thought it might be a lark to make a hook out of that horse-shoe. So I put it right in the coals and set to crankin' on the bellows, and she stood and watched. I drawed out one of the prongs and wrapped it to make an eye, then heated up the other one, chiseled it off about halfway down, and drawed out what was left into a point. I changed the bend in the shoe a little to get it right and there! A wicked big hook. I thought I was done and could give her the horse-shoe-hook and get back to work, but she looks it over and keeps askin' me can't I do this? and can't I do that? She wanted a barb on the hook the first thing, so I done that; then wanted the point so it didn't taper so quick. The bend suited her fine, but the eye must of took me twenty min-utes more before I got it right — right accordin' to her! She wanted the eye smooth as a bottle — claimed it'd cut the line if it wasn't. Well I tell you by the time I got that hook squared away to where she was happy with it, all the fun was gone out of the work for me. Then she asks what does she owe for the hook, and for a little I don't know what to say. Started the thing as a lark, you know, and wasn't goin' to charge her for playin' around with an old horseshoe, but then pretty quick it'd turned into real work — her bein' so fussy and all. She had coins right there in her hand ready to pay me. Well I'm in business to make a livin', I told myself, so I did charge her for the work. She paid right off and thanked me for the hook and seemed awful happy with it. Imagine that: a fishhook made out of a horseshoe!

"Then I was gettin' set to sit down and have a good laugh after she left, but on her way out the door she thought of somethin' else and come right back. Now this is the good part. Here I just went and made this fishhook out of a horseshoe — silliest project I ever had at my forge — and the thing must weigh upwards of a couple pounds. And she asks me, serious as can be, don't I have some old iron around with a hole in it she can use for a weight to get the bait down! Didn't I laugh then! Couldn't help it. Needin' a weight with that hook that'd sink faster 'n a rock all by itself. I laughed, but she was serious as can be, so I look around and find some old scrap and give it to her. She wants to pay for that too, but I just waved her out the door. Soon as she left I sat down and laughed 'til it hurt. Took me a while before I could get back to work. I still have to chuckle at it."

"Ha!" Steve said. "That ain't but about half of it, George! You should see the line they're gettin' from me. And it ain't line — it's rope! Malik and the girl, well they trade here a fair amount — bring me fish or what they get for tradin' fish with other folks. Regular customers, I'd call 'em. She was comin' in every afternoon with things and then every mornin' with a bottle for me to fill up to a mark with rum. That was Malik's rum, and she had him down to just so much a day. Quite a difference from how much he used to drink. And now, if you can believe it, she's got him so he don't ..."

"The rope," George interrupted. "Tell me about the rope, Steve."

"Oh well, let's see. The two of 'em come in here together and ask me about fishlines again — same as not long ago when they got a good one from me. Well they had that same one with 'em and wanted to trade it towards the price of a better one. Now that one they wanted to trade back was the heaviest fishline I carry — good solid cord, tough and thick. I started showin' 'em what else I had that was heavier but was never meant for fishline. What they finally settled on was some half-inch rope! Can you believe that?"

"Just the thing for haulin' perch out of the Connecticut, I'd say," George said. "Put my hook on it and a good weight so the bait don't float up on top of the water. Just the thing. Catch a couple dozen perch with it, and they might weigh as much as the hook!"

"And the best part was how much rope they wanted!" Steve continued. "There was a couple hundred yards here at least, and they wanted all that and asked me if I was goin' to get any more soon. Imagine that! Course that much rope runs into a pretty fair expense. I could see right away they wouldn't have the price of it and didn't feel very good tellin' 'em they couldn't take it with 'em 'til they could pay me for it. Well, they didn't expect to! Wanted me to keep accounts for 'em — keep a tally of what they gave me and have me tell 'em when I had enough from 'em to pay for the rope. And that was the last day the girl got rum for Malik. He ain't had a drop since unless somebody gave it to him. It's awful strange, is what I say."

"They made the price of the rope yet?" George asked.

"Few more days they will — 'bout three hundred yards in all I guess, countin' some more I just got yesterday. They worked hard fishin' for perch to earn it, let me tell you."

"Well, it's harmless," George said. "They can play around with it for a while. Then I expect they'll try sellin' it and put you out of the half-inch-rope business for a time."

"I s'pose they will if the rope's still good."

"Think of that, Steve — Malik not drinkin' any rum. Givin' it up just so's he can get as much half-inch rope as he can carry and so's he can tie a horseshoe-hook to it and heave it out into the Connecticut. Waste of time of course, but I tell you it's good for him fishin' with that girl. Don't you think so?"

"I s'pose it is," Steve said. "Look, George, could it be there's somethin' else they know? Sounds almost like they was tryin' to drag the river for a body. They could haul in a drownded cow on that rope or a drownded person. Could it be somethin' like that?"

"No, Steve. It ain't but a couple of kids playin' around — even if one of 'em is seventy or eighty years old. Malik is like a ten-year-old boy on a lot of things, and this is one of 'em. It's a harmless way for him to have fun. No. It's better 'n that if it keeps him from drinkin' too much. Maybe it'll keep him away from the blue paint too."

Steve laughed.

"You know, George, I got to admit I'm grateful to old Malik. There's still enough blue in his hair to make me laugh every time I look at him. And now when I can think about him out there goin' to fish with half-inch rope and a hook that'd kill a fish if it landed on it, I have to laugh some more. Yes sir. I'm grateful to that old cuss for entertainin' me and all the rest of the village. If I get bored, I might even let him have that rope early and trust him for the rest. Give me more time to laugh."

George got down from the counter, carried the sack over to Steve, and handed it to him.

"Well, I could talk all day, I expect, but I got to get back before the forge goes out and before somebody comes in with some work. Keep the sack for a while if you want. I'll get the rest of the candlesticks to you when I can."

"I know you will," Steve said. "No hurry. Say hello to Annie for me."

"Sure, Steve. And you say hello to Emma for us."

George went back to his forge, dumped more charcoal onto the coals, fired it by pumping his bellows, and launched into his work for the rest of the day.

* * * * *

She had frightened him doubly, that huge girl. First she'd startled him by sneaking up behind him and talking right into his ear — made him jump and whirl around towards her. Then just by standing in front of him, she'd made him feel about half as big as she was. He'd been wary and frightened because he remembered some of the insults he'd shouted at her in the past.

"Benjie Barston," she had said. "Malik wants me to ask if you got a woodchuck now or if you can get one for us. It don't have to be fresh — better if it ain't, he says — and we'll pay you for it."

Feeling ill at ease, he had mumbled something about knowing where he could get one. (Had he looked at the girl's face more instead of at her feet, he might have noticed how embarrassed she was, but his gaze had scarcely left the ground.) She had told him to take the woodchuck to Malik at the point when he had it, and Malik would pay him. Then she had left.

Benjie decided quickly that he needed a woodchuck. What had once been a stark fear of Malik, beginning the day the old Indian's grip had left such a bruise on his arm and fed largely by nightmares and by Benjie's active, daytime imagination, had gradually diminished to uneasiness as each new day came and he, Foss, and Tom had awakened unharmed. The three of them together had ridiculed Malik among themselves and had told one another time and again that his threat had been nothing more than the ranting of an old man and that they were certainly safe from him. Nonetheless, doubts raged through Benjie's mind. Harsh dreams each night kept him from convincing himself that it would be just as safe to sleep in his bed as underneath it. Yes, he certainly needed to get a woodchuck for Malik. He would see if he could find Foss and Tom. If he couldn't, he would go by himself to set the deadfalls. Then he would go get his bow and arrows and see if he could shoot a woodchuck before he caught one under a deadfall.

* * * * *

Two days later Benjie had a woodchuck. Carrying it on a cord, he led Foss and Tom down to where Sue and Malik were fishing at the point. The three boys stood and watched for a moment before Benjie called out. When Sue and Malik turned, he held up the woodchuck for them to see, and the two waded back in to the shore.

"We got a woodchuck for you, Malik," Benjie said. "She said you needed one. Caught it under a deadfall."

"Yes," Malik said. "It is what we need."

Malik glanced at the woodchuck as he took it from Benjie and then looked coldly at the three boys who stood before him in silent embarrassment. He remembered the other woodchuck, the one he had found on the end of his handline one day, after he had awakened from a nap, and remembered the taunts the three boys had made for days afterwards. And he needed only to glance down at the front of his clothes to remind himself that these same three boys had put blue paint all over him while he was sleeping. He glared at them for a long moment before he spoke again.

"We will pay for the woodchuck," Malik said. "What is the price?"

The boys darted glances at one another before Benjie finally spoke.

"We want to give it to you, Malik. We don't want to sell it. It's a gift."

"A gift?" Malik said. He brushed his hand through the hair on his forehead and looked at the three boys in surprise.

"A gift to you, Malik," Foss said.

"Yes, " Tom said. "And if you want another one, we'll try to get that one for you too — another gift, I mean."

Malik continued to stare at the boys.

"We should go now," Benjie said. "If you need another one, Malik, just let us know."

The boys turned quickly away, but Malik halted them before they'd gone a dozen steps.

"You boys!"

They looked back, frozen for a moment.

"Thank you," Malik said.

They nodded at him and left. Malik watched them until they were out of sight.

The boys slowed their steps as they neared the village square.

"You never asked him to show us those things about trappin', Benjie," Tom said.

"Well you didn't neither," Benjie said. "There's prob'ly a few things we need to let him forget before we start askin' him to teach us things."

"Benjie's right," Foss said. "I hope he needs more woodchucks and maybe some other things we can give him. We'll wait."

"Well, one thing sure feels better," Benjie said.

"What's that?" Foss asked.

"Givin' him somethin' instead of just playin' tricks on

him all the time. You see how surprised he was when we wouldn't let him pay for the woodchuck?"

"Sure," Tom said. "And if we give him a couple more, maybe then we can get him to show us some of his old Injun tricks about trappin'."

"Fishin' and huntin' too," Foss said. "And I think we got a better chance now when he starts thankin' us instead of pukin' out that silly, old-man talk about bashin' heads in at night."

"Ha," Benjie said. "Stupid old threats. Silly. Had to laugh every time I thought about 'em."

"Me too," Tom said. "Just thinkin' about that old wreck of an Injun sneakin' around at night. You know, I bet he has a hard time stayin' up much past sunset every day. And a man that old likely sleeps straight through the night."

"Bet the old goat 'd have a hard time even liftin' up a club now," Foss said. "Just tryin' to 'd prob'ly strain him."

"Course," Benjie said. "Why do you s'pose he needs us to get him woodchucks now? Can't do it any more by himself is why. But he knows things that we need him to teach us. And it is good to have him thank us instead of makin' those silly old threats. If we do some more nice things for him, I bet he'll be glad to teach us things."

Foss and Tom agreed.

That night for the first time in many days Benjie slept in his bed rather than underneath it, Foss didn't bother stringing up the ankle-high spider's web of rope meant to trip anyone sneaking around during the night, and Tom put a missing knife back in his mother's kitchen rather than keeping it under his pillow. All three boys slept well.

XXIII

Joe Reckford finished his supper, propped his elbows up on the table, and gazed at his daughter for a moment before he began speaking.

"Now we'll talk, Sue. There was somethin' I heard from Mark Hosmer today — somethin' that bothered me."

"What's that, Pa?"

"Well, he claims the whole village is chatterin' about you and the old Injun and about a rope and a hook huge enough to catch a whale on. Thought I might find out just what you and the old Injun are up to."

"Malik, Pa."

"All right. You and Malik, then. Are you fishin' with a rope? Got a hook made out of a horseshoe the way Mark says?"

"We got the hook," Sue said, "but we ain't got the rope yet. Mr. Danforth says we can have it tomorrow after we give him a few more fish."

"But why are you doin' somethin' so silly — somethin' folks was bound to notice? Everybody's laughin' at you and the old Injun on account of it. How come you're doin' it, Sue?"

"To catch somethin' bigger 'n those little perch," Sue said. "Old Sam Barston says he'll give Malik a silver dollar if he can catch a fish over ten pounds out of the Connecticut."

"Ha! Are you daft, girl? With a hook made out of a horseshoe? And Mark says it's half-inch rope. 'Three hundred yards of half-inch rope,' he says. That true?"

"Well, yes."

"Then he's right after all. I never would of believed it," Joe said, shaking his head.

Sue was silent; embarrassed that George Ballard had told people about the hook and that Steve Danforth had told them about the rope. She hadn't wanted the attention; had wanted to catch the big fish before anyone knew what she and Malik were up to. Now, she realized, everyone in the village must know what her father knew.

"Don't it seem silly wastin' your time like that?" Joe asked. "Seems to me you could play at a lot of other things that don't cost so much and that don't have all the folks in the village laughin' at you. That rope must come to quite a bit, and there's no tellin' how much you had to pay for a hook made out of a horseshoe."

"It ain't costin' you anythin', Pa."

"I don't care about that," Joe said, "but, now you mention it, you could get clothes, food, furniture, or a lot of other things instead. You could take hard coin and save it, too. What bothers me is that you're wastin' your time playin' silly games and that the whole village is noticin'. Don't you understand that, Sue?"

"It ain't a waste of time, and even if it was, can't I do what I want with my own earnin's?"

"Course you can. Strikes me as foolish is all, and I don't like havin' the whole village laughin' at you. I know you got more sense than that, Sue, and I just wish you'd get somebody your own age to play with — somebody that don't lead you around with such rabbit-brained ideas as that old Injun. I just wish ..."

"Malik ain't rabbit-brained, Pa!" Sue snapped. "And we ain't just playin' around and wastin' our time. We really are goin' to catch a big fish! That's how come we got the hook and the rope and how come we ..."

"Oh come, Sue," Joe said. "With a rope and a horseshoe? Might as well crack an egg with a post maul or shoot a squirrel with a cannon. I thought I raised a daughter with more sense than that. You're spendin' too much time with that old Injun instead of friends your own age. That's what the problem is. I think it'd be better if you ..."

"Malik," Sue said. "I wish you'd call him that instead of 'that old Injun' all the time. He's got a name just like anybody else. And I do have sense, Pa, and I know what I'm doin'. Can't you see that?"

"What I see, Sue, is a girl actin' silly in front of the whole village," Joe said. "Now I ain't goin' to order you to do anythin', but I want you to think about what I have to say. I think you been seein' too much of that old ... of Malik. Even if you don't realize it, you're gettin' all wrapped up in his way of seein' things. You'd be better off leavin' Malik alone. That's all."

Sue brushed at a tear, rose from the table, busied herself clearing off the dishes, and then began washing them. Joe came up behind her and stood awkwardly as he tried to think of the right words.

"I'm just tryin' to save you some pain, Sue. Everybody in the village is already laughin' at your hook and your rope, and they'll be laughin' even more if you start fishin' with 'em. Folks can be cruel with their talkin' and their laughin' and sometimes with just the way they look at you. They'll say a lot of things behind your back, too. If you go out of your way to draw attention, you got to expect that. Just think about what you're doin', Sue."

"I already did!" Sue snapped.

"Well make sure it ain't some foolishness that might hurt you later on. That's all I'm goin' to say about it, Sue. I don't want to talk about it any more."

Joe sat down to smoke his pipe, lighting it from a candle. Sue cleaned up from supper, not saying so much as a word. Joe kept looking over at her wondering whether he should say more or if he had already said too much.

When her work was done, Sue announced that she was going to bed.

"So soon?"

"Yes, Pa."

After she had gone upstairs, Joe smoked a second pipeful of tobacco and thought about her for a long time. She was upset. He blamed himself for that. It was another failure, he was certain; another attempt at being a good father, which had fallen flat. And he'd only been trying to help her! Well, he'd done a poor job. He'd seen her hands go up to brush away tears while she'd been washing the wooden bowls and plates and mugs. Then she had gone straight to bed, neglecting even to kiss him goodnight. Perhaps right then she was in bed crying to herself; miserable. What should he have done? He didn't know. He was caught between not wanting other people to hurt her feelings and not wanting to hurt them himself. He knew from the few words he had exchanged with Mark Hosmer that already Sue and the old Indian were being ridiculed behind their backs for their outrageous fishing gear. He guessed that when they actually began to use it, they would be the center of attention, laughingstocks, the butts of many jokes. That would hurt Sue badly. He might spare her if he simply ordered her to stop fishing with the old Indian, but he wasn't strong enough to do that. She would blame Joe harshly if he ended their fishing together, perhaps even hate him. It was a situation he couldn't win; couldn't do the right thing. He didn't even know what the right thing was. A good father would have known.

When Joe finally did go up to bed, his thoughts kept him from sleep until after midnight. He awoke in the morning tired and unhappy.

* * * * *

The next day Malik and Sue fished until mid morning at the point, cleaned the fish they had caught, and took them to Danforth's store. Steve Danforth gave them four coils of half-inch rope. Sue was excited as they carried the rope back to the river; eager to begin fishing with it. She thought they would start right away, but instead Malik made her sit down and talk.

"We must discover the best way to catch the fish for Sam Barston," Malik said. "The line and the hook took us many days to earn with our fishing, and we must not lose them by doing something wrong. We will talk and decide the best way."

"All right," Sue said. "And when we catch it, Malik, that'll give you plenty of food for the winter."

"The woodchuck will begin to smell in the heat, but I think that will be better than a fresh bait," Malik said. "If later we want a fresh woodchuck, we will speak to Benjie Barston again."

From his basket he took the hook George Ballard had made and kept turning it over in his hands and examining it. He felt particularly the smoothness of the eye and the sharpness of the point before he passed the hook to Sue.

"The hook is good," Malik said. "But see for yourself again."

Sue glanced at the hook, thinking the effort a waste of time.

"Now the weight," Malik said. He took from his basket a piece of scrap iron with a hole in it. "I do not like this weight."

"Why not?" Sue asked.

"It is because there is a roughness to the hole and a roughness to the edges. If the line tangles on the weight, the line might be cut. Here. You see."

Sue took the piece of iron from Malik.

"You're right, Malik. I didn't notice that before."

"That is why we must talk now and find the best way. The best weight is a sack of rocks," Malik said. "It will not cut the line. Do you agree?"

"Yes."

"Now the line. We must look at it all to see if there is a weakness, and we must tie together the four lines to make one very long line. Here. We will look at it and coil it carefully so that it does not tangle. I will show you a knot to tie the ends together."

They spent a long time on the rope, inspecting it foot-by-foot and tying the four lengths together. Sue and Malik pulled hard against each other on the rope to tighten the knots. Then Malik tied on the hook and tested that knot by putting the bend of the hook around the base of a young birch and pulling on the rope. Next they tied on a short dropper-line about ten feet above the hook and put a sack of rocks on the end of it. The dropper-line was an old, thin length of cord Malik had made years earlier by twisting together fibers from the inner bark of a basswood tree.

"It does not matter if we lose the weight," Malik said. "We can make another sack of rocks. If the great fish for Sam Barston, the *kabassa*, is on the hook and the weight tangles, we want the weight to break off."

They quickly agreed that the willow stick needed to be lashed to the plank-rig more strongly so that the heavier hook, line, bait, and weight wouldn't pull free by themselves. Then they sat and talked about how to fight the big fish once it was hooked. They spoke of many ideas because neither of them knew the best way. Sue suggested using a whole tree as a fishpole: cutting off its branches and lashing a pulley to its top with the rope passing through the pulley. The springiness in the tree, she thought, would help to tire the fish. Malik pointed out to her that the knots in their rope wouldn't pass through a pulley. He himself wondered about running their rope up among the young trees in a long loop to increase the friction as the fish pulled against the line. Sue told him that it would be just as hard for them to pull the rope in as it would be for the fish to pull it out. They kept talking and thinking, still not satisfied with their ideas about fighting the fish.

For a long time they discussed how to keep their reserve line from tangling. Sue talked about making a windlass, such as was used to haul a heavy water bucket up from a well, and keeping the rope wound on the windlass. However, Malik thought that would be a waste of time; that keeping the rope in coils on the ground or in loops which didn't overlap one another would be better than a windlass. They talked further, trying to decide.

Both agreed that the plank-rig and the rope tethering it to the tree up above should remain where they were. However, for fighting the fish Sue and Malik decided that they needed to move away from where their tripod was and down as close to the point as they could get. Wherever the hooked fish might run in the eddy or in the fast water above or below the point, the rope needed to swing freely without tangling in brush or dragging across rocks and dirt, as it had when they had seen the fish.

The first of many spectators appeared, drawn by the news they had heard in the village square that Malik and "the big girl" had their rope and were planning to start fishing with a hook made from a horseshoe. The curious came down to have a look, ask questions, laugh among themselves, and carry back word to others. By early afternoon, when Sue and Malik actually began fishing (both of them sitting up on a ledge back a ways from the point and a dozen feet above the level of the water), the numbers of people coming and going had increased considerably. Word spread quickly among them that the horseshoe hook was baited with a woodchuck. Perhaps a score of villagers at a time stood watching, talking, and laughing. Malik said little. Sue burned with embarrassment at being the center of attention.

Sue was angry when she saw the three boys — Benjie, Tom, and Foss. She expected streams of derision from them and began hating them in anticipation. When they said nothing, but merely sat at a distance and watched, that too somehow angered her. People came and looked around for a while and talked to others there and then left. The three boys stayed.

Towards the end of the afternoon Sue's heart gave a leap when she saw her father moving around on the edges of the crowd. Although she kept her attention on the line she held, she glanced at him frequently. She watched him studying the plank-rig up above out in the current, looking over the long, parallel loops of rope spread out on the bare ledge behind Malik and her, and standing beside other people from the village as they talked about the five-foot-tall stump of a birch. The stump was half a dozen paces in front of Sue and rose up out of a break in the ledge. It had four loops of their rope thrown around it. Malik had studied the lone birch growing there and had realized how he and Sue could use it to fight the great fish. Sue had chopped down the tree at shoulder height and had cleared away all the nearby brush from where it grew out of cracks in the ledge. Malik had explained to her that when the fish was pulling out the rope too quickly, they needed only to throw additional loops around the stump to increase the friction. They could regain rope quickly by lifting the loops off the stump and pulling the rope in directly; throw new loops back on when they had recovered the slack. The tree Sue had cut had been the one closest to the river, growing on a slight rise just above the spring flood level and allowing the line a clear swing both up the river and down through the eddy. Only if the great fish swam over right next to the canal and the lower warehouse would the rope drag across the ground.

Sue hoped her father would be impressed with the cleverness of all the arrangements, but the talk he was listening to among the men around him had nothing to do with Malik's and Sue's cleverness. She reddened with shame as her father overheard the same kinds of shouted comments people had thrown at Malik and her all afternoon:

"Hey Malik! You're wastin' your time with that rope. Do it right and get yourself a whaleboat and a harpoon!"

"Might as well feed all the candles and the tallow to the pigs! We ain't goin' to burn nothin' but whale oil lamps from now on, just as soon as they haul the thing in!"

"Naw, he ain't fishin' for a whale, you ignorant cuss! Rope that big, he's usin' a whale for bait!"

"How many perch you two caught on that whale-rig?"

"Haul it in so we can see the horseshoe and the woodchuck!"

"Hey, wake up you two! I think you caught a couple of planks!"

"If you hook into New Hampshire, don't pull her in too hard or you'll slam the river shut!"

"Hey Malik! Swim out and put yourself on that hook and let's see if whales like blue hair!"

Sue cringed at each loud comment. People one at a time shouted out their bits of supposed cleverness. All the others would laugh and keep talking among themselves for a while, and then somebody else would shout out another comment. Sue kept glancing over at her father as he stood and watched and listened. When he'd had enough, he walked away without once having waved, nodded, or spoken to Sue. She watched him go, carrying back with him his own axe, which she had borrowed from home, and felt very unhappy.

At the end of the afternoon Old Sam arrived at the point to see what was happening. He hobbled up beside Malik and Sue and looked over their rope, the stump, and the planks out in the river.

"Just ten pounds was what I said, Malik," Old Sam said. "I don't expect you to catch a fish big enough to feed the whole village for the winter."

"I have ears, Sam Barston, and my memory has not yet fled. There are things Sue and I know that you do not know. Fat as you are, Sam Barston, we will catch a fish bigger than you."

Old Sam laughed.

"How much rum you had today, Malik?" he asked.

"I had no rum today, Sam Barston."

"Well no wonder then. That ain't nearly enough. Got to get some rum in you quick as we can. Can't have you ravin' around here with your mind shrivelin' up from lack of rum. I got to take care of you, Malik. I'll run up and see if I can't get you some rum."

"I do not want your rum, Sam Barston. If you get it, I will not drink it. I will not drink rum from you until I catch your fish."

"Oh, come on, Malik. I want to give you just a ..."

"I do not want your gifts, Sam Barston. There are always too many gifts from you."

"Well you are quite an ornery old cuss today, Malik. Is that the way it's goin' to be?"

"Yes, Sam Barston. I spoke it once, and you have ears. If I speak it again, it will be the same."

The smile left Old Sam's face.

"Guess it's close enough to supper so I'm wastin' my time around here," he muttered.

Old Sam left. The numbers of other people from the village thinned as the sun dropped behind Barston Hill. Foss and Tom left.

"I got to go cook supper for my pa," Sue said to Malik. "You goin' to fish much longer?"

"Yes. I will stay until I catch the fish. It takes the bait before at night, and perhaps will take it again tonight. I must be here so that I may pull the hook deep into the jaw of the fish."

"You're right, Malik. Maybe I can come tonight for a while so you can get some sleep."

"If you cannot, Sue, do not worry."

Sue left. Malik stood up and stretched for a moment, pleased at the prospect of a quiet night without annoying questions and laughter. Just as he thought he was alone, however, someone stood up from the shadow of a big rock and came down towards him. He saw it was Benjie Barston. The boy stopped right beside him.

"Malik," he said.

"What is it, Benjie Barston?"

"Are you goin' to fish all night, the way you told her?"

"Yes."

"Well, I hope you catch your fish," Benjie said. "That's all I wanted to tell you. Now I got to go home."

He turned and left. Malik was at last alone and free to think his thoughts about a great fish out in the Connecticut. No one would bother him now.

XXIV

Sue finished putting supper onto the table, puzzling about where her father was. She went outside into the twilight and looked down the street, but there was no sign of him.

"Now what's keepin' him?"

Back inside she lighted candles, sat at the table, and waited. She wondered about putting the food back onto the stove to keep it warm, but made no move to get up. Instead she propped her elbows up on the table, cradled her chin in her hands, and thought about the day she'd just been through. It had started well enough. She and Malik had finally caught enough fish so that Steve Danforth had given them the rope. Next they had taken the time to plan how they could best use the rope and the hook and the weight to catch the big fish. Then, unfortunately, all those people had spoiled the day — all the people coming to stare and ask questions and yell out their comments. She and Malik had ignored them as best they could and had gone ahead to chop down the birch for its five-foot stump, lay out the half-inch rope, lash a larger stick into the plank-rig, tie a sack of rocks to the drop line, bait the hook with the woodchuck, and send the hook, weight, and bait out with the plank-rig close to the middle of the river. They had carefully let out their half-inch rope, dropping the bait down further out of the fast current; holding it at last where they wanted by throwing a few loops around the five-foot stump. And for that whole time those people had been underfoot and annoying. How she had wanted to hook into the fish then! Wouldn't that have changed those comments! But the bait had been untouched. Then her father had come. She would have given anything if the fish had taken the bait before Joe had turned and gone away without even speaking to her. She supposed that he hadn't even wanted people to know that he was her father; that he was ashamed and embarrassed by her. Afterwards Malik had been quite abrupt with Old Sam Barston, who left with a bitterness between them. No, it had not been a good day for her or for Malik even though it had started out so well.

Sue put the food back onto the stove. A few moments later, as she was sitting at the table trying to think how she would ask her father's permission about what she wanted to do that night, Joe came in through the door.

"Supper's all set, Pa," she said. "I was just rewarmin' it a little."

"I didn't mean to be so late, but I got started walkin' and thinkin'," Joe said. "Thinkin' about this afternoon."

Joe paused and looked hard at his daughter.

"I think that maybe I should of asked you not to fish with ... with Malik any more. He's a laughin'stock all through the village now, and so ain't you. I think that hurt you today, the way I told you it would, and I think it'll keep on hurtin' you just so long as you keep fishin' with him. I never saw the hook — the horseshoe — but others did, and I overheard 'em tell that you baited it with a whole woodchuck. It's stupid, is what I say. You'll gain nothin' from it but scorn. People will come to gape and stare and shout out their rudeness at you, and they'll keep doin' it just so long as you keep fishin' with that rope and that horseshoe. I'm disappointed in you, Sue."

Sue stood up from the table, forcing herself, for a moment, not to blink. Then the tears fell, even as she tried to hold them back. Sue brushed at them and took a step towards the stove, but her father's hands on her shoulders kept her from going any further.

"Well, I was hopin' I wouldn't upset you, but I guess I just blundered right into it again anyways. Tell me what's wrong, Sue."

"I want to help Malik, Pa. If he can salt down or smoke enough fish, then he'll have food for the whole winter. I want to keep fishin' with him."

"Then you will, if that's what you want. I was only tryin' to spare you pain, Sue. I went down there today to see you fishin' and heard the things folks said, and I know it couldn't of been much fun for you. I was thinkin' that if you hadn't of been there fishin' with him, nobody would of said any of those things to you. You can't get burned where there ain't a fire, Sue. I know it'd be better for you not to be there fishin' with Malik, but you're the one that's got to decide that."

Joe's hands dropped from her shoulders, and she went about getting the food from the stove. Joe sat at the table and watched her. Just as she was sitting down, he spoke to her again.

"Don't it seem even a little bit odd to you fishin' with a rope and a horseshoe? Can't you understand why somebody watchin' you might think it was strange?"

"Yes, I s'pose so," Sue said.

"Then why are you doin' it?"

She looked straight at him.

"To catch the fish, Pa."

"Oh come, Sue. Ain't we been through this before? I don't see how you can possibly think ..."

"We saw it, Pa. We saw the fish, and it's so big that we need the rope. We need that huge hook."

"You saw it? With your own two eyes you saw a fish that ..."

"Yes."

"You saw a fish ... a fish that ..." Joe faltered and then recovered. "Just how big is this fish you saw?"

"Bigger 'n you, Pa. A lot bigger."

Joe sputtered out a laugh and shook his head.

"Ain't it a fish you maybe dreamed about or that Malik saw through the bottom of a glass rum bottle?"

"No, Pa!" Sue said, beginning to anger. "We both saw it jump out of the water many times. It took out all our line, and then it got away when the hook bent out straight. That's how come we got the big hook now and how come we got the rope instead of a regular fishline."

Joe slumped back at the table and shook his head slowly for a long time.

"I'm surely cursed," he said at last.

"You don't believe me!" Sue said. "I told you I saw somethin' with my own two eyes, and you don't believe me!"

"Course I don't believe you," Joe said. "I don't believe you 'cause there ain't such a fish — not in the Connecticut River there ain't."

"But we saw it! We saw ..."

"You might think you saw somethin' down there, Sue, but it wasn't a fish. Nobody else but you and Malik see it?"

"No. It was rainin' and nobody else ..."

"Likely you hooked into a big log."

"We saw it, Pa!" Sue said angrily. "A fish! It jumped and ran with our line, and it stole bait and straightened hooks before!"

"Well, it's your imagination or else somebody's playin' tricks on the two of you. Now Sue, Malik ain't been givin' you rum, has he?"

"No! Why won't you believe me, Pa? Malik ain't been givin' me rum, and he ain't had any himself since we began payin' for the rope! Why can't you just believe what I'm tellin' you?"

"Because ... well, because," Joe began. "No, Sue. I think that's enough. We'll just upset each other even more with this talk. Let's sit down to supper and talk about somethin' else."

Sue ate, red-faced and sullen. Joe strained hard to talk about the weather, but finally he gave up, and they ate in silence.

Later, as Sue was clearing the table, she and her father were both startled by a loud knock at the door.

"Now who can that be?" Joe said, getting up and going to the door.

Sue looked up, wondering who might have reason to see them.

"Evenin', Joe," came the voice.

"Well, hello."

Her father stood in awkward silence for a moment before he found his tongue again.

"What can I do for you?" Joe asked.

"Well, it's your daughter I want to see. She at home?"

"Course she is," Joe said. "Wouldn't be anyplace else. Come in."

It was George Ballard. Sue rose from the table wondering what he could want with her.

"Hello, Sue," George said.

Sue nodded at him, not knowing what to say.

"Sue, I'm here to apologize," George said.

"What on earth for?" Joe asked.

"For havin' the biggest mouth in the village, I s'pose," George said.

"Well I surely don't know what you're talkin' about," Joe said. "Don't you want to sit down?"

"No. I won't stay but a minute," George said. "It's my flappin' tongue I ought to peg up. Sue had me make her a big hook at the forge. Well, I never made a hook before and never saw one anyplace that was so big. I thought it was funny, so I told other folks about it when they stopped by to have work done. It wasn't in my mind to hurt anybody with idle chatter, but I think that's just what I done, Sue. I was workin' all day at the forge today and didn't get down to where you and Malik was fishin', but plenty of folks dropped in to ask about the hook, to laugh, and to talk about you and Malik. From what I heard there was quite a crowd down there watchin', and I imagine they was makin' the same kinds of jokes I heard in the shop. I see now that I shouldn't of said anythin' about the hook. It won't do much good to tell you I'm sorry, but here I am anyways to tell you just that."

"But surely what other folks say ain't your fault," Joe said. "They'd of found out about the hook even if you didn't tell 'em a thing."

"Not nearly so quick," George said. "I'm the one that told 'em about it in the first place. If I caused you any grief, Sue, then I'm sorry for it. I didn't mean no harm."

The three of them stood in awkward silence for a moment glancing at one another, but mostly looking at the floor.

"Well, that was all I had to say," George said. "Now I best get home before Annie wonders where I am, and I already took enough of your time. Maybe I shouldn't of come, but when I realized what I done with my big mouth, it weighed on me hard enough so I had to tell you I was sorry. Well ... good night."

George went out the door without either Sue or Joe saying anything. Sue went back to cleaning up from supper, grateful to have chores to do just then. Joe sat at the table in silence for several minutes.

"You know," he said at last, "that was wicked decent of him to come. He could of just stayed at home and told himself that other folks' rudeness to you wasn't his fault. That's what I would of done, I think. And then we let him go out the door without even thankin' him. I should see him about that sometime."

Joe got out his pipe and packed it with tobacco. Though he often lighted his pipe directly from a candle, this time, to avoid the taste of tallow with his smoke, he used a long splinter of pine and sucked the flame down into the bowl. When the tobacco was burning, he tossed the burning pine over into the fireplace. Puffing on the pipe, he sat back down at the table and watched the wisps of smoke twist and curl and stretch out in the candlelight until they finally disappeared.

Yes. That George Ballard was a decent man, as good a man as Joe had ever run into. How many other men would have come to apologize for something like that — something that hadn't really been his fault? Perhaps one in a thousand, Joe thought. And he and Sue hadn't even thanked him for coming. Well, maybe he should get up and ask Sue where George lived and go thank him right away. Maybe he should ... The image of Annie Ballard sneaked into his thoughts for a moment. No. He'd go see George at the blacksmith shop. That would be a better place to thank him. It was something he should just do without thinking about; without giving himself a chance to come up with reasons for not going. He'd try to do that in the morning if he could get a few free moments.

Joe got up and walked over to the shelf where he kept the short stub of a peeled twig about the size of his little finger. He tamped the burning tobacco in his pipe with it, gave a few more puffs, and sat back down at the table.

He watched Sue for a moment, cleaning the dishes with her back to him, and thought about her fishing with the old Indian. Next, he thought again about George Ballard's visit. Then his thoughts went to Annie Ballard and stayed there for some time. He thought of her and of Sue's long-dead mother and after a while had difficulty keeping them apart in his mind. George Ballard was a lucky man. It would be worth whatever effort it cost to make the man his friend,

Joe thought. Then Annie would be just the wife of a friend. That might help control his thoughts about her.

The pipe went out, but Joe continued to suck at it absentmindedly. He felt tired from his day's work. It was a relief to sit still; to end the ceaseless, back-and-forth moving of boxes, kegs, and lumber. It felt good to sit and slouch and daydream.

Sue dried her hands on a cloth, went over to the table, and put a hand on her father's shoulder.

"Pa, there's somethin' I need to ask you," she said.

"What is it?"

"Well, I told you I want to keep fishin' with Malik."

"Yes, I know."

"I know you think it's silly, and you don't believe me when I tell you that we saw the fish."

"It's common sense, Sue, but I don't want to talk about it. We'll only start arguin' again. Let's leave that alone. You keep fishin' with Malik if you want. Fish with him and expect that folks will keep botherin' you because you are fishin' with him. Maybe some day you'll grow tired of it, but I'll leave that to you. I just don't want us to be cross with each other about it."

"All right, Pa. We won't argue about it. Now I wanted to ask you about Malik."

"What about him?"

"He's fishin' now, Pa. He's down watchin' the rope in case somethin' takes our bait tonight. He's all alone, and he won't get any sleep tonight."

"Well that's his choice. He can do what he wants."

"I was wonderin' if ... well, I was wonderin' if I can go down there and help him fish tonight so he can get some rest. If we take turns watchin' the rope, then we ..."

"Ha!" Joe said. "You want to go down there now in the dark alone with that old Injun and fish right there by the fast water? Fish like that at night?"

"Yes, Pa. Malik needs help. When it's dark, there's a better chance the fish ..."

"No. The answer is no. I won't have you wanderin' around alone in the dark. There's no tellin' what might happen to you. You need your rest at night. If you're worried about him gettin' rest, then tell him to sleep at night like everybody else."

"Please let me, Pa."

"No. You stay here at night, and that's my final word."

"Well if ..." Sue began.

"I don't want you back down there 'til after breakfast tomorrow, Sue. You understand?"

"Yes."

"Give me your word?"

"Yes, Pa, but I wish you'd let me go."

"No. I can't have you wanderin' around at night. I don't want to talk about it any more, Sue."

"I wouldn't be wanderin'. I'd be right down there fishin'."

"I told you you can't go, Sue!" Joe said, raising his voice. "How many times do I have to say it?"

"But please, Pa. Malik 'll have to stay awake all ..."

"That's enough, Sue!" Joe shouted, slamming his open hand down onto the table and rising to his feet. "Go up to bed! Right now!"

Sue pounded up the stairs two steps at a time. The door to her room slammed. In anger Joe raised his pipe and came close to smashing it on the floor. However, he caught himself in time. Very carefully he set the pipe down on the table. Then he slammed his right fist into his left palm and strode back and forth through the house. His heart pounded. His teeth ground together. His face burned.

Slowly he calmed. Finally he stopped walking. He brushed his forearm across his forehead, breathed deeply, and shook his head in disbelief. Why had he become so angry with Sue? It was the first time he could remember shouting at her like that. It was the first time in years that he had felt angry with anyone other than himself. What had caused that anger? He sat down and tried to think. His mind whirled from one thought to another and found nothing but remorse in any of them; found nothing but more reasons to be disgusted with himself for his poorness as a father.

Joe stepped outside and stood half a dozen paces from his door. There were stars overhead. He stretched his neck back and gazed at them and breathed the night air deeply in hopes that it would purge the polluting sourness from him. However, he found no comfort; no balm in the night.

He went back inside and blew out all but one of the candles. That one he carried up the stairs. He paused for a moment by Sue's closed door and in the stillness of the house heard her muffled sobs. The sound weighed his heart down with lead. He dragged himself into his own room, undressed, and got into bed. He stared at the ceiling for a while before he blew out the candle. Gazing wide-eyed into the darkness and tormented by many thoughts, he wondered if he would get any sleep at all that night.

XXV

Midnight came and went. Joe Reckford's eyes burned with exhaustion, and his muscles ached from his work of the day before, but still he could not sleep. He lay on his back with his hands folded behind his head and sighed. The more he thought about getting to sleep, the wider awake he became.

The moon rose. A little of its softened light filtered in through Joe's window and gave his eyes vague forms and outlines to rest on. He shifted his gaze around the room as the night dragged on.

Finally Joe gave up and got out of bed. He yawned and shook his head and went to the window. Out beyond the mills by the canal and out across the Connecticut he saw an enormous half moon. Low on the horizon and nearly a week past full, it was partly shrouded by the summer-night haze over the river. Joe knelt and leaned his upper body against the sill of the open window and gazed out at the moon, the obscured south slope of Rattlesnake Hill, the river, and part of the village of Barston Falls.

Water, he thought to himself. *If I have some water, maybe I can get to sleep. Wonder if it's worth the bother.* He stayed at the window a while longer, but then started to feel a chill on his bare skin. *Water.* He got to his feet, groped for his britches and shirt, and put them on.

Out in the hallway he stopped in front of the door to Sue's room and listened. He heard her shift on her bed, sigh, and then shift again. He continued down the hall, felt for the railing to the stairs, and descended. By the sink he found the oak water bucket. Holding it up with both hands, he drank from the rim — splashing the front of his shirt when he tilted the bucket too far. He drank all he wanted. Still sleep seemed far away. He shook his head and muttered. No, it didn't seem as if he'd get any rest at all that night. It was completely hopeless.

He felt his way back up the stairs, keeping a tight grip on the railing. In the hallway he again paused at Sue's door. He heard her shift on her bed. Very quietly he eased the door open and stuck his head inside.

"Sue," he whispered. "You awake?"

"Yes," she said in a whisper, but raised her voice as she continued. "Can't sleep tonight."

Joe opened the door wide and walked in.

"Me neither," he said.

He went over and sat on the side of her bed.

"Can I talk to you now?"

"Sure, Pa. Course."

"Sue, I don't know how come I lost my temper tonight. I'm sorry. It ain't like me."

"I know, Pa. And I shouldn't of kept after you about goin' down there tonight with Malik."

"Well I shouldn't of shouted at you, but I didn't want you down there wanderin' around at night. I don't ever mean to hurt you, Sue, but it happens anyways 'cause I don't know the right thing to do. I did hurt you tonight, didn't I? I shouldn't of sent you off to bed like that."

"It wasn't that, Pa. What hurt me was when I told you we saw the fish, and you didn't believe me."

"Well I know you thought you saw a big fish, Sue, but it just ..."

"We did see it, Pa — clear as you saw the table tonight at supper. And you still don't believe me, do you?"

"Well that's somethin' I don't want to answer, but let me just ask you this. Would you ever guess there was a frog, let's say, that was big as a sheep? That be reasonable?"

"No."

"Now then. What if I told you I saw a frog today that was big as a sheep? What would you say to that?"

"Well it'd surprise me."

"And if maybe it was a rock I saw or a stump that was shaped like a frog, and it looked so real that I was sure I saw a real frog. I was wrong, you see, but I didn't know it — didn't know anythin' 'cept that I saw a frog big as a sheep. Now it's the same for that fish that you and Malik think ..."

"No, Pa. It ain't the same. We saw it! It wasn't a stump or a rock or a log that took our bait and jumped out of the water and straightened our hook. I saw it! Can't you believe me?"

Joe laughed.

"This was right about where we was tonight after supper — just goin' around and around. We won't settle it, Sue."

"But can't you take my word that I ..."

"Ha!" Joe said as he got to his feet and stood with his hands on his hips. "Well, no. You're wrong. There ain't a fish in the Connecticut bigger 'n me. But hold on, Sue, before you get all worked up again. You know what we're goin' to do?"

"What?" Sue said after a pause.

"We're goin' fishin'. That's what. Get up and get dressed, and we'll go down to where Malik is and spend as long as you want down there. I ain't goin' to sleep tonight anyways, and I'm tired of lyin' in bed just waitin' for the night to end. No. I don't believe there's a fish bigger 'n me in the river. But I do believe I'm goin' to let you haul me down there so you can fish for the rest of the night, if that's what you want."

Sue jumped up out of bed.

"I really can go?"

"Now it's you who ain't believin' me. I'm tellin' you to get up and get dressed. I'll go get my shoes on and meet you downstairs. And, Sue, bring along a couple blankets 'cause it'll be damp down there. Now hurry up, and we'll go find Malik."

* * * * *

A dog snarled off in the shadows and then set up a loud barking. Joe jerked Sue around behind him and faced the sound of the barking: half-crouched, his hands stiffened in readiness, his heart pounding, his eyes straining towards the barking in the shadows beyond the dim moonlight. The barking continued, upsetting dogs in the distance, but no dog emerged from the shadows.

"Must be tied," Joe whispered. "Well come on so we don't wake up the whole village."

He fumbled for Sue's hand in the moonlight, forcing her to shift both blankets to her other arm. Then he hurried her along down the middle of the road, where they could see well enough not to trip over anything. After they had left the unseen dog far behind, Joe slowed his steps. Before long the peace and calm of the night had buried even the memory of the barking.

It was a strange, soft world in the moonlight. Joe tried to remember the last time he'd been outside walking in the middle of the night. Years, he thought. It was surely before Sue had been born; most likely when he'd been courting her mother. No. After that too, for they'd carried Sue out with them a few times, but still it had been a long time. He had forgotten how moonlight leached the substance from ordinary objects and replaced it with shadows and memories. It was almost like a dream. He and Sue crossed the canal on the lower bridge, able to see every plank clearly, but the canal itself was in complete darkness. A few rods past the canal they turned onto the road that passed along the east side of the mills. The tops of the buildings themselves were bright in the moonlight. Down low there were many shadows. Joe and Sue stuck to the middle of the road and followed it to the end. Then Joe let Sue lead him down through the small trees to meet the river not far from where the lower end of the canal joined the Connecticut. She tugged at his hand to move him along towards the point, but he held her back.

"Stop here, Sue," he said. "Old Malik don't even know we're comin'. He can wait a little more while we have a look. See how pretty it is."

They gazed out over the broad bay of the eddy. Moonlight reflected off small waves down below, where currents met. The crests of the waves stood out sharply against the darkness of the rest of the water. In the upper part of the bay over against the east bank all was lost in shadow, for the moon had yet to poke up high enough over the south slope of Rattlesnake Hill. Joe looked off to his right over past the entrance to the canal and saw the glow of the lower warehouse and the lower wharf, where he had worked for so many hours. In daylight they were quite familiar to him, but they looked strange in the moonlight. He shook his head and laughed at himself, feeling drunk with the moonlight and his lack of sleep and thinking that in just a few hours he would be back working with Mark Hosmer. He'd have to keep moving all day, he knew, or else he would fall asleep.

"Well, I s'pose I'll sleep tomorrow night," he said.

"Pa," Sue said. "Thanks for comin' out with me tonight."

"Should of been out earlier," Joe said. "This is much better 'n lyin' in bed and not gettin' to sleep. You know, Sue, your ma and me used to come out like this in the moonlight, and I recall carryin' you along with us a few times. That was long ago now."

"Pa, what was Ma like?"

Joe paused before he spoke.

"A wonderful woman, Sue. The best wife a man could have. There ain't a day goes by but that I think about her and miss her."

"Well I wish you'd talk more about her. I can barely remember her."

"Maybe I will," Joe said. "But for now you got to get down and help Malik."

Sue led him along the riverbank. All the way to the point they stumbled in the shadows in front of rocks. At the point Sue quickly found Malik just up beyond the tall stump with loops of rope around it. He was sitting in the moonlight and gazing out over the water.

"I got down here to help you after all, Malik," Sue said.

"Yes," Malik replied. "I did not think you would come tonight, Sue."

"I brought my pa with me," Sue said. "He don't believe there's a big fish, but he's here anyways. His name is Joe, Malik."

"Yes," Malik said, nodding at Joe. "Sam Barston does not think there is a big fish either, but it is no matter. We will catch the fish, and he will change his mind."

"Anythin' been after the bait tonight?" Sue asked.

"No. We must wait."

"Sue brought along two blankets, Malik," Joe said. "If you want, she can watch the line while you sleep. That's how come she's here anyways."

"Good," Malik said. "I will sleep. Then later I will watch the line again."

Malik took a blanket from Sue and without further words walked up among the young trees beyond the ledges. Joe watched him go, his eyes lingering on the strangeness of Malik's hair in the moonlight. After Malik went out of sight, Joe turned back and looked at the haze-shrouded moon poking up over the side of Rattlesnake Hill and then gazed at the river. His eyes stopped on the planks floating out in the current and on the moonlit rope by his feet leading up to them. Beyond the planks the shadow of Rattlesnake Hill obscured the eastern side of the river; would keep the river and the hill slope indistinguishable until the moon had risen further.

"Now explain how that thing works," Joe said, pointing up towards the plank-rig.

"The top plank's got boards under it, Pa, like fins and set in on edge at an angle. The current catches 'em and pushes the plank over towards the other side. The lower plank just keeps the other one straight in the water so the current can catch the fins right. Look up there at the rope, and you can see how much the plank with the fins pulls out into the current."

She swept her arm out several times, tracing the diagonal of the rope linking the planks with the red maple up above, before Joe saw that rope through the light mist.

"We rigged it so a hard pull 'll free the fishline from the planks," Sue continued. "Then we got extra rope to fight the fish with and that tall stump to wrap the rope around and slow down the fish when it's pullin' hard. All the extra rope is laid out up behind. Long as it don't tangle, I think we'll be all right."

Joe laughed.

"Well the two of you got it all thought out," he said. "All you need now's a fish to swallow a dead woodchuck and a horseshoe."

"Yes," Sue said. "That's just what we need, Pa."

Joe sat in silence with his daughter looking out over the Connecticut and watching the moonlit water creep towards the east bank as the moon rose further above the south slope of Rattlesnake Hill. Joe gazed out and thought back over the years. He thought of Betsy and of the ways Sue reminded him of her. Perhaps now would be a good time to tell Sue more about her mother. However, Sue kept yawning. She closed her eyes several times, and her chin drooped down onto her chest, but she gave a start each time and jerked her eyes open and her chin up.

"Here, Sue," Joe said. "Wrap up in the blanket and sleep for a little. If the woodchuck raises up from the dead, I'll give you a call."

"I wish you believed me about the fish," Sue said.

"Well now, I guess that don't make much difference, Sue. We're out here fishin' anyways so it don't matter what I believe. Here, give me that blanket."

Sue handed the blanket to her father. He unfolded it and tucked it around her shoulders.

"Now lie back and get comfortable and go to sleep," he said. "Dream about a big fish, and maybe it'll bring you luck. I'll wake you in a while."

"All right. Thanks, Pa. And thanks specially for bringin' me down here fishin'."

"Might just as well be down here not sleepin' as up in the house not sleepin'. All the same to me."

"Well, thanks anyways."

Joe watched over his daughter, pleased at how quickly she fell asleep. He smiled and shook his head to think of himself sitting down by the river in the middle of the night on a fool's errand. And yet he was happy to be there because it was what Sue wanted. For once, perhaps, he had blundered into doing the right thing as a father. He was glad, too, that Sue and Malik were asleep because he wanted to be alone with his thoughts just then. He gazed up at the moon. Moonlight softened him, he thought. He listened to the muted rush of the water and imagined the gentle touch of moonlight settling into him; stilling regrets and bringing on a feeling of peace which he hadn't had for years. He knew that everything would be different in the morning light and that he would be exhausted even before he began work, but for the time being he enjoyed the night and wished it could go on and on. He stared out at the broken reflection of the moon, listened to the Connecticut, and let his mind drift where it would, never once giving a thought to the half-inch-thick fishline beside him.

Two hours later Sue's shifting in her sleep brought Joe back from his reveries. He looked down on her in the moonlight and felt happy and content; pleased anew to have thought of accompanying her down to the river. He yawned and shook his head and laughed to think of Sue and Malik sleeping away the night and of himself supposedly watching the line for them; laughed at himself again for checking the line just then as if there weren't anything ridiculous about fishing in the Connecticut with a woodchuck for bait on a hook made from a horseshoe. Sue stirred at the second laugh, and he silenced himself immediately. However, she continued to move, and after a while she sat up.

"For a little I thought I was at home, Pa. I forgot about fishin'. Anythin' go after the bait?"

"No. I watched it like a hawk, and nothin' went after it. Like a hawk, mind you Sue, and not a owl. Hawks got more sense about what they do at night. But nothin' went after the bait near as I can tell."

"Well thank ..." Sue began, distorting the words so much with a yawn that she began again. "Well thanks for sittin' up, but now it's my turn. You got work in the mornin', Pa, and you ain't slept yet tonight. There, take the blanket. I'll watch the line."

"Guess I will sleep," Joe said. "Didn't feel much like it earlier, but I sure do now. Yes. I'll see if I can't get a little sleep before dawn."

"Did Malik come down?"

"No. Ain't seen him. Guess he's still asleep."

"Good. He needs the rest."

"It's a wonder he's fishin' at all," Joe said. "Man his age

shouldn't be out in the night air. Not many that old 'd even be out fishin' in the daylight."

"Yes, but he really wants to catch that big fish for Old Sam Barston. He'll keep fishin' hard 'til he catches it."

"Might be a while," Joe said.

"Well, he'll keep fishin' anyways. Now you get some sleep, Pa. I'll take care of the fishin'."

"All right. I ain't goin' to fight you for it."

Joe wrapped himself in the blanket and lay down a few yards from Sue. Several lumps of rock poking into his back made him roll around to find a more comfortable position. Then he let out a long sigh and quickly fell asleep.

* * * * *

How long he slept, Joe had no idea. He dreamed that someone had screamed, and then he awoke abruptly from a deep sleep, overwhelmed with confusion. Half a dozen dogs barked in the distance. He didn't know where he was. He stared stupidly at the moon, trying to gather his thoughts. *The river. I'm by the river.* Then he heard the low, strained voice of his daughter.

"Pa! Pa!"

Malik loomed over him in the moonlight. Then Joe was suddenly awake.

"What is it?" he shouted, sitting up. "What is it, Sue?"

"The fish!" she rasped. "The fish!"

Joe exploded up onto his feet.

XXVI

"Help us Pa!"

Joe lurched towards Sue, stumbled on a shifting rock, and sprawled hard on the ground. Back on his feet quickly, he held his leg as he hobbled over to Sue and Malik. He caught hold of the rope in front of them and, astonished at the force of the pull against him, forgot about his bruised thigh. He leaned against the rope with his full strength, but still it pulled him forward. He watched as the tight loops of rope around the birch stump further shredded the tatters of bark, exposing more of the white wood to the moonlight. When Joe was right up next to the stump, he let the rope slide through his hands for a brief instant, but dropped it as quickly as he would have dropped a hot iron bar. Taking up the rope again, he let it out hand-over-hand, as Sue and Malik were doing.

"We need more loops around the stump," Sue said.

"Yes," Joe said, without any idea how to put additional loops around the stump while there was so much tension on the rope. He continued to pay it out hand-over-hand; continued to strain hard as its tight coils stripped off bark to leave a solid band of bare wood on the birch stump. Then the outgoing rope slowed and at last stopped. Joe called for slack from Sue and Malik and threw two more loops around the stump. The rope stayed still for only a moment before it began to slide out once again, but far more slowly than before and without so brutal a pull against Joe's arms.

"That's better," Sue said. "What do you think now, Pa?"

"I think I'm either crazy or dreamin'," Joe said, "unless maybe you just hooked into a washed-down tree, but I ..."

"It is the fish for Sam Barston," Malik said. "The *kabassa*."

"Got me shakin' anyways, whatever it is," Joe said. "Look at this."

He held one hand off the rope in the moonlight to show the trembling in his fingers.

"It stopped takin' out line," Sue said. "Let's see if we can't get some of it back."

"No, Sue," Malik said. "Pull in the rope only if there is slack. It is a big fish — strong and fresh now — and we cannot see enough in the moonlight to fight it hard. We must tire Sam Barston's fish slowly. We will save our strength for the daylight and fight it hard then."

"Either of you see a fish on the end of this rope?" Joe asked.

Neither had. Joe wondered to himself again if an uprooted tree might be tangled with the hook and rope; whirling to and fro in the irregular currents below the falls and on the edges of the eddy.

"Here," Joe said. "You two take care of the rope while I go have a closer look."

Joe walked right down to the point. He saw the rope readily in the moonlight, but really had no better a view than when he'd been with Sue and Malik. He looked beyond where the rope sank into the black water, staring in vain for a glimpse of whatever was on the other end. The rope disappeared just to the right of the raised wave where the eddy came back into the main current. Then as Joe watched, the rope swung towards the west. He saw clearly a white spot where the moving line cut a froth into the water. He kept his eyes on that spot until it disappeared halfway over towards the canal. Joe kept scanning the water until the same white spot reappeared, this time headed back towards the east bank of the river, but angling further downriver than it had before.

The rope, in its slow swing, touched Joe on the side. He grabbed it and pulled against a pulsing, downward throb of resistance. To see what would happen, Joe jerked hard several times. Immediately the rope began sliding out. Joe strained against it, but was forced to give line hand-over-hand to keep from being pulled into the river. Finally he let go.

"Ha!" he said, as he rubbed his palms together. "That ain't a driftin' tree! I'll be hanged if I know what is out there, but it surely ain't a tree."

Joe stood and looked out beyond where the rope disappeared. He stared hard across the black water, waiting for a glimpse of whatever might be on the hook. He stared and muttered for nearly ten minutes.

"Well Betsy," he said aloud as he turned to leave the point. "I wish you could see what your daughter is up to tonight. I surely wish you could see this."

Joe rejoined Sue and Malik.

"You see it, Pa?" Sue asked. "You see our fish?"

"No," Joe said. "But I know it ain't a tree you hooked into."

"It made another long run," Sue said. "Took out some rope, but we still got a lot left. I just hope it don't decide to go straight down the river and keep right on goin'."

"Yes," Malik said. "Unless it does that, we have enough line. And we have all the daylight to tire the fish and bring it to shore. If the hook holds, we will catch the fish for Sam Barston."

"Well I hope you do," Joe said. "Both of you. Now listen. I been thinkin'. If it's a fish out there on the end of your line, it's your fish, and I want the two of you to catch it without any help from me. I'll be right here for as long as it takes you to bring it in, just in case you do need help. Otherwise I'll let the two of you fight it yourselves. I want everybody in the village to know that it's your fish."

"You can help catch it if you want, Pa," Sue said.

"Well I ain't goin' to. You don't need me to help right now and unless you decide you need me later on, I'm just goin' to wait close by. I can get water and food for you and anythin' else you need. If you want, I can even go get Old Sam Barston."

"Yes," Malik said. "We will fight the great fish, Sue and I. And perhaps we will get Sam Barston down here to watch. But now ..."

Malik cut off his words as the rope pulled out in a short surge.

"It will be a long time before the fish is ready," Malik said. "We will fight it through the night, but not make it run in panic. Be gentle on the line, Sue, and do not pull too hard against the fish."

"All right," said Sue. "You rested from your sleep, Malik?"

"Yes. I am rested."

Joe sat and pulled a blanket over his shoulders. Sue and Malik stood holding the line. The three of them settled into a silence broken only by occasional murmurings.

The time passed slowly for Sue. She felt the steady pull on the rope and imagined the great fish with the hook deep in its jaw; imagined it swimming in the eddy. When she and Malik lost rope, she prayed to herself that the fish wouldn't keep going down the river with the current. When they regained the slack, she pictured the fish swimming back up towards them in the wide circle of the eddy. Occasionally fear gripped her: an image of the hook held in the great fish by the merest flap of skin and on the verge of pulling free; a vision of the fish tearing off straight down the Connecticut without stopping as their reserve line disappeared, the end of the rope circled the stump, and she and Malik were dragged perhaps even into the water before they let go. She thought of them fighting the great fish for many hours and then losing it, their line, and their hook. The fear arose each time she and Malik began to lose line and subsided each time they freed the loops from the stump and regained the slack. Sue spoke little to Malik or her father; thought of nothing but the line and the fish.

Malik leaned against the rope and wished he weren't so old or so light. If only he could have been fighting the great fish ten or twenty or thirty years earlier, when he had been a heavier man and a lot stronger, he would have been content. Old age had turned him into a husk of what he had been, he thought. It had robbed him of the strength he needed to fight the fish. His weakness would leave more work to Sue, but impatience was the way of the young, and he didn't trust her to save her strength. They would need to be patient and smart in the way they fought the great fish, or it would beat them. As his muscles began to ache, he thought of Sam Barston to give himself more strength. Yes, he needed to show that Sam Barston was wrong. He needed to catch the great fish so that he and Sue could give it to Sam Barston. He envied Joe Reckford's size and strength. At the same time he was glad that Joe wasn't helping to fight the fish, for if he helped them land it, then what would Sam Barston say? He would scoff and claim that Joe Reckford had caught the fish and that Malik had merely touched the rope. It would be a long struggle against the fish, Malik knew, but he vowed not to quit unless his body failed him.

Joe sat with the blanket hanging down from his shoulders. All his fatigue had vanished. For the first half hour after he had sat down, he was completely alert: ready in an instant to bound up and grab hold of the rope. And yet neither Sue nor Malik had asked him to help. Joe kept glancing at Malik with increasing respect for the stubborn determination of the old Indian. Mostly, however, he watched Sue. He saw her give out rope grudgingly and move quickly

to regain it whenever there was slack. Joe felt surges of pride in his daughter and was glad for his decision to let Malik and Sue battle by themselves whatever was on the other end of the line. Yet bewilderment lingered and gnawed at him about what might be so powerful, a fear of something unknown and unnamed which couldn't logically be in the Connecticut River.

After the first hour the urgency began to fade from Joe's excitement. It seemed likely that Sue and Malik would be hauling on the rope for many hours to come. Joe stood up and stretched and began looking around at the night. The mist had thinned. The moon was high and brighter than it had been. Except for when a rare scattering of clouds drifted across its face, it cast a brilliant glow over everything. Joe wandered down to the water again. As before, he saw where the rope entered the river and watched its movement across the eddy, but still couldn't see what was on the hook. When he tired of watching the rope and his gaze roamed else-where over the Connecticut, his attention suddenly fixed on the two planks floating end to end.

"Well there's somethin' I can do," he said.

He walked up along the riverbank until he got to where the rope down to the planks was tied. He pulled the rope in hand-over-hand and then dragged the planks up onto the bank.

"Now if the thing runs up the river, at least it won't tangle the line in this," he said to himself.

Then as Joe stood next to the river, he gazed all around. There was Barston Hill behind him and Rattlesnake Hill across the river in New Hampshire. Up above was the fast water of Barston Falls; down below the outrun and that part of the eddy he could see to the left of the point. In front of Barston Hill the tops of the mills and of several other buildings in the village rose above the growth of young trees. Joe stared at the moonlight reflected from the fast water and felt filled with the beauty and peace of the scene.

"Just let her land whatever they hooked," Joe murmured. "That's all I ask. Just let her bring the thing in."

He went back down below and spoke to Sue and Malik. They said they were all right. Joe sat and watched, and time dragged by slowly for him.

XXVII

Benjie Barston awoke slowly. For the second night in a row he'd slept in his bed rather than underneath it, and he was reluctant to leave its comfort. When he had gone to bed, he'd had it in mind to get up in the middle of the night and sneak out of the house down to where Malik was fishing. He had planned to sit by the old Indian and offer to help him. If he got his courage up enough, he would tell Malik that he was sorry he had painted him blue and that he would like to learn anything Malik could teach him about hunting or fishing or trapping. He would sit with Malik in the darkness even if he shivered and suffered; would make Malik think differently of him. However, in spite of Benjie's intentions, he had slept soundly through the night. The first time he opened his eyes, he saw that it was already getting light outside. Even then he hadn't sprung out of bed. He had turned his face away from the light and had enjoyed the comfort a while longer. When at last he did get up, the sun was just on the verge of rising.

Benjie yawned and rubbed his eyes, picked up his clothes from where they lay on the floor, and put them on. He started towards the door, but stopped abruptly. No. It wouldn't do to go out through the door. His mother's hearing was too good. That was the problem. He would creak a floorboard in the hall, and she would come charging out of the bedroom, catch him, and force him to sit through the agony of a slow breakfast. No. That simply would not do. He'd stay out of the hall. This would be a good time to use the ash tree outside his window. He'd been meaning to try it for some time.

Benjie opened the window wide and eased himself up to crouch on the sill. He made the mistake of glancing down and shrank back so quickly that he nearly fell into the room.

"If you ain't goin' to jump down there, don't look down there," he muttered. "Look at the tree. That's where you're plannin' to jump. That branch right there for my foot and grab the trunk right there. If I was on the ground, it'd only be a quick hop, just like ... one, two, three ... this!"

Benjie sprang and grabbed hold of the tree, banging his left knee hard against the trunk and knocking half the air from his lungs. He muffled a groan and a fledgling curse. After a moment he lowered himself from branch to branch until he was on the ground. There he sat and rubbed his knee. Then he hobbled off down Tannery Road. By the time he'd crossed the upper bridge, his knee had loosened up and felt almost as good as new.

Though it was early, people were already stirring in the village square. Benjie waved off to his right to George Ballard, who had fired up his forge and was just coming out of his blacksmith shop to go home for breakfast. Through the windows of the Eagle Hotel, up in the northeast corner of the square, Benjie could see people moving around. A horse and wagon stood in front of the stables next to the hotel — ready for a day's work. Someone in the square was frying pork, and the smell lingered in the air. Benjie sniffed several times, but still was glad to have escaped his mother's breakfast, for it always took ten times longer than he was willing to spend. Breakfast was something you bolted down as you were on your way to the day's work. It wasn't something you waited around for and then lingered over. Wasted time the first thing in the morning could spoil a whole day. Women — mothers anyway — never seemed to realize that. There would be plenty of time to eat later. For now he wanted to go down and be with Malik.

Benjie walked on the path of hard-packed dirt which split the large rectangle of grass and young elms in the center of the square. Mid way along the path Benjie paused briefly. Off to his left he saw that the door to Steve Danforth's store stood open, though he couldn't see anyone stirring there. To his right, on the opposite side of the square, the Catamount Tavern had yet to show any signs of life. However, Bickford House, the hotel adjoining the tavern, was as busy as usual. It was much frequented by teamsters in transit. As Benjie looked, two men who might have been teamsters themselves came out the door and headed toward the stables on the other side of the Catamount Tavern. Benjie saw four freight wagons in the carriage shed of the stables — none thusfar with horses hitched to them.

Benjie glanced over at the shed for the fire carriage just before he left the square. He followed the road south out of the square the short distance until it turned abruptly west to pass the head of the mill row and cross the lower bridge. At the turn Benjie went straight and picked his way along the footpath through the young trees. The path dropped down towards the ledges by the point, and Benjie hoped to find Malik still fishing there. He wondered if Malik had indeed fished the whole night. Benjie halted as he began to emerge from the trees and had a partial view of the river. His gaze wandered here and there, searching. The emptiness of the water puzzled him.

"Thought it was right out about there," he said aloud. "Thought they had the two planks floatin' right out about there."

A few yards further down the slope only a scattering of young trees stood between Benjie and the river. Immediately he saw Malik and the girl leaning back against their rope as they let it out hand-over-hand. Benjie hurried down over the ledges to them.

"What's goin' on, Malik?" Benjie demanded to know.

"The big fish for Sam Barston," Malik said in a strained voice.

"What? You seen it?" Benjie asked as he jerked his head several times to scan the river.

"You seen it?" he repeated, this time looking at Malik.

Malik's mere nod seemed to push Benjie down along the rope to the water's edge, where he soon stood beside the girl's father — the big man who worked with Mark Hosmer; the boy and the man both staring out beyond where the rope entered the river.

"They catch a fish?" Benjie asked.

"They sure hooked somethin'," the man said. "Been fightin' it three or four or five hours now I guess — don't know for sure how long. And it goes back and forth out there both with the current and against it too so I know it ain't just a tree driftin' in the eddy. I saw a couple splashes so far, but nothin' else. Keep your eyes out there past the end of the rope, and we might see somethin'."

Benjie's eyes widened as he saw the rope change direction twice out in the river. He followed the rope closely and gazed out beyond it. For a long time there was nothing. Then there was a splash that he and the man both exclaimed at and pointed to at the same time, but they didn't see what had caused the splash.

"That's what I saw before," the man said. "Just the splashes. Keep lookin'."

They both looked. They saw several large swirls which might have been strange motions of the eddy currents and another splash which definitely wasn't caused by the current.

"I know you're Benjie Barston," the man said.

"Yes."

"I'm Joe Reckford, Benjie. I work for your pa down at the lower warehouse. That's my Sue fishin' with Malik."

"Oh, I know," Benjie said. "She's the ... look at that!"

Benjie jabbed his finger out towards the eddy, where a strange, dark object pointed up out of the water. It looked like a shaved, tapered plank standing on end. It wavered for a moment and then sank out of sight.

"Now what on earth ...?" Joe said, but never finished what he was saying.

A dark bulk rolled on the surface: wide and long and thick. Joe and Benjie gasped through a series of exclamations. Joe sat right down on the ground. Benjie's mouth stayed open, and his wide eyes didn't seem as if they would ever blink again.

"If that's ... if that's a fish," Joe whispered. "Oh my ... my."

He shook his head slowly and stayed seated.

Benjie's hair prickled on the back of his neck, giving him the sensation that he had suddenly grown a foot taller. He scarcely believed his eyes when he saw the wide body roll a second time — an unbelievably long creature with a monstrous fish tail and a large fin just in front of the tail. Without waiting an instant longer, Benjie turned and ran and never stopped until he got to the village square.

* * * * *

George Ballard finished his eggs and potatoes, ate three more slabs of toasted bread, and reached for another chunk of ham. Annie, standing by the cookstove, glanced over at his plate.

"More dried apple pie, George?"

"I could stand it."

"Well there's only half a pie left. You might as well finish it."

"Don't you want some?"

"No. It'll give me an excuse to make some more today

if you finish that off now. That one's already three days old anyways and prob'ly not fit to eat."

"The other half was," George said. "But I'll try out the unfit half too if you want."

"Sorry there ain't fish too, George. I know how you like fish in the mornin', but Malik and Sue didn't have 'em in the square yesterday the way they usually do. They only caught a few and took those to Steve in the mornin', and he traded 'em all away before I got there."

"Fish 'd be nice," George said, "but I'll try and make do with just this and hope I don't faint away before noon time."

Annie set the half pie down next to him on the table.

"They used to catch an awful lot of fish," she said.

"Well they got tired of catchin' little ones all the time," George said. "Rather fish for a whale than a perch right now. I expect they'll do as they please for a little and then go back to catchin' perch."

George turned his attention to the pie and had eaten most of it when suddenly he and Annie heard a loud clanging noise.

"Is that ..." Annie began.

"Fire bell!" George bellowed with his mouth full of pie.

He sprang up from the table, tore down his fire bucket from beside the door, and was outside running south along the road before his chair had stopped clattering on the floor. He thought immediately of his blacksmith shop and wondered in a panic if the fire in his forge had somehow set the whole place on fire. He sprinted down to the square, turned a sharp right towards the shop, and then slowed when he saw no cloud of smoke billowing from it. Pausing only for a moment to poke his head inside and see that everything was all right, he then skirted Israel Barston's park running as hard as he could down the west side of the square. At the foot of the square he halted by Benjie Barston, who was pulling the bell rope at the brick shed for the fire carriage.

"Where is it, Benjie?" George shouted as he threw his bucket onto the fire carriage and heaved against it to start it out of the shed. "Whose place?"

"Down to the point!" Benjie shouted back over his shoulder.

George was so keyed up to take a few words from Benjie and then explode off to fight a house fire that he practically tripped over his own legs in confusion. There were no buildings anywhere near the point; nothing but ledges and young, green trees. George stopped dead, panting hard; fragments of pie still in the corners of his mouth; the fire carriage already half out of the shed. Other people came running in towards him, buckets in hand; grabbing holds to help pull the fire carriage. George brushed past them, went over to Benjie, and grabbed the rope so the bell couldn't ring any more.

"What do you mean 'down to the point'? What's to burn down to the point?" George demanded.

"Where's the fire? Where's the fire?" other voices clamored as the fire carriage rolled the rest of the way out of the shed. People surged into the south end of the square from every direction. The Eagle Hotel and Bickford House poured people out their front doors. Benjie was quickly surrounded by a crush of bucket-carrying, panting men and women with more arriving all the time, most of them shouting questions about where the fire was. All was noise and confusion and urgency. Few heard Benjie speak.

"It's a fish!" Benjie said. "A fish, not a fire! Down to the point!"

"What?" George shouted. He let go of the rope, grabbed Benjie by the shoulders, and thrust his face right in front of the boy's. "Is there a fire, Benjie?"

"No, it's a fish!" Benjie said.

George let go of Benjie, bolted upright, and cupped his hands around his mouth.

"No fire! No fire!" he bellowed out above the other noise and confusion.

Others took up George's cry and kept yelling it out as more people came running to the square, themselves clamoring for directions until they realized there was no fire. Then anger swelled through the crowd of men and women, whose slow, morning pace had been shattered by a false alarm. Many of them were furious. They demanded to know who had rung the bell and held onto all their fury after they had found out. Steve Danforth seemed to have the loudest voice of anyone.

"Shut up! Shut up, everybody!" he kept shouting until the crowd quieted. Then he turned towards Benjie, pointed his finger at him, glared, and in a voice of barely controlled anger began speaking.

"Benjie Barston," he thundered. "If your pa don't beat you 'til you can't set down for a week, I'll have hard words for him. That is a fire bell, and nobody ... Nobody! ... is to touch it ever unless there's a fire. Nobody! Ever! What's got into you, boy?"

"The fish," Benjie said, barely able to keep from crying. "The fish."

"What on earth are you talkin' about?" Steve asked in a far quieter voice than before.

"Malik and the girl hooked a huge fish on the whale-rig," Benjie said.

George's hands caught Benjie's shoulders again and spun the boy towards him.

"What, Benjie? Sue and Malik hooked somethin' on that hook of mine? That hook made out of a horseshoe?"

"Yes!" Benjie said. "Her pa's down there with 'em. The girl ... Sue ... and Malik hooked it in the middle of the night, and they been fightin' it for hours. I seen the fish, and it's wicked huge — huger than a man!"

Scornful laughter and mumbled curses swept through the crowd. Someone called out, "Have some more rum, Benjie!" Men and women shook their heads and began milling around muttering to one another. In voices filled with disgust several of them loudly told latecomers what had happened. A few, having decided that they had wasted enough time, turned abruptly and went home. Most of them, however, wanted at least enough time together to share their outrage and disgust. When George Ballard announced he was going down to the point and left with Benjie, some in the crowd drifted after them "to have a look," though not too quickly and not too eagerly and with many of them, before they went, casting glances out across the crowd to make sure they were as unconcerned as anyone else.

Twenty minutes later the fire bell again began ringing. Those who gathered around it the second time heard the news that Sue Reckford and Malik had hooked into the biggest fish in the world. A few of them headed home to spread the news. All the rest hurried down towards the point.

XXVIII

Old Sam Barston moved slowly in the mornings, more slowly the older he got. Five years earlier he had sold his horse because getting food and water to it first thing every morning had become too much of a chore. The year after that he had given up keeping hens. ("Now I'm the only livestock I got to feed," he had said.) He joked that his pace in the morning for an hour or so after he arose was the same as when he was asleep. Usually, Old Sam claimed, he wasn't fully awake until the middle of the morning.

Old Sam sat eating oatmeal porridge and wondering about the fire bell he had heard. Ten years earlier he might have charged out to fight the fire, but now he only sat and wondered about it. He would leave the fighting of fires to young men with strong legs and strong backs. He himself would be useless. Curiosity might still draw him to watch a fire if he had nothing better to do, but the time had passed when the alarm bell could summon him instantly from a meal, from his bed, or from fishing for trout. When breakfast was done, he thought, he would get his cane and go down to see where the fire was.

When the fire bell rang a second time, Old Sam began to eat his porridge more quickly. It was unheard of for it to ring twice like that in all the years since Old Sam's brother, Israel, had given the fire bell to the village. He guessed there must be a huge fire and with consternation recalled the great fire of 1804. Bowl in hand, Old Sam shuffled out of the room and into the hallway and then out the door and down the front steps. He stood in the middle of Tannery Road and looked down towards the village, eating a few spoonfuls right there in the middle of the road as he looked. No, he couldn't see any smoke. He smelled smoke, but that could easily be from the cook fires in the Barstons' brick houses. Anyway the wind was out of the northwest — towards the village. Well, he'd have to go down and have a look. Two different ringings of the alarm bell probably meant that a fire had spread and that more people were needed. Yet there hadn't been any great cloud of smoke over the village, at least not that he could see. Curiosity began to nag at him.

Old Sam was back sitting at his table working down towards the bottom of his bowl of porridge when he heard a clattering at his front door and then Benjie shouting for him out in the hallway.

"In here," Old Sam called back.

An instant later his great-grandnephew stood beside him, sweating hard and gasping for breath.

"Now to look at you, Benjie, a man might get the idea there was a fire someplace."

"No, Grampy Sam, it's Malik and the girl! They hooked a fish big as a whale!"

"No fire then? The bell ..."

"No, it was on account of the fish!"

"Now that must be a mighty big fish if it gets two alarm bells, young Benjie. I don't know as I recall any fish in the village gettin' so much as one before. Must be two-alarm big, or else it must be a small fish that's on fire."

"It's wicked huge!" Benjie said. "They been fightin' it for hours on that big rope! Everybody's down there watchin' 'em!"

Old Sam's spoon clattered down onto the table.

"On that big rig of theirs? Had a fish on that thing for hours you say?"

"Yes Grampy Sam! I had to tell you, but I got to get back 'fore they bring it in! Come down and see, Grampy Sam!"

Benjie was quickly gone. Old Sam rested his fingers on the edge of the table with his thumbs gripping underneath. He shook his head slowly and then picked up his spoon to finish his porridge.

"No," he said to himself. "It can't be. It's just a log Malik's hooked into out in the current, and the old cuss is too stubborn to admit it. And if he's got a crowd down there watchin' him, he's too embarrassed to land it in front of them. He'll likely fight it 'til dark and then figure out a convenient way to lose it. Stubborn old cuss."

Old Sam finished his porridge, thinking about Malik and Sue. He smiled and shook his head. Then he got up slowly from the table and went over to the cupboard in the corner of the room. From the back of one of the shelves he took a pair of wrought-iron spikes with the last half inch of their points bent over at right angles. He took the two spikes to the hearth and knelt down stiffly. With them he gradually raised a brick out of the hearth, burrowed into loose sand underneath, and pulled out a small, leather bag. Untying a cord from around the neck of the bag, he reached into it, pulled out a large coin, and put the coin into his pocket. After he had replaced the bag, the brick, and the spikes, he took his walking stick and went down Tannery Road on his way to the point.

Proud and ornery old cuss, Old Sam thought, swinging his cane as he walked and poking a trail of marks into the dirt of the road. *Won't live with me, but makes a point of askin' permission to live on my land in a woodchuck hole up on the hill every summer. Don't take food from me but once in a long time, even though he's skinny enough so that every time a breeze comes up I want to slide a couple bricks in his pockets to keep him from blowin' away. Likes his rum maybe too well — tradin' fish for it and all — but when I offer to get him some, he won't have it from me. Too many gifts from me already, he says. And don't you s'pose the old cuss would realize the two of us ain't got a lot of time left?*

Don't you s'pose he'd heave away his pride so we could have some fun durin' our last few years? No, not Malik. We're friends, or we used to be. He ain't got enough of food or drink or lodgin', and I got more than I can use. But he lets his silly old pride get in the way, and he won't take anythin' from me. Just a stubborn and proud and ornery old Injun.

Old Sam stopped in surprise as he walked into the village square. At that time of the morning, it should have been bustling with activity. Half a dozen horses, two of them hitched to wagons, stood tied on the edges of the square, but not a man, woman, or child was anywhere in sight. Old Sam gazed around in the quiet stillness, remarked aloud at the strangeness of the scene, and stood resting for a moment. His hand closed on the coin in his pocket — the silver dollar. He pulled it out and turned it over several times looking at it.

"Eighteen — aught — four," Old Sam said. "You know you ain't a bad lookin' woman for eighteen years old, Miss Liberty. You're a lot prettier than the bird on the back. Don't know as they'd let you into church in a dress like that, but I don't s'pose I'd ever try and take you there anyway. You stick with Old Sam now. This is where you belong. I'll take good care of you. Don't go runnin' off to that ornery old Injun. He'd sell you in half a minute for rum. You stay with me."

Old Sam put the dollar back into his pocket and continued on his way. At the south end of the square he paused again at the sight of the fire carriage out of its shed. The ground around it was covered with the fire buckets his brother, Israel, had given to the village — one for each able-bodied adult to keep in readiness at home. Many people had hurried there with their fire buckets. It must have been quite a crowd, Old Sam thought, but now the square was completely deserted. He kept walking and was down nearly to where the road turned right to cross the lower bridge before he saw anyone. George Ballard emerged from among the trees on the path up from the point. He seemed to be in a hurry.

"Well, Old Sam," George said. "I thought the whole world was down there, but I guess it ain't. We must be the last two, though."

"Not a soul in the square," Old Sam said.

"No, and ain't likely to be. Ain't likely anybody 'll do a lick of work today neither. But I'm in a hurry, Old Sam. You go on down there quick as you can, and I'll be back in a little."

"But what's all the fuss ..."

"Can't talk now, Old Sam. Go on down there and be surprised," George said over his shoulder. He hurried up towards the square.

Old Sam quickened his steps, picking his way as best he could along the path down to the point. Curiosity hurried him on as he heard occasional shouts and cheers down below. He stumbled and came close to falling several times before he finally laughed at himself and slowed down for the last part of the path.

As Old Sam emerged from the young trees, it seemed to him that he hadn't seen such a crowd even on the Fourth of July. Most people were clustered along the sides of the point in two separate groups. A few stood further up the slope close to Malik and Sue. He watched the two of them let out rope hand-over-hand. The rope passed around a tall stump and then ran about four feet above the ground between the groups of spectators. Benjie, Foss, and Tom were immediately in front of Old Sam, a little to his left, tending to loose rope spread out across the ledges. All three cautioned him not to step on it or near it. They seemed to be making overly intense efforts to keep the rope from tangling as they paid it out to Malik and Sue. Old Sam watched the old Indian and the girl for a moment. Then, keeping wide of both them and the rope, he went down to the right side of the point. He stood on the edge of the crowd and stared out to where the taut rope disappeared into the water. There was nothing there that Old Sam could see. He walked over a few steps to where Steve Danforth was standing.

"So Steve," Old Sam said. "How many sawlogs you s'pose are in her if she's still sound?"

Steve Danforth turned, in confusion for a moment, but saw Old Sam's nod out towards the river and broke into a smile.

"Just what I thought when I got down here," Steve said. "And now I know there ain't so much as one sawlog in it, Old Sam. You keep your eyes out there for a little. Look sharp and tell me if that thing acts like any waterlogged drift tree you ever saw before."

Old Sam watched for several minutes. The rope moved slightly from side to side, but did no more than that. Finally he spoke to Steve again.

"Well I looked sharp, Steve, and I'm tellin' you she acts just exactly like every big, waterlogged hunk of dead tree I ever saw. Like an old pine, near as I can tell, but I might be wrong and it may be a yellow birch. My guess is Malik will keep haulin' on that rope 'til it gets dark, and then he'll find some way to let the log break off. Might even be a swamp maple, but it's hard to tell from here."

Steve laughed.

"Look a while longer, Old Sam, and watch out if the rope sweeps over towards us 'cause you'll have to duck under."

"If it's contrary enough wood to drift around that far, then it's definitely elm," Old Sam said.

Steve laughed again. They stood together for a few more minutes before Steve suddenly nudged Old Sam and pointed.

"Out there. See it?"

Old Sam saw a splash and nothing more and was about to speak to Steve again, but the words stopped before they left his mouth. A broad and dark back rolled up out of the Connecticut and then sank beneath the surface again with a tremendous sickle-like tail thrust out of the water at the end of the roll. Old Sam sat right down on a rock and stared out over the water.

"So, Old Sam," Steve said. "What do you think now?

"Shadbush," Old Sam whispered. "A shadbush comes closest if it's got leaves, but I don't believe it's got leaves."

"Well, so it ..." Steve began. "But look out now, Old Sam. The rope's swingin', and you don't want to be against it if it's runnin' out or you'll get a bad burn. Move over or else go under the rope."

Old Sam rose awkwardly from the rock and stepped back from the rope as it came towards him. He watched it over his shoulder as he retreated a few yards towards the canal and lower warehouse. It stopped right about where he'd been talking with Steve and then began to swing back the other way. Old Sam watched the rope for a moment. His hands were shaking, and weakness crept over him. He sat down on another rock to recover, breathed deeply, and looked up at Malik and Sue holding on to the rope.

* * * * *

Joe Reckford stood with his hands thrust into his britches' pockets and looked out over the crowd. He thought it strange how his daughter had drawn so many people together; that villagers who hadn't even known her at dawn that day now called out her name and shouted encouragement to her. And Joe, pointed out as being her father, had shared some of the attention. He still wasn't used to the novelty of having strangers talk to him about

Sue, about his work, about where he lived, how long he had been in Barston Falls, and where he had come from. Some people introduced themselves; others simply sidled up to him and talked in general. It gave him a feeling he hadn't had since the time before Betsy had died: the feeling that he fit in and belonged where he was.

Joe was happy when he watched Sue, who was as much the center of attention as whatever was on the hook at the end of the rope. The three boys — Benjie, Foss, and Tom — certainly were attentive keeping the loose, reserve rope free from tangles and screaming at people to walk around it rather than over it. If they wound up being Sue's friends after the day was over, Joe knew he'd worry about her a lot less. Perhaps this would mark the start of Sue's breaking out of her loneliness; perhaps a start for himself too, he thought. He looked around at the people who had already spoken to him about Sue. Most of them hadn't known who he was before then. Now it seemed that nearly all of them did, even if it was just as Sue's father. Right at that moment he saw one man point him out to another. It made Joe feel a little embarrassed, but pleased nonetheless.

Joe saw Old Sam Barston sitting on a rock over at the far edge of the crowd. Old Sam looked overheated, but there was quite a smile on his face as he talked to a woman standing next to him. He seemed ready to break into laughter. When the woman glanced up towards Malik and Sue, Joe realized she was Annie Ballard. Suddenly she looked straight at him. As Joe turned away, the heat came into his face in what he knew must have been a violent red. He felt his insides crumbling with embarrassment. When he peered over his shoulder a moment later, she was still staring at him. He jolted his head back around and stumbled for a few steps, nearly falling against Mark Hosmer in his haste.

"Joe," Mark said and nodded to him. "You look mighty het up, Joe. Feelin' all right?"

"Yes. Just a little excited, I guess," Joe said.

"Don't know as I blame you. If it was my girl that hooked into whatever that critter out there is, I'd be more 'n just a little excited. Ho! No, just a little splash out there," Mark said, pointing out past the end of the rope. "Thought it might come out of the water so we could get a better look, but it wasn't but a little splash."

The two men stood side-by-side looking out over the river. After a while Mark spoke again.

"There's a flatboat needs to go up, you know. Jared told me a half hour ago, I s'pose it was."

"Should we go do ..." Joe began.

"Ha!" Mark interrupted. "I ain't movin' a step 'til I see what kind of critter they got on the hook. Told Jared that, and he laughs and says he ain't neither. Whole flatboat crew's watchin' too, and they won't budge. Jared says it'll surprise him if anybody in the village does a lick of work today, and I don't know but what he's right."

"Fine with me," Joe said. "Don't know as I'd earn my money workin' today anyways. I was down here most of last night with Sue and Malik and ain't slept much."

"When was it they hooked the thing?" Mark asked.

"Can't say for sure," Joe said. "Sue woke me up then, and I think they must of had it on at least a couple hours before dawn. But things got confusin' then, awful confusin'. Can't tell you anythin' about it for sure. They had it on for quite some time thrashin' around in the moonlight and, believe me, I was glad to see the sun come up."

"How old's your girl, Joe?"

"Twelve now."

"Fine-lookin' rugged girl for twelve," Mark said. "I been watchin' how she heaves on that rope, and there ain't many girls — or boys neither — could keep that up the way she does. Bet you're wicked proud of her, Joe. I sure would be if she was my daughter."

"Well, yes," Joe said. "Yes. I s'pose I am."

"Shy ain't she? My wife sees her up in the square tradin' fish, and that's what she says."

"I guess she always was."

"Shy and quiet, just like you," Mark said.

"Yes. That's a curse she got from me. Her ma was different, but she died when Sue was two, and I ain't done much of a job raisin' her by myself."

"What? Just on account of she turned out quiet?"

"Yes. I didn't want her to be ..."

"Ha!" Mark said. "Wake up and count your blessin's, man! Be thankful she's quiet and that you got some peace at home. And you yourself, I am surely thankful that you're a quiet man. You should of seen the last feller Jared had me workin' with — man that was here before you. Couldn't hardly breathe without talkin', talkin', talkin'! Drove me close to crazy on account of he just wouldn't shut up. I told Jared I couldn't work with him, so Jared picked me over him — I was a better worker — and sent the other feller off down the river someplace. A quiet man like you wears good week after week, 'specially if he hops right to the work and gets it done without a lot of talk and fuss. What I'm sayin', Joe, is I like workin' with you."

"Well I ..." Joe began. "Well thanks, Mark. I like workin' with you too."

"And I hope that girl of yours and Malik can ... Oh, now what's this she could want?"

Down by the tip of the point a woman waved repeatedly up at Mark and Joe.

"It's my wife after me for one thing or another," Mark said. "Be best for me to hop right down there and see what it is — hop right down there if I want her to keep feedin' me, that is. I got to go now. But look here, Joe. Let's get out and do some things together when we ain't workin'. A feller has a need to get out of the house now and again so him and his wife don't pester each other to death. We could go off fishin' someplace maybe. I got a rowboat up on Eagle Pond that I don't get out in near enough. Or we could just set and talk and do some damage to a jug of rum; be fun to get Old Sam to help us and tell us lies about the early days. Let's get together, Joe."

"Suits me, Mark," Joe said.

"Now I got to go. That woman of mine waves much harder, she's goin' to flap right on up into the air."

Mark went down towards his wife. Joe stared at him, feeling such warmth inside that he started to follow Mark down to the point. He was already halfway there when he looked up at Annie Ballard. She was about two rods away and was staring straight into his eyes. He stopped dead, as if he had run into a tree on a dark night; confused that she should be where she was when it seemed that a mere moment earlier she'd been way over talking with Old Sam. He'd lost track of the time while he'd been with Mark Hosmer, he realized. Annie smiled at him. He stared right back at her with his mouth open. Then in a surge of embarrassment he turned abruptly away. This time he didn't look back at her. He walked up beyond the crowd and kept going all the way to where he'd hauled the plank-rig out of the water. When he got there, he lay down on the ground and watched the river go by. He was in no hurry to do anything else.

XXIX

Sue squinted into the glare down below until she saw the long belly of slack rope in the water. Yes, just as she had thought, the fish was angling back up the river. She left Malik, walked down just beyond the tall stump, and began hauling in the rope — gaining a few feet each time she heaved against it. As she worked, she glanced back first at Malik, who was pulling in the slack through a single loop around the tall stump, and then at the three boys, who were laying the slack they got from Malik out neatly across the ledges in long, parallel rows. After that she kept her attention on the rope in the river so she'd be able to warn Malik to put the loops back around the stump before the fish began running again.

She tried to guess what time it was from the height of the sun; tried to cipher how many hours they'd been fighting the fish. If, as she supposed, they had hooked it about three o'clock and if the height of the sun now made it close to noon, then that would mean nine hours already — long, difficult, and unrewarding hours. The fish had enormous, unending power. Sue wondered how Malik, so old and frail-looking, had endured thusfar; wondered how much longer the two of them could keep fighting the fish. It had been discouraging to work so hard regaining rope and then to have the fish so easily take it out again time after time. Even pulling in slack, because of the current's drag on it, was hard work. When the rope began to come in easily, it was time to pay close attention so that she and Malik wouldn't be caught unprepared when the fish began another run.

"Now, Malik!" she said, looking back at him.

Sue watched him throw more loops around the stump and then take up the rope again. She went back and grabbed it behind him. For a moment they simply held tension. Then, slowly at first, the rope began to pull out. Sue let it slide through her hands, thankful for the leather gloves which she and Malik now both wore. With them she no longer had to be so constantly watchful about the rope cutting and burning her flesh. She could let it slide across her palms and closed fingers rather than paying it out hand-over-hand. She wished she'd had the gloves right from the beginning, for the coarse rope had cut her hands badly while she'd been fighting the fish before dawn. Inside the gloves her fingers were sticky with clotted blood and stung from the sweat.

The use of the gloves had been a kindness she hadn't expected. Indeed, she'd been overwhelmed by offers of food and water, by the many words of encouragement, by the sheer numbers of people she didn't even know who wished her luck. Many of them had seemed as excited about the fish as she was herself. They had wrenched her out of her loneliness and isolation and had thrust her suddenly into being the center of attention. It had embarrassed her deeply. Never before had so many people called her by name; known who she was. She kept thinking about that as she fought the fish. Then at the end of the morning — as she'd been looking down at what must have been all the people of the village crowded together at the point talking, laughing, and gazing out over the river for glimpses of the fish — a strange and giddy feeling had suddenly replaced the embarrassment: a feeling of happiness at being known by name; a sense that the people of Barston Falls were good people; the realization that never again would she be a stranger to them. She recognized all the people who had bought fish from her, the women and girls she had studied in silence trying to decide if she would like to be in their places, Steve Danforth, George and Annie Ballard, familiar faces of people whose names she didn't know, but whom she'd seen many times up in the village square. And now it was likely that every single one of the people there knew her name. An awareness crept over her that with a little effort she could learn their names too, either by asking them outright or by asking Old Sam, Steve Danforth, or George or Annie Ballard. Then she'd be able to greet them by name every day as she happened across them in the village, just as they greeted one another. She could stand and talk with them and have them for friends.

Sue looked down at Old Sam, sitting on the same rock he'd been on for quite a while. He watched Malik and her most of the time, giving only occasional glances out over the river. She thought about how much fun it was to be with Old Sam and listen to his teasing and joking. She had never known her own grandfathers. Very well then, she would adopt Old Sam as one of them; Malik would be the other. She would make them forget their silly quarrel so that they could be friends again. Very soon she would cook supper for both of them at her house.

The three boys, whom she'd hated so much, had surprised her most of all. Benjie and Foss and Tom. She repeated the names to herself several times. They had made a great deal of noise as they went about their self-appointed work, but she admitted that they had helped Malik and her a lot by taking care of the reserve rope. They had laid it all out on the ledges in long, parallel rows a foot apart. Nowhere did it cross itself. When the fish made its sudden, long runs, the rope ran out smoothly. Never once did it tangle. When she and Malik regained the lost rope, the boys set it back down carefully into the parallel rows. Loudly, far more loudly than necessary, they had shouted for people to walk around the reserve rope rather than over it. She would have to thank the boys later, Sue thought.

Much of the time the dull ache and sting of her gloved hands and the increasing pain of her exhausted muscles kept Sue murmuring prayers that the fight would end soon. She wanted the fish up on dry ground so that she could quit her ordeal. Occasionally, when the continuing strength of the fish seemed overwhelming, she thought it might be a blessing if the fish broke off. Sometimes, however, Sue thought that in spite of her pain she didn't want the battle with the great fish ever to end. She didn't want all the people there at the point to stop calling her by name, to stop wishing her luck, to stop paying attention to her. She didn't ever want to go back to the loneliness and isolation she had known as long as she could remember; didn't want to end what so far was the best day of her life.

Sue wondered where her father was, hoping he hadn't had to go to work at the lower warehouse that day. So many times she'd wished he'd been fighting the fish alongside Malik and her; pulling on the rope with his great strength. However, she thought too of his words that the fish belonged to her and to Malik and that he wanted the two of them to catch it without his help. He didn't want people to say that Joe Reckford had caught the fish; he wanted them to say it had been Sue Reckford and Malik — a girl and an old man. She thought back — how long ago now it seemed — to when he had told her in the middle of the night to get up and get dressed for fishing with Malik. He hadn't even believed that the fish existed, but he'd been willing to take her down to the point so that she could help Malik fish. She wondered how many other fathers would have done that. Again she wondered where he had gone off to; wished he could be right there watching and encouraging her.

Malik interrupted her thoughts.

"It is a strong fish," he said.

"Think it's tirin' at all?" she asked.

"The fish is not as strong as it once was, but it has much

strength left. We must find a way to tire it faster, but not ourselves."

"How are you?"

"I am a tired, old man, but I will keep fighting the fish as long as I must. I will have much time to rest later, but I want to have the great fish to remember and to talk about while I have my rest."

"Folks will help us if we ask 'em," Sue said.

"No," Malik said. "It is our fish, Sue. It belongs to no one else. No one believed there was a fish — not Sam Barston and not your father. Perhaps Benjie Barston only. Perhaps he wanted there to be a fish, but still I don't know if he believed there was. He helps us now by keeping the loose line in order, but he must not pull on the line with us. That work is ours only, so that when at last we catch the *kabassa,* all the village will know Sue Reckford and old Malik caught it."

"Good," Sue said. "We'll catch it by ourselves then. I just wish it wasn't so strong."

"We will be tired. There will be more pain," Malik said. "But the honor will be great when at last we catch the fish for Sam Barston."

The fish ran again for a few rods. Sue and Malik let the rope slide through their hands until the run stopped. Then they set back to work regaining the line. Both of them were sweating hard in the sun when Joe Reckford appeared.

"You two all right?" Joe asked.

"We are tired," Malik said. "But we will catch the fish."

"I wondered where you went to, Pa," Sue said. "What time is it now?"

"I'm guessin' it's one o'clock," Joe said. "You been fightin' the fish for a long, long time. Is the fish ... Oh, good. Where'd you get the gloves?"

"From George Ballard, Pa. He got 'em from his black-smith shop."

"We'll have to thank him for that," Joe said. "Now tell me if you're tirin' that fish at all."

"A little, but it's still wicked strong," Sue said.

"Well, I'm thinkin' that if it keeps goin' the way it has, you might run out of daylight. Maybe I'm worryin' too early, but if it ain't tirin' in another couple hours, we might find some pine knots or roll some birch bark for torches. Be better if you could just tire it faster and bring it in."

"That's what Malik says, Pa."

"Do what you want," Joe said. "Just remember that you're fishin' with quite a large rope and that your hook ain't goin' to straighten. You can lean into that rope just as hard as you got the strength to, and nothin's likely to break."

"Yes," Malik said. "We must tire the fish better. We must eat something and then fight the fish harder. Many people offer food. I will send Benjie Barston to get some."

Malik slid his gloved hands back along the rope to where Benjie, Foss, and Tom were sitting. In a moment Benjie was hurrying down into the crowd.

* * * * *

With food in her stomach Sue moved out in front of the stump and began pulling hard on the taut rope. She pulled steadily against the weight of the fish, surprised at how much she gained. Malik worked the rope through the slack loops around the stump without taking any of them off. Tom, Foss, and Benjie laid down the long loops on the ledges and began calling out encouragement to Sue and Malik, for they hadn't had so much rope in before. Two of them worked at a time; the third stood out of their way and watched the river for a glimpse of the fish. Sue increased her efforts.

Benjie, watching the river, echoed the sudden shouts from the crowd. He had a good view of the explosion of thrashings in the water just off the point. When he heard Sue cry out, he turned to see her hurrying back to hold the rope with Malik. Then he rejoined Tom and Foss as their long loops of rope sprang from the ledges one after another.

Sue looked over Malik's shoulder out across the wide bay of the eddy as the rope slid through her gloves. Since the only bad glare on the water then was over by the west shore of the bay, she could see clearly the occasional swirls out beyond where the rope entered the water. The swirls kept appearing further down the river and had a pronounced swing towards the east bank — out of the eddy and into the main current of the river.

"Hold, Sue," Malik said. "We must turn the fish away from the current."

Sue gripped the rope more tightly. Her hands began to burn even through the gloves. Still the rope swung out into the main current. The fish angled off down the river, and Sue felt the rope sliding out faster than before. Sudden shouts from the three boys made her glance behind. There Benjie, Foss, and Tom pointed to the last two loops of rope on the ledge.

"Malik!" she screamed. "We're runnin' out of rope!"

Malik shouted orders. Sue and the three boys leaped out in front of the stump, held the rope hard, and glanced back at Malik, who moved more quickly than any of them knew he could. He flung off his gloves and whipped the rope's free end around in a fury as he knotted it to the taut rope coming off the stump: one knot, two knots, and then he stood clear. The three boys jumped back away from the rope and began rubbing the pain from their hands.

The top of the stump lurched towards the river half a foot and then a foot as the stump itself protested with creaks and poppings. Without a word to one another Sue, Malik, and the boys all strained against the stump in an effort to keep it upright.

"Look! Look!" Benjie shrieked, pointing straight down the rope just as a tremendous clamor arose from the crowd.

The great fish twisted up into the air for a long moment, looking huge — an ox-like bulk — even at that distance. Sunlight glistened off the dark back, the white belly, and the splashes of spray. Then the fish fell back into the river in a confusion of white. Three more times it rose straight up thrashing the air with its sickle tail. The next leap was short and angled toward the west bank. Then the fish was off with unbelievable speed across the lower part of the eddy. The rope in the water curved in a long arc as the fish raced towards the west. The knot where two of the ropes were tied together plowed a white furrow.

The rope in the river straightened, and the fish made two more stump-twitching leaps before it reversed itself and headed back towards the east bank. For several minutes the fish pulled hard at the end of the arc: dragging the rope sideways through the river, leaping into the air, reversing direction, thrashing the surface, straining hard against the stump. In silence Sue and Malik pushed against the stump and watched the surges of the great fish. Benjie, Foss, and Tom were reduced to mere gasps and whimperings.

Then the line slackened. Malik and Sue sprang out in front of the stump and began pulling in the rope as quickly as they could, leaving the accumulating slack in disarray. Not until they had reached the first knot which linked two ropes together did Malik have the three boys untie the rope from the stump and take the slack back up onto the ledges, telling them to tie the loose end around the nearest tree they could find up the slope. For a while as Sue pulled in the slack, she feared that somehow the great fish had broken off. A few moments later, however, she was reassured when once again she stood with Malik, the rope sliding through their gloves and around the loops on the stump.

The fish bolted, taking most of the line she and Malik had regained. They cast anxious glances up behind them until they were certain that the boys had indeed tied the end of the rope to a tree.

The fish took out every foot of rope and then set off on another series of leaps and runs. Malik stood back with a tremendous smile on his face; shaking his hands down at his sides.

"Good. We will tire the fish well this way, Sue," he said. "See that now it does not leap so far above the water. See that when it runs it does not move so quickly across the river. It is tiring while we take our rest, but we must tire it further. We must keep the *kabassa* pulling hard against the rope and moving always."

For well over an hour the fish kept fighting way down in the eddy. Malik and Sue goaded the fish hard whenever it slowed down or left slack in the rope. They rarely gained more than a few yards before they quickly lost it again — all the way to the end. Then they stood and rested and watched the fish constantly moving back and forth; constantly straining against the stump and the tree up behind, where the boys had tied the end of the rope.

In the middle of the afternoon, as Sue was pulling in the slack quickly to goad the fish hard once again, she was surprised when it kept coming. The three boys were soon back at work laying out the rope in the long, parallel rows on the ledges. Sue and Malik both saw the fish at the same time, just as dozens of arms pointed at it surging straight up into the current. It passed the point and kept right on towards the faster water above. Sue redoubled her efforts to pull in the slack, but Malik stopped her.

"No, Sue. Rest. Let the fish swim up into the force of the current, for that will tire it better than we can. If it goes up too far, we will try to turn it, but let it swim against the current as long as it will."

They stood and watched as the fish took out the rest of the slack. Then they let the reserve rope slide out by itself. The resistance from the loops around the stump slowed and then halted the progress of the fish upriver. For a long time it hung even in the current, astounding Malik and Sue yet again with its strength.

Then, abruptly, the fish turned and shot back down with the current, leaving a great deal of slack rope. As the fish kept on down the river, the rope suddenly tightened and swept around the point so unexpectedly quickly that it knocked down several people. Sue and Malik kept the rope tight as the fish fought more slowly down in the eddy, not again taking out all the reserve rope. Time and again they goaded it, but it didn't respond as it had before. Occasionally it settled into what must have been a very deep hole at the foot of the fast water a little below and to the east of the point. With great efforts Sue and Malik kept forcing the fish from its deep refuge and sending it back out into its eddy circuits. They fought the fish steadily, tiring it and tiring themselves. Around it went in the eddy, moving more deliberately than before, without any panicked leaps or long runs; wallowing occasionally on the surface. Sue and Malik took in line as the fish swung toward them in the eddy and let it slide out grudgingly as the fish pulled against them.

The afternoon progressed. People sat down by the point and waited. There were no more great leaps to watch; nothing but the rope disappearing into the water and going around in the eddy. Many of the spectators began to realize how hungry and thirsty they were. Some left and before long were back with food and drink. People talked incessantly as they kept watch on the river. All the villagers of Barston Falls were there eating, drinking, enjoying the sun, laughing, and chatting among themselves. Many wondered out loud if Sue and Malik would ever bring in the great fish.

XXX

George Ballard stirred the ashes in his forge with a poker and then dropped the poker across them.

"Dead as ice," he said aloud. "I ain't goin' to burn the place down today. Better chance of settin' myself on fire, if I can find it."

He rummaged around in the dim light over in one corner of his shop, then hooked a finger into the loop on the neck of a small earthenware jug and lifted it out from among accumulations of iron scraps and old rags. Over in the better light by the doorway he blew the dust off the jug, unstoppered it, and drank.

"There," he said, as he re-stoppered the jug and carried it out of his blacksmith shop. "Now I'll have an easier look at that fish."

George laughed and shook his head at how deserted the village square was that day. In the middle of the square, as he was crossing Israel Barston's park, he met Jared Barston walking towards him.

"They ain't cheated me by catchin' the thing yet, have they Jared?" George asked.

"Not yet," Jared said. "I had a thirst naggin' at me and thought I'd do somethin' about it. See other folks had the same idea."

"Headed all the way up to your house?"

"Yes. I keep a jug there generally."

"But ain't the lower warehouse a lot closer 'n goin' all the way up onto Tannery Road? Seems like you got kegs and kegs of rum at the lower warehouse."

"That's right, but I don't want a whole keg. All I want is a jug, and the jug's at home, so that's where I'm headed."

"Well how do you know you won't die of thirst on the way?"

"I don't," Jared grinned. "Just have to take my chances."

George held the jug out to him.

"Don't want it on my conscience, Jared."

Jared drank and returned the jug to George.

"Thanks George. You're a good man. Now you get on down there to the point, and I'll join you after I get my jug. They had the fish on its side for a little and thought the fight was over, but then it went off again fresh as ever, and it may be hours yet. I don't know. Biggest thing I ever saw in the Connecticut."

"Me too. Hope they catch the thing. See you down there, Jared."

George kept on his way towards the point. He left the road and went down along the path. As he was emerging from the trees, half a dozen rods down to his left he saw Joe Reckford standing alone where he could keep an eye on his daughter. George stopped and watched Sue and Malik long enough to decide that they would be fighting the fish for some time yet. Then he turned his attention back to Joe.

"Joe Reckford," George murmured to himself. "Hard to get to know somebody like that. Stays to himself so much. Never even see him in church. Well, maybe after today's done, he won't be such a stranger."

George walked down the slope towards Joe. When he spoke, Joe turned in surprise.

"Big day for your daughter."

"Yes ... biggest one she ever had," Joe said, pausing awkwardly for a moment before he plunged on. "And I didn't even believe her when she said there was a big fish out there."

"Well, you wasn't the only one. Who'd of thought there was anythin' like that in the Connecticut? But I tell you it's made quite a day for us in the village. Best entertainment we ever had. Now I don't mean to insult you if you're temperance, Joe, but I got more 'n enough rum here for a couple of good men if you want any."

"Oh," Joe said, taking the jug. "I like rum."

Joe drank.

"How are Sue and Malik bearin' up?" George asked.

"Malik's about wore out, but Sue's holdin' out all right. Her hands and arms cramp sometimes, but that's all. She'll sleep tonight, let me tell you, if they ever get the fish in."

"They been at it a long time," George said. "And the three boys, too, takin' care of that extra rope. Guess they'll all feel good when it's over — just so long as they get the fish, of course."

The two men passed the jug for several minutes as they watched Malik and Sue and the three boys.

"So how's your work, Joe?"

"Can't complain," Joe said. "Mark Hosmer is an awful good man. I like workin' for Jared."

"Two good men," George said. "Jared's the best Barston around — best in that generation anyways. Course Old Sam and his brothers now, that's somethin' different. They don't make 'em like that any more. When he was young, people claimed that Old Sam was the strongest man in the whole Connecticut valley. Lot of stories about him then."

George held the jug out towards Joe, but Joe shook his head.

"I had enough, George," Joe said.

"Got plenty left here. No cause to be polite. That's what they make it for — drinkin'."

"Obliged to you, George, but it's an old promise, and I guess I had enough for today."

"Old promise?"

"Well, to my wife before she died. Told her I'd have one good measure of rum a day and no more 'n that. Just wouldn't seem right to me now if I had more."

"Hard to measure it when it comes straight out of the jug. Likely you short-measured yourself, Joe."

"I thank you, George, but I s'pose I had enough. You drink it for me, and enjoy it. It is good rum."

"How long you kept that promise, Joe?"

"A year or two while Betsy was still alive. Ten years now, I guess, since she died. Childbirth it was, tryin' to give me a son."

"And you kept your promise all these years?"

"Gave her my word. Be like spittin' on her grave to go back on my word like that."

"A long time, Joe," George said, shaking his head.

"Course not many days in all that time that I ain't filled that measure right up to the line," Joe said. "And I been known to stay up past midnight so's I could pour one day's measure down on top of the one from the day before. I do like my rum."

George laughed.

"I'll drink for both of us then." He tilted the jug and drank; wiped his mouth with the back of his hand. "You know, Joe, I'd of thought you might remarry. Ever thought about it?"

"Thought about it a lot, George. Sue needed a mother all those years."

"Why ain't you then?"

"Never found the right woman, I guess. Without Betsy I just didn't want to have much to do with other folks, and then I sort of crusted over that way. We moved around a lot too, Sue and me. I looked some, but I guess I never did find the right woman."

"Well some day maybe you will," George said. He drank again from the jug.

"You know, George, I been meanin' to thank you," Joe said.

"What for?"

"Well, a number of things. The gloves this mornin', for one. Sue said you went up and got gloves for her and Malik. Says they made quite a difference to 'em fightin' the fish."

"Ha!" George said. "Nobody else in town was goin' to use gloves today — not mine and not anybody else's. No sense lettin' all the idle gloves in Barston Falls just set and do nothin'. Glad mine could be of some use."

"That's just it," Joe said. "A lot of idle gloves in the village, but only you thought to bother with gettin' 'em down here to Sue and Malik, and I thank you for that if they ain't had a chance to yet."

"Nothin' at all," George said, "but you're welcome anyways."

"And then last night. I meant to thank you for comin' by last night and speakin' to Sue. Apologizin' to her like that. Took a man with some backbone to ..."

"Backbone nothin'," George said. "Took a man with solid bone all the way through his head. Who'd of thought there was a fish in the Connecticut that'd go after bait stuck onto what used to be a horseshoe? Not me and not anybody else in the village. Solid bone through an awful lot of heads around here, for that matter. Look how wrong all of us was."

"I didn't think there was a fish neither," Joe said. "But that ain't what I'm talkin' about. I mean to thank you for realizin' how the idle chatter about the horseshoe hook might hurt Sue and then for comin' around to talk to her about it. Few men would of done that."

"Ha," George said and took another drink from the jug. "And don't I look foolish now when I should of been braggin' about makin' that hook — braggin' about it instead of laughin' about it?"

"Well I'll give you my thanks anyways," Joe said, "even if you're tryin' to duck away from it. Truth is, George, I admire everythin' about you. I hope you're a happy man because I think you should be. You do good, honest work. Everybody in the village likes you. You got a wife that a lot of men would ..."

"My wife?" George interrupted.

"Annie," Joe said. "A lot of men 'd be happy to have a wife like her."

"Oh, my wife Annie," George said with a strange bluster in his voice. "Tell me all about my wife Annie now, Joe. Sure you don't want more rum?"

"I guess I won't, George."

"Well all right then," George said with a wide smile on his face. He tipped back the jug to drink again. "Now tell me all about my wife Annie, for the truth is that lately I've had a hard time seein' much good in her. Too big and too plain-lookin' to start off with."

"Oh no, George. She's healthy and strong. And there's a solid, clean look to her. She ain't just some rattlebrained piece of fluff like a lot of those short and scrawny women. There's somethin' to her — somethin' you can count on — and it ain't just her size and looks."

"Well, what else is there to her?" George asked.

"She's kind, for one thing. And for another, she's a much better cook than most women, which some men might think important, though it's not the most important thing. She's got a pretty smile too."

"I can't for the life of me guess how you know so much about her, Joe," George said and watched the color creep into Joe's face and neck. "She's told me herself that you scarcely will speak to her. Said this mornin' — just this mornin' — that you kept runnin' away from her like she was a catamount or a rattlesnake. What do you say to that?"

"Well ... well, I guess it's true," Joe said quietly.

"Now that ain't much of a way to treat her," George said. "There's a woman that sees you and Sue — both of you hangin' back from gettin' to know folks in the village — and she goes out of her way to be a good neighbor. Cooks food for you. Tries to be friendly and what do you do? Why, you run away from her! How come, Joe?"

George looked hard at Joe, now in full blush and staring down at the ground.

"Just afraid, I guess," Joe said.

"Afraid of Annie?"

"No, not of her. Just afraid ... afraid, well ... afraid I might get too attracted to her."

"Well, what 'd be wrong with that?" George asked.

"I don't want to be attracted to another man's wife is all," Joe said. He lifted his gaze and looked George squarely in the face. "I'll tell you this, George, on account of nothin' happened and nothin' is goin' to happen. You're a lucky man, George Ballard. I liked the looks of Annie the first time I saw her, but I won't chase after another man's wife."

"And that's how come you been runnin' away from her?"

"Yes. If I didn't, the temptation 'd make me ashamed. If it gets too strong, I'll move away. I promise you."

"You really would, wouldn't you?"

"I would. I want you to know you're a lucky man to have Annie, George. Hope you appreciate her."

"Well, might be too late, Joe," George said. "Truth is Annie's part of the problem too. She's been up to a lot more 'n just bein' a good neighbor. She's hurt that you ain't paid her more attention when she goes out of her way to do things for you. I think she's after you, Joe."

"And she said that? Come right out and told you?"

"Not exactly. But she don't have to. I can tell from seein' the way she acts. But no doubt about it: she's got her eye on you."

"I'll leave then, George. I won't do anythin' that ..."

"Oh, stick around. You might get to like it here in Barston Falls."

"No. I'll leave. This time next week I'll be gone. Wouldn't be decent to stay."

"You're makin' too much of it, Joe. No need to move away just on account of a large, plain woman tryin' to chase after you. Maybe she can cook. Maybe there are a few other things about her that some men might admire, but, for me, I'd rather have a woman with a little bit of fluff to her. Not that I like the rattle-brained kind of fluff, but I like a woman to be a little more delicate — always have."

"Well then, you're the biggest fool in the world, George Ballard! Can't even appreciate what you got! That's the way you feel, how come you went and married her?"

"Ain't."

"What?" Joe demanded. His mouth dropped open.

"Annie ain't really my wife. Never did marry her. We ... we just live together is all."

Joe shook his head for a long moment.

"Well," he said. "Well ... it ... it ain't proper. It ain't fair to Annie. Marry her, George."

"Don't want to, and I ain't goin' to. Got my eye out to catch one of those small, fluffy women. That's what I want. I like a little woman with some softness to her — maybe straw-colored hair with some curls and some dimples in her cheeks when she smiles. Somebody with some nice blue or green eyes. Why on earth would I want to marry an ox like Annie when I could have a pretty little ..."

Joe Reckford's fist smashed into George's cheek with the full force of his body behind it; the power twisting all the way up from his legs and through his hips and back. George crumpled backward onto the ground. He lay dazed for a moment, holding his cheek with one hand and the rum jug with the other. The look of surprise slowly drained from his face. Then, suddenly, laughter poured out of him wave on wave. Joe stood over George in complete confusion. His fists wilted; his arms hung at his sides. George laughed until tears came into his eyes. When he took his hand off his cheek, Joe saw the already huge swelling which made the smile behind it look ridiculous. The swelling was as red as the birthmark poking up out of George's shirt onto the right side of his neck.

"Oh, I guess you'll do, Joe Reckford," George said, at last in control of his laughter. "We're goin' to change you around just a bit, but you're goin' to do just fine."

"You all right?" Joe asked.

"Long as you ain't goin' to hit me again, Joe. That's quite a fist you got there. I was wonderin' how far I could string you along, and I guess I just found out."

George sat up and checked to make sure the rum jug wasn't broken. Then abruptly he pointed a finger at Joe, who was leaning down towards him.

"Now, Joe Reckford," George said. "Now the first thing we're goin' to do is get you out of your cave or out from under your rock or wherever else you been hidin'. You ain't goin' to live like a dead man any more. You're goin' to get to know the folks of Barston Falls and let them get to know you. You're goin' to learn what's happenin' in the village. I don't care how you been used to livin'. Those days are over for good, startin' today. From now on you ain't to hide from anybody and you ain't to run away either.

"Listen to me. How can you live right in Barston Falls for however many weeks you been here and not know that Annie ain't my wife? Listen to me, you old hermit, and promise me you'll start talkin' with people! Annie and I been livin' in that house together ever since our ma died three years ago. She's my sister, Joe. You understand that?"

Joe looked dazed.

"Your sister?" he whispered.

"My sister. Is it safe to get up now?"

Joe helped George to his feet, scarcely knowing what he was doing. He was suddenly very pale.

"Your sister?" Joe murmured. "Your sister ... I ... I'm sorry I hit you, George. Your sister, you say? Well I'm sorry. I ... I don't know what come over me. I don't think I hit anybody like that since I was a boy."

"I don't imagine you ever hit anybody like that before," George said. "I hope you never do again. And I know exactly what come over you. As for hittin' me, you're in more trouble than you know, only not from me. I think she'll be quite interested when she gets a look at my cheek and hears you try and explain. You got apologies to make to her, Joe, and I think that soon as you open your mouth tryin' to tell her, there ain't any turnin' back."

"Your sister?" Joe said.

"Exactly."

"And she ain't married?"

"Not yet, Joe."

"Your sister," Joe murmured again. "Why, I made a terrible mistake! I got to tell her!"

"Yes you do, Joe, and I think she's right down there by the point. We'll go find her together. I want her to see my face before you start explainin' things."

"Yes. I need to tell her a lot of things," Joe said. Suddenly he clutched at George's arm. "George? Can I borrow some rum?"

"Thought you had your measure for today, Joe."

"I think I short-measured myself," Joe said. "That's what it feels like anyways. Hard to measure when it comes straight out of the jug."

George handed him the jug. Joe took a long drink and gave the jug back.

"Ready Joe?"

"I guess I am."

"You know, Joe, I'm goin' to remember this day for the rest of my life."

"Yes. I will too. Let's go, George."

Joe led the way down towards the point. Before following him, George glanced over at Sue and Malik where they were holding onto the rope. They were busy and didn't notice him. However, Benjie, Foss, and Tom stared at him, all looking alarmed. Old Sam Barston gazed up at him too. George laughed, waved to all of them, and then hurried ahead to catch up with Joe. He threw an arm over Joe's shoulder, and together they walked down towards the point.

XXXI

Malik knew that the fish was tired. Hours had passed since it had last leaped clear of the water. Its recent runs had been short and feeble compared to earlier ones. There was still strength in the fish to be respected, but Malik had seen the strength only in the panicked thrashings the fish made when, wallowing on its side, it would right itself and take out some of the rope he and Sue had gained. He hoped that the fish's exhaustion and defeat would come before he himself collapsed. Pain ran all through his body — not the sharp, demanding pain of a wound or injury, but rather a grinding, overall aching of his muscles and joints. He bore it, though the aching grew worse with each passing hour. His old body could keep working a while longer, he thought, but he was uncertain just how much longer.

Malik turned his gaze away from the river and studied Sue. During the last hour cramps had repeatedly stabbed into the muscles of her arms and hands. She hadn't controlled the tears — a girl's weakness, Malik thought — but she had shaken out the cramps as best she could and had kept fighting the fish. He regarded her with growing respect and thought of things he might later tell Joe Reckford about his daughter.

He looked back at the three boys standing by the neat rows of rope they had laid down. The three had been tending the rope for a long time. Though the fish's failing strength had left them with little to do, still they waited patiently: talking among themselves on the ledges or talking one at a time with Old Sam Barston down by the rock where he had sat for many hours. Malik watched and thought and then suddenly beckoned to them. Foss Richardson came over to him quickly.

"What is it, Malik?" Foss asked.

"Another rope," Malik said. "We must have a long rope to tie around the great fish when it comes near the shore. We will not pull the *kabassa* from the river with this rope lest the hook tear free or a sharp rock cut the line as the fish struggles. Up above there is the rope to the planks. I need you to go and bring it to me."

"All right, Malik," Foss said.

Foss hurried back to speak with Tom and Benjie. Then Malik watched him run up along the riverbank. When Malik turned his attention to the rope again, he saw Old Sam Barston hobbling towards him with his cane. A moment later, red-faced and slightly out of breath, Old Sam stood beside Malik and Sue in silence looking down at the river with them.

Five rods from the point the great fish lay on its side, unbelievably huge. The three of them saw where the rope disappeared into its mouth, underneath the rounded snout — a mouth underslung like that of a sucker from a brook, but on a fish a hundred times heavier than any sucker they'd ever seen. A line of diamond-shaped patterns ran down its side all the way to the pointed, sickle tail. Up by the heaving gills a fin waved feebly for a moment. The fish thrashed, disappeared beneath the surface, and pulled hard against the rope. Sue and Malik let the rope slide out through their gloved hands as the fish made a short swim across the eddy; regained some of what they'd lost as the fish came back up in the eddy current.

"Plenty of life in it still," Old Sam said. "It's tired but ain't ready to give up yet. You two all right? Can I get anythin' for you?"

"I'm all right, Old Sam," Sue said.

Malik looked down at the river and didn't speak.

"Say Malik," Old Sam said. "Think that thing weighs more 'n ten pounds?"

"Yes, Sam Barston. I think the hook and the bait weigh ten pounds."

"Well, I might owe you a dollar then, if you can land the thing."

"Yes," Malik said. "You will give me a dollar."

Sue and Malik pulled against the rope in silence as Old Sam watched. He looked out at the fish thrashing on the surface again, at the people down below by the point, and then back at Malik. His gaze rested on the old Abenaki for some time.

"Hard luck for the fish that you're such a stubborn old cuss," Old Sam said at last. "Any other old man would of pastured himself out into a rockin' chair on a porch by now, but there you go, ornery and stubborn as ever, pretendin' you're a young man again. If Nabatis was still alive and challenged you to canoe-race him down to the mouth of the Connecticut, I think you'd hop right to it. You remember that, Malik? And you remember racin' right back down there a second time just as soon as you and Nabatis got back?"

"Yes, Sam Barston," Malik said. "I remember many things from the old days."

"Well, I hope you remember your friends from the old days on account of hardly any of 'em are still alive and pretty soon none of 'em will be. One of these days you'll find yourself all alone, Malik. Too much talk for you yet?"

"Yes, Sam Barston."

"I'll shut up then. But I'll be right here."

Old Sam sat on a rock and watched the fish down below. Sue and Malik kept fighting the fish, slowly losing and gaining back rope; wondering how much longer the tired fish could go on and wondering how much longer they themselves could last. Malik glanced over at Old Sam now and then, but didn't speak. He fought the fish in silence until Foss returned with a coil of rope over his shoulder.

"Good," Malik said. "That is what we need. Now bring the other two boys here, and I will tell you what we must do."

Foss took a few steps toward Benjie and Tom; waved and shouted. They joined him. The three boys then stood and waited as Sue and Malik grudgingly yielded rope until the fish had finished another short run.

"There you see that the great fish is tired," Malik said. "The fish was strong, but we fought for many hours and tired it. Soon we will finish the battle with the *kabassa* and pull it up onto the riverbank, but we will not pull it with the line and the hook, for there is a danger that the hook might come out as we pull. We must put another rope onto the fish instead. When we do, then many people down at the point will help us pull the great fish from the water. The other rope must be tied well. It must be tied by those not afraid of the water or of the thrashings of the fish while they are tying the rope. The knot must tighten when many men and women pull on the rope, and it must be around the head of the great fish and under the gill covers. If the work is not done well, then the rope will pull free. Will you boys do it, or are you afraid?"

Benjie, Tom, and Foss glanced at one another.

"We'll do it," Benjie said. "But you got to show us the knot."

The fish thrashed again on the surface. Malik leaned back. The rope slid out, but only a few feet.

"I can show the boys a slip-knot," Old Sam said. "You got your hands full already, Malik."

Malik nodded without saying anything. He and Sue strained against the fish. Old Sam took the coil of rope Foss had carried down and showed the boys a simple knot; then had them practice tying it around one another and pulling to see how well it would slip. The boys stood and talked nervously, watched the fish down below, and fussed with the rope.

"They're ready, Malik," Old Sam said.

"Good," Malik said. "Take the rope down by the point and wait. When the fish is ready, Sue and I will come down and tell you."

"All right," Old Sam said. "But you boys give me that rope. I see your ma down there, Benjie, and there's Tom's pa over to her right. If you go down there carryin' a rope and start braggin' about how you're goin' to go out and tie it around the fish, I think you might discover your folks have different ideas. Give me the rope to carry. When we're down there, don't hang around me or they might get suspicious. Just be close by so you can hop in the river with the rope soon as Malik gives the word. That sound about right to you, Malik?"

"Yes, Sam Barston."

The boys went down to the point. Old Sam followed them with the rope several minutes later. Sue watched him go and then gazed out over the crowd. Off to one side she was surprised to see her father standing so close to Annie Ballard as they talked. Their heads were scarcely a foot apart. For as long as she watched, neither of them so much as glanced at her or the river. A short run of the fish pulled her attention back to the rope and then to the fish itself after it had stopped. It lay on its side with its gill-plate heaving. It struggled and succeeded in righting itself and going underwater, but then the pressure she and Malik put on the rope easily pulled it back to the surface again and over onto its side.

"See that it is nearly ready, Sue," Malik said. "We will keep the great fish on its side a while longer, and then it will be ready."

"Ain't it dangerous for the boys when they try and put the rope around the fish?" Sue asked.

"Only if they are foolish and become tangled," Malik said.

"But if the fish bites them, ain't that ...?"

Malik interrupted her with his short laughter.

"It is good for the boys if they have that to worry about. It is good if they have that fear, but the great fish has no teeth."

"You know that for sure?" Sue asked.

"Yes," Malik said. "Far down the Connecticut when I was young there were many such fish — *kabassa*. They were taken often by the spear, but they were far smaller than Sam Barston's great fish. Perhaps this is the greatest *kabassa* ever in the river. And none of the others ever had teeth. Unless teeth have sprouted in the great fish's mouth in its old age, there will be none in this one either. Look now, Sue. The whiteness of the belly. Pull hard on the line and let us see if there is any strength left in the great *kabassa*."

The two pulled on the rope out in front of the stump. The great fish turned over with its belly up and then rolled over onto its side again. Sue and Malik watched the heaving gill-plate and the feeble twitching of fins up by the head and halfway down the body. The tail flopped powerlessly in and out of the water. They pulled the fish closer to shore and watched it for several more minutes. It made no more attempts to run. No longer could it even right itself in the water.

"It is ready," Malik said. He gathered a long loop of slack in the rope and knotted it around the stump. Then he put his hand on Sue's shoulder.

"Come, Sue. At last the fight is over. Let us go and bring in Sam Barston's fish."

The two walked arm-in-arm down beside the rope; down through the strangely silent crowd until they stood at the water's edge. Malik gazed at the fish for a moment, then turned and nodded to Old Sam.

"All right, boys," Old Sam said quietly.

Benjie, Foss, and Tom were instantly in the water carrying one end of the rope to the fish; wading out over their waists and up to their armpits. Their movements gave the crowd back its voice. Shouts of encouragement obscured whatever Benjie's mother kept shrieking at him. Benjie himself swam underneath the fish with the rope, came up on the far side, and flung the loose end back over at Tom and Foss. The two of them struggled together to tie the slip-knot, more hindrance than help to each other; taking twice as long at the simple task as either of them alone would have done. Then the three boys worked the rope down under the gill-plates and finally snugged the loop tight. With whoops of glee they thrashed away from the fish and didn't look back until they were out of the river.

Old Sam Barston stood in the midst of the crowd with his hands on his hips.

"All right, folks!" he bellowed. "Grab the rope and pull the thing in! Everybody grab hold and heave!"

Sue and Malik stood apart from the crowd and watched. They felt no sense of triumph after their long efforts; felt nothing but overwhelming exhaustion and relief. They watched the rope stretch out through the crowd with nearly everyone scrambling for a grip. Then people hauled on the rope, stumbling here and there because they were so crowded in against one another, but the rope kept coming in. In staggered movements the fish nosed up out of the shallows and slid onto the riverbank and further up across the ledges. The pullers let go of the rope randomly, and the fish came to a halt. Someone tied the free end of the rope to a tree far above. Everyone began shouting and laughing and cheering as they milled around admiring the great fish.

It lay there in its hugeness, twitching and shuddering its life away. From the round snout hung a whisker-like appendage. Below it the rope disappeared into the huge, sucker-mouth with no sign of the hook or of the wood-chuck-bait. The one visible gill plate flared out, forced open by the tight rope, with trickles of blood around its edges. A bony shield covered the surface of the plate. Rows of similar bony shields ran down along the fish's back and stomach. A silver line stretched along the side from the gill-plate to the tail right through the center of a row of diamond-shaped, bony plates. Otherwise the skin was smooth and scaleless; dark on the back and white on the stomach. The upper half of the tail tapered into a long point; the lower, shorter part curved down nearly at a right angle to it. People gaped at the hugeness of the creature. George Ballard stepped off five paces for its length, and people soon took up the cry that the fish was a rod long. They were talking about how they might find its weight when Malik approached with his knife in one hand and his gloves in the other. Conversations dwindled as increasing numbers of people turned their attention to the old Indian.

The crowd hushed as Malik knelt by the fish. He seemed to be speaking to it as he set the gloves down. People strained to hear what he might be saying. They wondered at the gestures he made with his knife to the fish, to the sky, and to the river. They scarcely breathed when he bowed his head down briefly to touch the fish and when he began singing in a whispery chant. Then he himself was silent and still. After a long moment he laid his free hand over the fish's eye and slid the knife blade deep into the flesh at the back of the head, right where the line of bony shields began. He twisted the knife. The fish shuddered and then lay still. Malik cut the rope where it disappeared into the fish's mouth, cut the other rope away from its gills, wiped the blade on his britches, and re-sheathed his knife. Then he picked up his gloves and walked back over to stand by Sue. Benjie, Foss, and Tom joined them, and after a moment Old Sam shuffled over too.

"It's done," Old Sam said, "and I never expected to see such a thing at Barston Falls. It's nothin' you youngsters would have any reason to know about, but that fish is called a sturgeon. I never knew one to be this far up the Connecticut before. They're common down at the lower part of the river, and I saw them there many times when I was younger and down workin' on the mast drives and the log drives. This is the biggest one I ever saw, though there was one nearly as big caught down by the mouth of the Connecticut more than forty years ago. Folks used to spear the littler ones or net them, and you have to watch out for the young fish on account of the little bony things on the back and sides and stomach are awful sharp. But this one here is so old that the sharpness on the bony things is all wore off. This sturgeon is prob'ly older 'n me by quite a bit. Wouldn't surprise me if it was a hundred or a hundred and fifty years old, or maybe more. Have to be to grow so big."

"Yes," Malik said "An old *kabassa* — sturgeon — that has lived here for many years."

"That's right," Old Sam said. "That fish had to get up above the dams before they went in. And let's see. That one at South Hadley Falls. That was the first as I recall, and that went in ... must of been '92 or '94. Yes, '94 it was. They tore it out later on account of the fever it caused upriver in the flooded land, but other dams were in by then. So it's close to thirty years anyways that this fish has been in the upper river. And not a soul's known it all these years. Quite a surprise for me, let me tell you. And I was so pig-headed that I wouldn't even believe Malik when he told me about it straight out. I wouldn't believe him, and he never told me a lie in his life. Well, I believe you now, Old Malik. And givin' you the benefit of the doubt — even if the fish ain't been weighed yet — I believe that I owe you a dollar."

"Yes, Sam Barston. You owe me a dollar. You were wrong about the big fish in the river, and you owe me a dollar."

"Well I got it here, Malik. I hate to let a debt stand too long."

Old Sam reached into his pocket and pulled out the dollar. He handed it to Malik.

"Here it is, old-timer. I was wrong, and you were right. Here's your dollar."

Malik took the dollar in his palm and stared at it for several moments as he kept turning it over. Then he looked up at Old Sam.

"I thank you Sam Barston for paying the dollar so quickly."

"Well, I'm glad you finally ... " Old Sam began.

A sharp yell from Malik silenced him — followed by a drawn-out scream of yips and wails which turned every head in the crowd toward the old Indian. At the end of his cry Malik drew back his arm and flung the silver dollar as far as he could out into the Connecticut.

"Why ... why ..." Benjie sputtered. "You threw a whole dollar in the river!"

Malik nodded. His washed-out, exhausted look had completely disappeared. He turned and stared at Old Sam. Old Sam stared back with a smile on his face that slowly grew into a laugh.

"Sam Barston," Malik said. "I have a gift for you. Here is a fish I caught from the Connecticut — a fish that weighs more than ten pounds. It is your fish now, Sam Barston. You will take it as a gift, and you will have me at your house so that we may eat the fish together. It is a gift to you, Sam Barston. A gift from a friend."

"All right you skinny old cuss," Old Sam said. "I thank you as a friend for your gift, but see if I don't hold you right to what you just said. You are comin' home with me, and you'll stay and help me eat that fish. I don't care if it takes all winter or all the rest of your life. We'll salt the fish down and pack it in barrels, and together we'll eat the whole infernal thing! And you ain't goin' to skip off after we finish it because I'll need a chance to give you somethin' then in return. Understand that, you old cuss?"

"Yes, Sam Barston. I understand," Malik said.

Thereafter, the crowd pressed in so eagerly around Sue and Malik that there was no peace. Seemingly everyone wanted to touch them and congratulate them. They felt all but overwhelmed by the attention. George Ballard offered to buy the hook back from Sue for a dollar. She agreed and told Old Sam to save the hook for George. Sue looked all around for her father and finally spotted him trying to get through the throng. It seemed to take him forever, but at last he wrapped his arms around her in a huge hug and lifted her from the ground. As she was in the air, she saw Annie Ballard over her father's shoulder and felt Annie's arm on her back. When her feet touched the ground again, her father loosened his grip enough to capture Annie in a joyous, three-person hug. Loud cheering and laughter arose from all over the point. Rum jugs circulated freely.

Later, after much of the excitement had died down, George Ballard and Steve Danforth organized the people to take the great fish up to the village square. There was talk about weighing it, tracing it, skinning it. Jared Barston promised a horse and wagon and went off to get it himself. The others at the point rigged slings and, amid a great deal of confusion and disagreement over the best way to go about moving the fish, finally succeeded in dragging and carrying it up the path to where the road came in. There they loaded the sturgeon into Jared's wagon and accompanied it up to the square amid loud singing, cheering, and laughter.

All of the townspeople gathered in the village square and surrounded the great fish in Jared's wagon. Someone began ringing the fire bell. Many took turns pulling the bell rope and would keep up the ringing nearly until dark. With a chisel George Ballard freed the hook from the fish's throat. He left the short length of rope attached to the hook and then took the hook and rope over to his blacksmith shop and clenched them into the upper trim board of his doorframe with bent-over spikes. (The rope would slowly rot away over the years, until nest-building swallows finally carried the last of it off. The rusted hook would remain until long after George Ballard had died of old age.)

As supper time approached, there was a great deal of talk about the best way of preserving the memory of Sue's and Malik's feat. Old Sam decided that he would do his best to tan the skin of the fish, though he had never tried tanning anything like that before. He announced that he would skin and butcher the fish the next day and that if anyone wanted to make a tracing of it, that he needed only to appear at Old Sam's house early in the morning with a big enough plank. He and Malik rode with Jared on the wagon with the fish and with some empty barrels Old Sam had bought from Steve Danforth. At Old Sam's house Jared unloaded the fish by tying it to a tree and driving the wagon out from underneath it. Old Sam and Malik ate their supper sitting on empty barrels right beside the fish. Benjie joined them and convinced his mother to let him stay the night with Old Sam and Malik. Sue and her father ate supper with George and Annie Ballard.

The next morning several people made tracings of the sturgeon on planks before Old Sam and Malik set to work. As the two of them began a careful job of skinning the fish and cutting up the flesh to pack into barrels of brine, they discovered a huge mass of eggs inside the sturgeon. They shook their heads in astonishment at the quantity, put them aside for a time as a curiosity to show to spectators, and then at the end of the afternoon had Benjie take them next door in a wheelbarrow along with the guts and give them to Seth Barston's pigs.

The skin and the tracings of the sturgeon survived for many years. The skin hung on the wall of the Catamount Tavern for decades until, falling apart from age, it was put into storage somewhere and forgotten. Perhaps it waits now in a barrel or box off in an obscure corner of someone's attic, ready to be discovered and wondered at. At least two of the tracings have survived to the present day — faded outlines in blue paint on planks of a width not often seen in recent years; still bearing stains of blood up by the head, right where clots from the gills had ruptured during the tracing and had dried afterwards. Though people spoke of the sturgeon for years as "a rod long," the tracings on the planks are just a few inches over fourteen feet. The weight was never taken. Not until after the fish had been cut up and put into barrels, the guts and eggs eaten by Seth Barston's pigs, and the skin set to soaking in a vat at the tannery did someone comment that the parts could have been weighed separately and their weights totaled. Consequently, there were only estimates of the weight. They ranged all the way from six hundred pounds on up to a thousand.

No one ever fished for sturgeon again down by the point. There was talk of it, but no one ever went beyond the talk to cajole George Ballard into making a new hook or lending the one clenched into the trim board covering the granite door lintel of his blacksmith shop. Malik later tore the plank-rig apart to make a box; he and Sue sold the rope back to Steve Danforth. Neither of them had any intention of repeating the long ordeal of battling the sturgeon. No one else was willing to go to the trouble of getting a hook, trading for enough thick rope, and making a plank-rig. Besides, it was common knowledge that the presence of the sturgeon had been an outrageous fluke: none had been there before and, because of the dams across the Connecticut, none would be there again.

And thus during the day several shadowy forms in the deep hole at the foot of the fast water went unmolested; at night they cruised freely through the eddy. They were there once — the sturgeon — many years ago. Perhaps some have lingered even to the present day.

ATTENTION

ORGANIZATIONS, SCHOOLS, GROUPS:

Quantity discounts are available on
bulk purchases of this book for
educational purposes,
fund raising, or gift giving.

For information, contact

MOOSE COUNTRY PRESS

TOLL FREE 1-800-34-MOOSE.
(1-800-346-6673)

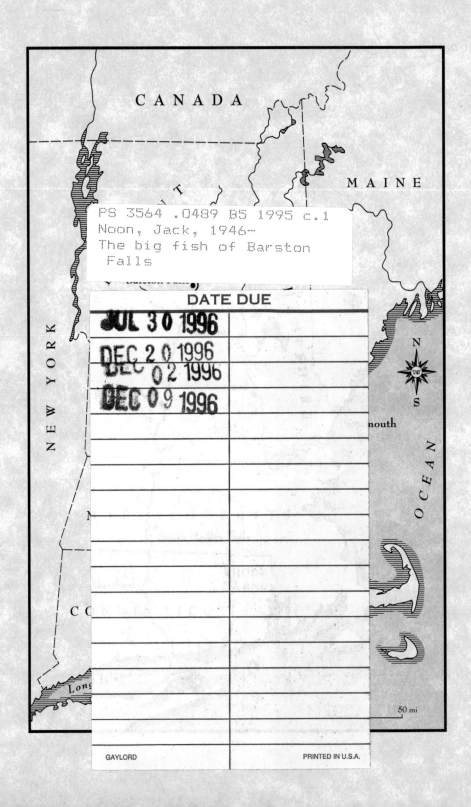